A former journalist, media executive and screenwriter, Thomas Greanias is the founder and CEO of Atlantis Interactive Inc., a Beverly Hills-based entertainment company that has created some of the Web's most groundbreaking entertainment.
Visit www.atlantisprophecy.com

ALSO BY THOMAS GREANIAS

Raising Atlantis

THOMAS GREANIAS

THE ATLANTIS

P R O P H E C Y

POCKET BOOKS

LONDON • SYDNEY • NEW YORK • TORONTO

First published in the United States of America by Pocket Star Books, 2008
First published in Great Britain by Pocket Books UK, 2008
An imprint of Simon & Schuster UK Ltd
A CBS COMPANY

London WC1X 8HB

www.simonsays.co.uk

Simon & Schuster Australia
Sydney

A CIP catalogue record for this book
is available from the British Library

ISBN 978-1-4165-2233-1

Printed and bound in Great Britain by
Cox & Wyman Ltd, Reading, Berks

For Alex & Jake

ACKNOWLEDGMENTS

Thanks to Emily Bestler, my editor, and to Sarah Branham and the rest of the family at Atria and Pocket. Many thanks to certain daughters of Freemasons and Air Force officers, certain syndicated Washington columnists, and certain congressional and White House officials. Special thanks to the staff and docents at Mount Vernon, Library of Congress, U.S. Capitol, and National Archives for their generous assistance and outstanding public service; you are a national treasure. And an extra-special thanks to my son, Alex, president of the student body at his elementary school, for his research on Benjamin Banneker, and for his example in looking out for the interests not just of his friends and little brother, Jake, but of everyone on the school yard. America needs more leaders like you.

'The only new thing in the world is the history you don't know'

—Harry S. Truman
33rd American President
33rd Degree Freemason

George Town

P O T O M A K   R I V E R

Lat. Capitol 38. 53. N.
Long. 0. 0.

THE FEDERAL DISTRICT

FIVE SOLDIERS of the U.S. Provisional Army came to an abrupt halt at the Georgetown wharf and dismounted their horses. The sleet had stopped, but it was bitter cold outside. The commanding officer looked out across the water at Suter's Tavern. It was the middle of the night, but he could hear music from inside. A lone lantern flickered in the middle window of the second floor.

That was the sign.

The man they were after was inside.

The officer signaled his men. They moved quickly toward the front door in single file. Their boots splashed lightly in the moonlit puddles, the bayonets at the end of their muskets glinting. Two soldiers went around the back to take positions behind the kitchen. The other two pounded the front door with the butts of their muskets.

"Open in the name of the United States of America!"

The door opened a crack to reveal the face of a small boy, who fell back in alarm as the soldiers pushed their way inside. The thirty or so revelers in the tavern sat fast in their chairs, their mugs of ale midair and their mouths open. The music stopped, the sudden silence broken only by the crackling of the fireplace flames.

The commanding officer, a head taller than most in the room, grabbed the boy by his collar and demanded, "We are looking for a runaway slave, a cook who goes by the name Hercules."

Hercules was in the kitchen, chopping onions for one last serving of his popular stew. His wiry dark hair was pulled tight to his scalp and stuck straight back like the handle of an iron skillet. Rules of the house. But he had refused to shave his beard. As his stew rose to a slow boil he suddenly realized that the noise in the tavern had died down. He cocked his ear.

The kitchen door flew open, and in stormed four Green Coats. Their commanding officer, who identified himself as Major Cornelius Temple of the U.S. Provisional Army, shouted, "Which of you is Hercules?"

Hercules froze. So did the other kitchen staff, all slaves. None of them said a word, but their anxious gazes drifted toward Hercules.

Hercules had been a slave until he ran away from his master two years ago. He had been making his way as a cook ever since, having perfected his renowned Southern dishes at the General's homes in New York, Philadelphia, and Virginia. If all he ever did was cook for his master, he would never have left. But his master made him carry out other missions, too. Secret missions. Dangerous missions. Now his past had finally caught up with him.

He just hadn't expected it to come so soon.

Hercules laid down his chopping knife on the table

and stepped forward, praying that the only thing the soldiers were after tonight was a runaway slave, and not the secret his master had him bury years ago.

The major looked down his nose at Hercules. "Come with us, slave."

Hercules was only average in height, but he was as muscular as his namesake. Standing proud, he gazed directly at the commanding officer. The major's green coat reached the knee and sported yellow lapels and cuffs. His vest was white, single breasted, with white buttons. The white fringed strap epaulette on his right shoulder designated his rank. But it was the major's black three-cornered hat that had transfixed Hercules, specifically its small but spellbinding silver insignia.

The Regiment of Riflemen.

Hercules understood then that he was in the presence of killers, sanctioned by the new federal government. Until now Hercules knew of the Regiment of Riflemen by reputation only. Earlier that year Congress authorized the formation of a specialized unit of snipers that engaged in unconventional tactics. "The first in the field and last out" was the regiment's motto, and their tactics borrowed heavily from the Light Infantry and even Indians. That much was clear from the major's belt, which along with a leather cartridge and bullet cases held a tomahawk and scalping knife.

Hercules would not resist arrest, if only for the sake of the other slaves.

He turned to open a small closet door and heard the *click* of a musket hammer behind him.

"Slowly, slave."

"Jus' gettin' my coat."

Hercules calmly removed his herringbone overcoat with ivory buttons from its hook. The wool was so finely woven it gave the whole coat a glossy sheen.

The young soldier released the cocked flintlock and lowered his special model French Charleville. But before Hercules could button up, the butt of another musket smacked him in the side of his head and he went down on all fours.

"You run away with that coat, slave?" the major snarled, as he kicked Hercules in the side like an animal.

Hercules knew the drill. The major had no feelings for him one way or another. He simply needed to make him an example to any other slaves in the kitchen who might think that they, too, could one day run away.

"I bought it righteously, suh," Hercules managed to say with a grunt before four strong arms pushed him outside.

"He's a freedman by law in Pennsylvania!" cried one of the cooks.

"He's not in Pennsylvania anymore," the major barked as the door slammed shut behind him.

A flat-bottom boat, manned by four boatmen, waited at the wharf, the icy waters of the Potomac lapping at its sides. The sleet had returned, coming down even harder than before. The soldiers pushed Hercules to the stern. A moment later he was sitting between two soldiers and opposite the major and two others as they shoved off into the dark.

"The General is looking for you, slave."

Hercules shivered. The General, his master, was a just man and a great leader. But he had burdened Hercules with secrets too heavy for any American patriot to bear, let alone a slave.

Lord, please don't let this be about the globe.

Hercules gazed at the white exterior of the Presidential Palace as they floated by. Now in its seventh year of construction, it was still unoccupied; President Adams lived in Philadelphia with his family. In the distance loomed Jenkins Hill and on top of it the new U.S. Capitol Building, or at least part of it.

The General had once told him that more than a century ago the hill was called Rome and the Potomac the Tiber, because the property owner, a man named Francis Pope, had a dream that one day a great empire to rival ancient Rome would rise on these banks. But all Hercules could see was marshland, half-finished buildings, and tree stumps along what was supposed to be a grand thoroughfare—Pennsylvania Avenue—linking the great white Presidential Palace to what they were now calling Capitol Hill.

The boatmen were rowing vigorously now, as a few floating chunks of ice struck the sides of the boat. Even the major had to grab an oar. Hercules at first wondered why they didn't make him row too. But he figured they didn't want to hand a runaway slave an oar only to have him swing it at them.

Hercules pulled at the collar of his coat as pellets of sleet slapped his face. He felt the stare of the major in the bow, whose own coat was not so heavy. But Hercules had paid for the coat himself, and his tailored wool trousers and buckled shoes, too. The General had allowed him to cook outside of the Philadelphia house in nearby taverns to earn extra money. Much of it he spent on fine clothing, which offended soldiers in the General's charge who were not paid nearly as much nor dressed as well.

Finally the sleet stopped and the boat struck the opposite shore. The soldiers pulled him out and escorted him toward steps that led up the hill to the General's estate.

Mount Vernon was ablaze with light. There were torches everywhere, and Hercules saw carriages and horsemen five deep in the court as he was marched toward the servants' entrance. An express courier galloped past on horseback, shouting for them to get out of the way, and almost trampled them.

Inside the manor, at the bottom of the back stairs, Hercules waited with several parties of private citizens and military officers and wondered what he was doing among such august company. The General's personal physician, the lanky Dr. Craik, was exchanging sharp words in hushed tones with a portly Catholic priest. Hercules couldn't hear what they were saying, and he was embarrassed by the curious glances from the others. They all seemed to know some terrible secret that he did not.

A few minutes later, a gaunt-looking man Hercules recognized as the General's chief of staff, Colonel Tobias Lear, plodded down the steps. Hercules anxiously watched the group part as Colonel Lear walked straight up to him. His military escort, seeing no chance for him to flee, stepped back and released him.

Lear looked him over. "My God, man, they were supposed to bring you, not beat you senseless."

Hercules didn't understand what Lear meant, nor Lear's glare at the major, whose expression remained emotionless.

"I been beaten worse," Hercules said.

Lear glanced about the room in search of Dr. Craik, but the General's physician was still occupied with the priest. He took out his own handkerchief and touched it to Hercules' temple. When Lear withdrew his hand, Hercules saw blood on the cloth. Instantly worried about his coat, Hercules glanced down and was relieved to find no soiling.

"His Excellency will see you now," Colonel Lear said.

Hercules glanced back at his military escort and then followed Lear up the stairs. Lear paused before the door to the General's chamber.

"Brace yourself, man," Lear said and opened the door.

Hercules at last beheld the cause of all the hue and cry: There, in his bed, writhing in pain and gasping for air, lay General George Washington, first president of the United States of America and current commander-in-chief of its armed forces. A string was tied around the great man's arm, where blood, thick and heavy, oozed from a vein.

They're bleeding him, Hercules realized. A bad sign.

Sobbing quietly at the foot of the bed was the General's wife, Martha, who rose to her feet and smiled weakly at Hercules. Young Christopher, the General's personal servant, helped her out of the room and shut the door, all the while averting his eyes from Hercules. The guilty look on his face made Hercules wonder if he was the servant who gave him up and told Washington his whereabouts.

"The General asked for you," Lear said now that they were alone. "As you can see, he's dying."

How can this be? Hercules wondered. The last time Hercules saw his master, he seemed as robust and regal a man in his 60s as he had ever laid eyes upon. That was shortly before Hercules had run away. Terror seized his heart as he approached the bed, anxious to know what punishment his master might have in store for him.

"Massa Washington," Hercules said. "I didn't mean no disrespect. I just wanna be free, like you said the law allowed back in Philly."

"Don't be alarmed, Hercules," Colonel Lear said. "His Excellency understands the reasons for your departure and apologizes for the abruptness of your summons. He wants you to know all is forgiven. But he asks one final favor of you, not as a slave but as a freedman and patriot. Apparently, you are the only man he trusts with it."

Astonished, Hercules drew himself up to his full stature, his pride mixed with fear. For years the General had trusted him with his life—every time he put a fork in his mouth—like the Pharaohs of Egypt and their taste-testers, paranoid of conspirators who would poison them. But this was different.

Washington tried to speak but struggled with it, forcing Hercules to bend his ear. "The republic requires your services," Washington gasped hoarsely, in so low and broken a voice that Hercules could hardly understand him. He could smell vapors of vinegar, molasses, and butter on the General's breath. "I would be most grateful."

Hercules, moved deeply, bowed low. "Massa Washington, I ain't up to something like this no more."

But the General seemed not to hear him and gestured to Colonel Lear, who held out an envelope for Hercules.

Despite his protest, Hercules took the yellowed envelope and saw the bold letters written across that spelled STARGAZER. Like most of Washington's slaves, Hercules couldn't read, and he often wondered if this was another reason why the General trusted him with these sorts of communiqués. But he knew the code name all too well.

Colonel Lear asked, "Do you know the Christian name of this patriot, this agent with the code name Stargazer?"

Hercules shook his head.

"Neither do I, and I know more about the General's military papers than anybody else," Lear said. "But you know where to find him?"

Hercules nodded.

"Very well then. Two of the General's officers will escort you to the woods outside the Federal District. From there you will take the route the General says you have taken before for him, and deliver the letter to its proper destination."

Hercules put the letter in his coat, aware of Washington's anguished eyes following the path of the letter closely. The General preferred his spies to carry secret communiqués at the bottom of their knee-high boots. But tonight Hercules was wearing his shiny buckled shoes, which the General considered far less secure, so that was not an option.

"One more thing," said Lear, and presented Hercules with a small dagger in a leather sheath. "As a token of his appreciation, the General would like you to have this. It's one of his favorites. During the Revolution you apparently proved yourself very good with a knife."

Hercules took the dagger in his hand. Engraved on the handle were strange symbols that Hercules would never understand but which, after decades in the service of his master, he recognized as Masonic. He slipped it under his coat and into his belt behind the small of his back.

The General seemed to approve and strained to say something. He gulped air to breathe and made a harsh, high-pitched respiratory noise that frightened Hercules.

"Hercules," he gasped. "There is one evil I dread, and that is their spies. You know whom I mean."

Hercules nodded.

"Deliver the letter," Washington hissed, his voice losing strength. "Rid the republic of this evil. Preserve America's destiny."

"Yessa."

Hercules rose and glanced at Lear.

"You have the final orders of His Excellency General

George Washington, commander-in-chief of the United States armed forces," Lear said. "Carry them out."

"Yessa."

Hercules bowed and walked out the door just as Dr. Craik and two consulting physicians rushed in with Martha. As Hercules stumbled down the stairs in a daze and stepped out into the bitter night, the cries of the servants rang in his ears:

"Massa Washington is dead! The General is dead!"

Outside, dispatches concerning the General's demise were already being handed to express couriers for delivery to President Adams and Generals Hamilton and Pinckney.

Two military aides, meanwhile, were waiting for Hercules with the horses. Hercules faintly recalled their faces. One was a former Son of Liberty. The other was an assassin and an original member of the Culper Spy Ring who helped Washington beat the British in New York. No words were exchanged as Hercules threw a leg over his chestnut-colored horse and they galloped away from Mount Vernon.

They avoided the main roads as they rode north through the outskirts of Alexandria, cutting across farms and orchards in a wide arc until they reached the nape of the Potomac and crossed a wooden bridge a few miles west of Georgetown. Ten minutes later they reached the great woods at the edge of the federal district and Hercules brought his horse to a halt.

"What are you waiting for?" asked the former Son of Liberty.

Hercules looked into the woods. The twisted trees and strange noises had always spooked him, even before that terrible night when he and the General buried the old globe.

Oh, Lord, not here! Please don't make me come back here!

Hercules remembered the stories about the ancient Algonquin Indians that old Benjamin Banneker, the General's Negro astronomer, used to tell him when the General used the stars to draw the boundaries for the federal district. According to Banneker, long before Europeans colonized the New World, the Algonquin held tribal grand councils both at the base of Jenkins Hill, where the new Capitol Building sat, and in the ravines of these woods. What they did during those councils, Banneker wouldn't say. But he did say that the Algonquin were linked by archaeology to the ancient Mayans and by legend to the descendents of Atlantis. The chiefs of their primary tribe, the Montauk Indians, were known as *Pharaoh*, like their ancient Egyptian cousins 10,000 years ago. Banneker told him the word Pharaoh meant "Star Child" or "Children of the Stars."

Hercules craned his head up to the stars. The clouds had parted like a frame around Virgo. A chill shook his bones. Hercules knew that, by making the layout of the new capital city mirror the constellation, the General benignly sought the blessings of the Blessed Virgin in heaven upon the new republic. But such mysteries spooked him, almost as much as words like *Pharaoh* and *Star Child*.

After all, slaves built the pyramids of Egypt. Would the same be true of America?

"Let's move," demanded the former assassin.

Hercules led his military escort into the woods. For several minutes he listened to the crunch of leaves beneath hooves as he weaved between the trees in the starlight, a bare branch or two scratching him along the way.

"Thro' many dangers, toils and snares, I have already come," he began to sing, repeating his favorite verse from the song "Amazing Grace." " 'Tis grace has brought me safe thus far, and grace will lead me home."

He tried not to think about old Banneker's otherworldly stories or, God forbid, the secret cave and the secret globe, which contained the greatest secret of them all. As he sang, his eyes darted back and forth, glancing at the dancing shadows all around. Then he heard the snap of a twig and stopped.

He glanced back at the two horses of his military escort in the darkness. But he could see only one rider—the former assassin. At that moment, he felt the muzzle of a pistol in his back and then heard the voice of the other escort, the former Son of Liberty.

"Get down here, slave."

Slowly Hercules dismounted and turned. Both soldiers, now standing before him, pointed their pistols at him.

"The communiqué," said the assassin. "Hand it over."

Hercules hesitated, staring down the long barrel of the French flintlock.

"The communiqué, slave!"

Hercules slowly put his hand into his coat and removed the letter. He handed it to the former Son of Liberty, who glanced at it and handed it to the assassin.

"Who is Stargazer?"

Hercules said nothing.

"Tell me or we kill your family, too, starting with your two-year-old bastard daughter. We know where to find her. She lives with her mother in Philadelphia. So, again, who is Stargazer?"

"I-I don't know," Hercules said.

The assassin's face turned red with rage and he tapped the barrel of his flintlock to Hercules' temple. "How can you not know, slave?"

"Because, be-because," Hercules stammered, "he ain't been born yet. Won't for a long, long time."

"What gibberish is this?" The assassin glanced at the other soldier and grimaced at Hercules. "Give me your coat."

Hercules stepped back, furious.

"Now, or I put a bullet hole in it."

Hercules shook his head, trying to understand what was happening. "The republic . . ."

"The republic dies tonight with the General, his slave, and this Stargazer," said the assassin. "Now give me my coat."

"*Your* coat?"

"That's right, slave. *My* coat."

Hercules suddenly felt the calm that often washed over him in moments of great danger, whenever the face behind his fear finally revealed itself. As he started to take off his coat, he used his free hand to reach into the small of his back and remove from its sheath the dagger that the General had given him. He held the coat in front of him.

"Throw it on the ground, slave."

The soldier might as well have asked him to soil the American flag. Hercules had worked too hard to buy this coat to give it up now, especially as they meant to kill him in the end. He had fed too many American soldiers with food his hands had prepared, and had sacrificed too much for his children and the General's dream of a free nation for men and women of all races and creeds.

Everything, Lord, but not my coat!

"For the last time, slave, throw it down."

"Not the ground," Hercules said. "It would get your coat dirty, sir."

Hercules tossed it through the air to the soldier. For a moment the soldier let his hand with the gun swing to the side to catch the coat, and in that moment Hercules turned to slit the throat of the soldier behind him, the blade slowed only by the catch of an artery. Before the man crumpled over, Hercules hurled the dagger at the assassin who held his coat. The blade struck him in the chest and drove him back against the trunk of a tree. The flintlock discharged aimlessly as he slid down to the ground.

A wisp of gunsmoke hung in the air as Hercules marched over to the assassin, who was gurgling up blood, his eyes rolling in surprise and fear. Hercules yanked the dagger out of his chest. The assassin opened his mouth to scream, but emitted only a low wheeze as the breath of life slowly escaped him.

"*My* coat, sir."

Hercules picked up his coat, mounted his horse, and looked up at the constellation of Virgo, the Blessed Virgin, watching over him. He slipped the letter to Stargazer into his coat and buttoned up. Then he kicked his horse to life and rode off into the night toward America's destiny.

PART ONE

PRESENT DAY

1

ARLINGTON NATIONAL CEMETERY
ARLINGTON, VIRGINIA

CONRAD YEATS kept a good three steps behind the flag-draped coffin. Six horses pulled the caisson toward the gravesite, their hooves clomping like a cosmic metronome in the heavy air. Each resounding clap proclaimed the march of time, the brevity of life. In the distance lightning flickered across the dark sky. But still no rain.

Conrad looked over at Marshall Packard. The secretary of defense walked beside him, his Secret Service agents a few paces behind with the other mourners from all branches of America's armed forces, umbrellas at the ready.

Conrad said, "It's not often you bury a soldier four years after his death."

"No, it's not," said Packard, a fireplug of a former pilot known for his unflagging intensity. "I wish it hadn't taken this long. But you're the only one who knows the extraordinary way in which your father met his end."

Packard had delivered a stirring eulogy for his old wingman "the Griffter" back at the military chapel up the hill. What Packard had failed to mention, Conrad knew, was that he hated the Griffter's guts. The two men had had a falling out over Conrad's unusual role at the Pentagon years ago, which involved identifying secret targets for bunker-busting cruise missiles: underground military installations and nuclear facilities in the Middle East that America's enemies were building beneath archaeological sites for protection. Packard couldn't believe that Conrad, the world's foremost expert on megalithic architecture, would risk destroying civilization's most ancient treasures. The Griffter couldn't believe that Packard would risk American lives to preserve a few unturned stones that had already yielded all the information that archaeologists like Conrad needed to know about the dead culture that built them. The clash ended with an aborted air strike on the pyramid at Ur in Iraq and the revocation of Conrad's Top Secret security clearance from the Department of Defense.

"He wasn't my biological father," Conrad reminded Packard. "I was adopted."

There was a lot more Conrad could say, none of it helpful right now. Especially about how he had nothing to do with the planning of this funeral, how the Pentagon wouldn't even let him see the tombstone his father had picked out for himself before he had died, and, most of all, how Conrad was certain that the man they were burying today could not possibly be his father.

"Level with me, son." Packard glanced to his left and right. "Did you kill him?"

Conrad locked eyes with Packard, the man he called "Uncle MP" as a child and feared more than anybody else except his father. "Your people performed the autopsy, Mr. Secretary. Why don't you tell me?"

The two men said nothing more on the way down the hill to the gravesite.

Conrad suspected that the DOD had spent tens of millions of American taxpayer dollars over the past four years to locate the remains of USAF Gen. Griffin Yeats. It was all in the vain hope of finding out what happened to the billions more his father had squandered in a black ops mission to Antarctica during which dozens of soldiers from various countries had perished.

What Conrad and his father had found was none other than the lost civilization of Atlantis. And just when they were about to uncover its secrets, that ancient world was destroyed in a massive explosion that purportedly killed his father, sank an ice shelf the size of California, and sent a catastrophic tsunami to Indonesia that killed thousands.

The only other survivor of the ill-fated Antarctica expedition besides Conrad was Sister Serena Serghetti, the famed Vatican linguist and environmental activist. But the impossibly beautiful Sister Serghetti, or "Mother Earth" as she was dubbed by the media, wasn't talking to the United States or U.N. about Antarctica or lost civilizations. Nor was she talking to Conrad.

The long, bitter road ended here, at a belated funeral ceremony for a general more feared than revered, and a corpse that finally allowed the Pentagon to save face and bury the whole affair with full military honors.

For Conrad it was a homecoming of sorts to the only family he had left: the U.S. Armed Forces, even if he was its black sheep.

At the gravesite stood a gray-haired U.S. Air Force

chaplain, an open Bible in hand. "I am the resurrection and the life," he said, quoting Jesus and gazing straight at Conrad. "He who believes in me, though he dies, yet shall he live."

Six Blue Angel fighter jets streaked overhead in a missing-man formation. As they peeled up into the dark skies, the thunder from their rainbow-colored vapor trails faded and an unearthly silence descended upon the gravesite.

As Conrad watched the flag being lifted off the coffin and folded, he remembered his school days as a military brat when his dad was a test pilot, like many of the other dads at the base. The sound of jets had filled the base playground. But every now and then there'd be a sputter or pop and all the kids would stop playing and listen to the long whistle, waiting to hear the poof of an ejector lid blowing. You knew who was flying that day just by looking at the faces. Ninety-nine times out of a hundred he would look up and see a chute open. But if it didn't, two days later he would be standing at a funeral just like this one, watching a friend's mom receive the flag and disappear from his life.

The miracle, he thought, was that it took this long for his turn to come.

Packard presented Conrad with his father's Legion of Merit award, his Purple Heart medal, some obscure medal from the Society of Cincinnati, and the flag from the coffin. The flag was folded neatly into a triangle of stars. The stars, so crisp and white against the dark navy blue, seemed to glow.

"On behalf of a grateful America," Packard told him, "our condolences."

The oppressive air was suddenly and violently broken by the crack of gunfire as the seven-member rifle team shot the first of three volleys.

A lone bugler played Taps, and Conrad looked on as the casket was lowered into the earth. He felt angry, empty and lost. Despite his doubts that his father was in that casket and his feeling that this whole charade was yet another attempt by the military to bring closure to a mission gone bad, the full weight of his father's death sank in, a sense of loss more profound than Conrad expected.

His father often spoke of fellow Apollo astronauts who had "been to the moon" and then came back to Earth only to find civilian life wanting. Now Conrad knew what his father had been talking about. Everything Conrad had been searching for his entire life he had discovered in Antarctica, including Serena. Now it was all lost.

Gone were the days when Conrad was a world-class archaeologist whose deconstructionist philosophy— namely, that ancient monuments weren't nearly so important as the information they yielded about their builders—led to mayhem and media coverage in many of the world's hot spots.

Gone, too, was his academic reputation after disastrous digs in Luxor and later Antarctica, where he had returned only to find that any traces of Atlantis had vanished.

Gone, last of all, was his relationship with Serena, the one ruin in his life he actually cared about.

Someone coughed and Conrad looked up in time to see the chaplain step aside from the grave, the sweep of his vestment parting like a curtain to unveil the tombstone behind him.

The sight sucked the air from Conrad's lungs.

Like some of the older stones in the cemetery, his father's tombstone was in the shape of an obelisk, just like the 555-foot-tall Washington Monument in the distance. This obelisk was a little over three feet tall. Inscribed in a circle near the top was a Christian cross. Beneath the cross were the words:

GRIFFIN W. YEATS
BRIG GEN
US AIR FORCE
BORN
MAY 4 1945
KILLED IN ACTION
EAST ANTARCTICA
SEPT 21 2004

Unlike any other obelisk at Arlington, however, this one had three constellations engraved on one side, and on the other a strange sequence of numbers he couldn't quite make out from where he was standing. The markings were bizarre by any measure, and yet familiar all the same. Four years ago in Antarctica Conrad had come across a similar obelisk.

Conrad stared at the tombstone, an uneasy feeling creeping up his spine.

It had to be a message from his father.

Conrad's heart pounded as he caught Packard watching him. Other mourners were staring, too, watching him. Belatedly, Conrad recognized the faces of five senior Pentagon code breakers and two hostage negotiators among the gathering. Then it dawned on him: This burial service wasn't meant for his father. And it wasn't meant for the DOD, to save face. It was meant for *him*. It was all some kind of setup.

They're gauging my reaction.

Conrad felt a surge of fight-or-flight in his veins, but he kept a poker face for the rest of the service. Afterward, the funeral party dispersed, and a few tourists drifted down the hillside from the Tomb of the Unknown Soldier to watch from a distance as the horses clomped away with the empty caisson. Only he and Packard were left at the grave, along with a younger man who looked vaguely familiar to Conrad.

"Conrad, I'd like you to meet Max Seavers," Packard said. "He's your father's acting replacement at DARPA."

DARPA stood for the Defense Advanced Research Projects Agency and was the Pentagon's research and development organization. Among other things, DARPA took credit for inventing stealth technology, the global positioning system, and the Internet. DARPA's mission was to maintain America's technological superiority and to prevent any other power on earth from challenging that superiority. That mission is what sent his father and, ultimately, Conrad to Antarctica four years ago.

Conrad looked at Seavers and remembered now where he had seen the sandy locks, the dimpled jaw, and the piercing blue eyes before. Seavers, barely 30, was the

Bill Gates of biotech and a fixture in business magazines. A few years ago Seavers had turned over his day job running his big pharma company, SeaGen, in order to devote himself to "a higher calling" by developing and distributing vaccines to fight disease in Third World countries. Now, it appeared, he had been called to public service.

"A younger and, hopefully, wiser DARPA, I see," Conrad said, offering his hand.

Seavers's iron grip as they shook hands felt like ice. And his gaze conveyed all the warmth of a scientist in a white lab coat studying a microscopic specimen of bacteria at the bottom of a petri dish.

"We still take America's technological superiority seriously, Dr. Yeats." Seavers spoke in a baritone voice that sounded too deep for his age. "And we could always use a man with your unique skills."

"And what skills would those be?"

"Cut the bullshit, Yeats." Packard glanced both ways to see if anybody was within earshot, leaned over and rasped. "Tell us the meaning of this."

"Meaning of what?"

"This." Packard pointed to the obelisk. "What's the deal?"

"I'm supposed to know?"

"Damn right you're supposed to know. Those astrological signs. The numbers. You're the world's foremost astro-archaeologist."

It sounded funny coming out of Packard's mouth: *astro-archaeologist.* But that's what he was these days, an archaeologist who used the astronomical alignments of pyramids, temples, and other ancient landmarks to date their construction and the civilizations that erected them. His specialty hadn't made him rich yet. But over the years it had given him his own now-canceled reality TV show called *Ancient Riddles*, exotic adventures with young female fans, and the expertise to spend an obscene amount of other people's money—mostly Uncle Packard's.

"Hey, your people handled all the funeral arrangements," Conrad said. "Couldn't your brilliant cryptologists at the Pentagon crack it?"

Seavers steamed but said nothing.

Conrad sighed. "For all we know, Mr. Secretary, this obelisk is probably another sick joke to send us around the world looking for clues that ultimately lead to a statue of Dad giving us all the finger."

"You know him better than that, son."

"Obviously a lot better than you did, sir, if you and your code breakers can't figure it out. Why do you even care?"

Packard glowered at him. "Your father was a test pilot, an astronaut, and the head of DARPA. If it involves him, it's vital to national security."

"Dr. Serghetti is the real expert on this sort of thing," Conrad said. "But I'm looking around and don't see any sign of her."

"And see that you don't, son," Packard said. "This is a state secret. And Sister Serghetti is an agent of a foreign power."

Conrad blinked. "So now the Vatican is a foreign power?"

"I don't see the pope taking orders from the president, do you?" Packard said. "You are to share nothing with that girl. And I expect you to report any attempt by her to reestablish contact with you."

If only, Conrad thought, as Packard walked away with Max Seavers.

It had started to drizzle, and Conrad watched the pair march down the hill to the secret service detail, which welcomed them with two open umbrellas and escorted them to the convoy of limousines, town cars, and SUVs. Conrad counted nine vehicles parked on the narrow road. Before the funeral procession he had counted eight.

One by one the cars left, until a single black limousine remained. He was certain it wasn't the cab he called for. He'd give it another two minutes to show up before he walked down to the main gate and hailed another.

Conrad studied the obelisk in the rain.

"Now what have you gotten me into, Dad?"

Whatever answers he was looking for, however, had apparently died with his father four years ago.

He turned again toward the road and splashed toward the limousine to tell Packard's boys to take the day off.

Conrad felt a strange electricity in the air even before he recognized beefy Benito behind the wheel. Then the window came down and he saw Serena Serghetti sitting in back. His blood jumped.

"Don't just stand there, mate," she told him in her bold Australian accent. "Get in."

2

As the limousine drove out the main gate at Arlington Cemetery, Conrad Yeats set aside the folded, starry flag that had draped his father's casket and stared at Serena Serghetti with a rage that surprised him. She was the only woman he ever truly loved, and she had made it clear to him on two separate occasions, each four years apart, that he was the only man she had ever loved. Conrad always had considered it a crime against humanity that God would create such an exquisite creature as Serena Serghetti and make her a nun, forever keeping them apart.

Now here she was again, Her Holiness, the picture of effortless, earth-tone elegance in a long, belted cardigan, plaid pants, and knee-high suede boots. A gold cross hung from the columned neck of her Edwardian top. She had pulled back her hair into a ponytail, revealing her high cheekbones, upturned nose, and pointed chin. She could have just come in from a polo match as easily as from the Vatican, where she was the Roman Catholic Church's top linguist—and cryptologist.

As always, it was incumbent upon him to cast the first

pebble and hope to see a ripple form across the smooth surface of her mirror-like calm.

"Ah, no medieval habit," he said. "So, you've finally come to your senses and quit that damn church."

She gave him that arch look of hers—raised eyebrow and smirk—but her brown eyes, soft as ever, told him she would if she could. She regarded his newly cut hair, dark jacket, white dress shirt, and khaki trousers approvingly.

"You clean up nice yourself, Conrad, for an archaeologist. Maybe one day you'll even discover the razor blade." She reached over and ran her soft hand across the stubble on his face. "I came because of your father."

Conrad felt her warm fingertips linger for a moment on his cheek. "Making sure he's really dead?"

"I was with you when he vanished from the face of the Earth in Antarctica, remember?" She removed her hand. "Although it's a mystery to me how anybody found his body."

"Me, too," Conrad said. "Maybe that's him following us."

Conrad looked out the rear window of the limousine, aware of Serena following his gaze. A black Ford Expedition was tailing them. Based on his reception at his father's funeral, it was obvious to Conrad that Packard thought he knew more than he was letting on—and was letting him know it.

"DOD cutouts," he said. "They're watching us."

"And we're watching them," Serena said, unruffled. "And God is watching over all of us. No worries. This passenger cabin is soundproof. They don't know who you're talking with now. When they trace the plates, they'll find a funeral home account rented out in your name for transportation to and from the service."

"I'm impressed," he said, "that you'd go to all this trouble to see me."

"Hardly." She turned from the window and looked him in the eye, all business. "I'm here to help you figure out the warning on your father's tombstone."

"Warning?" he repeated. "You're here to warn me about my father's warning?"

"That's right."

He suspected she must have had some kind of agenda all along but still he could not hide his disappointment and, again, his anger. "I don't know how I could have imagined that you came to pay respect to my father or offer me consolation for my loss."

Serena said, "I don't believe in mourning for those we may quickly follow."

Conrad settled back in the seat and folded his arms. "So our lives are in danger?"

"Ever since Antarctica."

"And you decided to tell me this, what, four years later? After you ran back to the safe confines of the Church?"

"It was the only way to gather the resources I needed to protect you."

"Protect me? You're the one I need to be protected from!" He glanced back out the rear window at the black SUV, which was doing a terrible job of trying to remain invisible three cars back. "The U.S. secretary of defense is going to string me up by my balls if he finds out I'm talking to you."

"Not until you give him what he's looking for."

Conrad sighed. "And what's that?"

She unbuttoned her jacket and slipped her hand inside her blouse.

Conrad lifted an eyebrow as she removed a key, leaned over to the soft leather attaché on the floor between her legs, and began to unlock it.

"Focus, Conrad." She removed a folder and handed it to him. "Seen this?"

He switched on the overhead reading lamp to get a better look. Upon opening the folder, Conrad saw four photos, one for each face of his father's tombstone.

"You move fast, Serena, I'll give you that."

There was the epitaph on the north face, the astronomical symbols on the east face, the set of five numerical strings on the west face, and, finally, an inscription on the back or south face of the obelisk he had missed: the number 763.

"How'd you get these? I just saw the tombstone myself."

"Max Seavers and two Homeland Security officials showed me these photos two days ago in New York," she said. "The United Nations is in session and I'm in the States for a couple of weeks. They cornered me outside the General Assembly, took me to the office of the United States Ambassador and briefed me."

Conrad considered his conversation with Seavers and Packard back at the cemetery just minutes ago. Apparently it was OK for them to talk to Serena but not him. Why was that? "You've got diplomatic immunity, and

U.N. Headquarters is international territory," he said. "You didn't have to go."

"I couldn't say no to Max."

"Oh, it's 'Max,' is it?"

"Before he put his personal fortune into a blind trust and stepped into your father's shoes at DARPA, Max Seavers donated millions in vaccines for my relief efforts in Africa and Asia, on top of the $2 billion he gave to the U.N."

Conrad looked at Serena and wondered: Did Seavers and Packard really think that he was going to spill national security secrets to a nun? Or were they worried that she was going to tell him something they didn't want him to know?

"So why did Saint Max show you these photos and what did you say?"

"He said that the DOD recovered your father's body in Antarctica, which as you can imagine came as quite a surprise to me," she said. "He also said once the burial arrangements at Arlington got under way, the designs your father left for his tombstone with the cemetery raised some eyebrows, and they certainly raised mine."

"Why's that?"

"Because your father chose to make his tombstone look like the Scepter of Osiris we found in Antarctica, and to engrave it with clues he knew that only you and I working together could make heads or tails of," she said. "The only problem is he submitted his designs to Arlington before Antarctica and our discovery."

They were driving over Memorial Bridge, and Conrad

could see the Lincoln Memorial, Washington Monument, and U.S. Capitol Building lined up before them on one axis, with the White House to the north and Jefferson Memorial to the south forming another axis. It looked like a model city under the stormy skies, configured like a giant white marble cross on the wet green lawns and reflecting pools of the National Mall.

He handed the sketch back to her. "Big deal. So my father obviously knew what we were looking for in Antarctica. For all I know, you probably did too. What else is new?"

"Your father's tombstone, Conrad. He wanted us to figure it out together."

"Us?"

"Why else would he leave his clue in the form of an obelisk that only you and I could decipher? You saw those astrological signs. They're celestial markers. They have terrestrial counterparts on the ground, as you bloody well know. It's a star map to lead us to a specific landmark."

"You told Seavers this?"

"Of course not, Conrad. I told him I didn't have a clue. That you're the only one on the planet who can figure it out."

Conrad grinned. "That's what I told him just now back at Arlington, but about you."

Serena didn't grin back. "He wanted me to tell him if you tried to contact me," she said. "To let him know what you tell me and what we find out."

"Thanks for the heads-up, Serena," Conrad said, the anger he had been suppressing now rising again. "But what are 'we' supposed to find at the end of this treasure trail? The lost treasure of the Knights Templar? A sinister secret that could destroy the republic? Or maybe you've forgotten that besides the occasional Discovery Channel documentary, I now make my living as a technical advisor for Hollywood movies about these sorts of fantasies? That's because nobody wants to fund any real-world digs for me anymore. You saw to that when you kept your mouth shut after Antarctica destroyed whatever reputation I had left as an archaeologist. So, Serena, what do you think my father wants 'us' to find?"

Serena listened to his outburst calmly. She had absorbed his fury like a palm tree planted firmly in the sands of some South Pacific island, bending gracefully in a monsoon only to rise taller in the sun afterward.

"I don't know," she said. "But it's obviously something important enough for the Pentagon to investigate. Something even my superiors in Rome won't reveal to me."

"Ooh, I have chills," Conrad deadpanned, although secretly he had been hooked from the second he saw the obelisk. "Guess the new pope isn't as fond of you as the old one, huh? But if you could just tell His Holiness the meaning of some cryptic ciphers on some dead American general's tombstone, then the Church would know what we'll find at the end of that celestial treasure trail and you'd be 'Mother Earth' again."

She frowned and said nothing, obviously not appreciating the dig.

"I have a deal to make with you, Conrad. You figure out the meaning of those astrological signs and numerical strings, and I'll help you figure out the meaning of 763."

"Or else?"

"Or else Max Seavers and the Pentagon will beat us to whatever secret your father left behind," she said, "at which point there's no reason to keep you around anymore—or the republic."

"The republic?" Conrad was incredulous. "What makes you think this has anything to do with the republic?"

"Fine," she said. "Then at least let me help you save your life. That's all you seem to care about these days." She gave him her card, which was blank except for a ten-digit number. "That's my private number, Conrad."

Conrad stared at it for a moment and didn't know which excited him more: seeing secret ciphers on his father's tombstone or securing Sister Serghetti's private number after all these years.

Serena said, "Call me if you figure something out."

Conrad realized the limo had stopped. He took her card and looked out to see that they were parked in front of Brooke's house at 3040 N Street. She knew where he lived.

"Too bad Ms. Scarborough couldn't make it to the funeral to offer her own condolences," Serena said.

And she also knew about Brooke. She probably knew a whole hell of a lot more than that, too.

"Just because you chose to be a nun doesn't mean I have to live like a monk," he told her and stepped out of the car into the rain, angry that he felt it necessary to justify himself to her, and even angrier that her opinion meant so much to him.

"I'm sorry, Conrad," she said through her lowered window, a single drop of rain falling on her face like a tear. "God called me. And now he's called you."

She raised her window and signaled her driver.

Conrad watched the limo drive away, aware of a black SUV slowly rounding the corner and parking across the street, its tinted windows too dark to see anybody inside.

3

CONRAD BOUNDED UP the front steps to Brooke's brownstone in two strides and unlocked the front door. She had given him the key to her place months before he agreed to move in with her, a decision made only after he had finally accepted that he would never get another chance with Serena Serghetti.

Inside the foyer, he threw his coat on the bench and began to disarm the alarm. His mind was already on the book that awaited him in the study, and he absently punched the wrong numeric code on the keypad.

As he cleared the alarm and put in the correct code, he wondered what kind of other surveillance besides the SUV outside the SecDef had on him. Probably audio but no video, he concluded, and even that from directional microphones in the SUV and not from any bugs in the house. Packard wouldn't risk the ire of Brooke's father, Senator Joseph Scarborough, who oversaw half of Packard's black ops appropriations from his seat on the Senate Armed Services Committee. Then again, Senator Scarborough had an even lower opinion of the man his daughter was living with than the Secretary of

Defense. "Never did any woman see so much in a man with so little," the Senator once mused. He wouldn't overlook any opportunity to terminate their relationship.

Conrad walked into Brooke's study and placed the flag from the funeral on the fireplace mantle. He pulled out an old, brown cloth hardcover book from the third shelf.

The title was gilt stamped on the book's spine—*The Adventures of Tom Sawyer* by Mark Twain. His father had given it to him when he was ten. It was the only thing his father had ever given him except pain and grief.

Conrad grabbed a pen and a pad of stationery that read *Brooke Scarborough / The Fox on Fox Sports* and dropped them with *Tom Sawyer* on the coffee table in the living room. He then went to the kitchen to heat up some leftover pasta from Café Milano before he sat down on the living room sofa with his bowl of carbs, bottle of Sam Adams, and *Tom Sawyer.*

He tore off three sheets from Brooke's notepad.

On the first sheet he wrote the number from the back of his father's tombstone: 763. He was clueless as to its meaning for now.

On the second sheet he wrote out the names of the constellations he had seen on the east face of the obelisk:

> Boötes
> Leo
> Virgo

Next to each constellation, he wrote down the name of its anchor or "alpha star," which was usually the brightest to the naked eye as seen from Earth:

> Boötes   (Arcturus)
> Leo   (Regulus)
> Virgo   (Spica)

In theory, each alpha star had a terrestrial counterpart or landmark. In places like Giza or Teotihuacán, the ancients placed their pyramids or ziggurats to point to key stars in the heavens. The effect was an astronomically aligned city that mirrored the heavens on the ground. Symbolically, it was intended to achieve some kind of cosmic harmony between man and the gods. Practically, it created a secret "treasure map" to the city known only to its founders.

He quickly drew the alpha stars in relation to each other from memory and came up with a triangle:

That makes no sense at all.

The way it worked in places like the pyramids in Egypt and the Way of the Dead in South America, each landmark linked to a star would lead to another landmark and then another. In theory, you could follow the star map written across the heavens on the ground until you reached a fixed destination. Usually it was a monument or shrine of some kind whose true meaning and purpose would finally be revealed—along with whatever treasure or secret knowledge it contained.

Unfortunately, this triangle of stars was no map at all. It had no direction. In effect, it was an endless loop, going in circles. This, too, would take time to crack.

Finally, on the third sheet, he quickly scribbled out the numeric code—a sequence of five numerical strings—he had memorized:

155.1.6

142.8.1

48.7.5

111.2.8

54.3.4

Ah, finally something familiar.

From the looks of them, Conrad guessed the numbers were in "book code." Each string of three numbers represented a word. The first number was the page of the book. The second was the line on that page. The third was the actual word on that line. So the five sets of numbers meant there were five words, which together formed a phrase or message. That message would be key to unlocking the meaning of the star coordinates.

The problem with book codes was that they were impossible to break—unless you had the book on which they were based, usually a specific book and edition possessed by both the sender and the recipient.

This has to be the book, Conrad thought as he picked

up *The Adventures of Tom Sawyer*. It was the only book his father ever gave him, and his father had taught him the cipher when Conrad was into codes as a Boy Scout at age ten, the same age as Tom Sawyer in the book.

Conrad sat back in the sofa and cracked open the front cover of the novel. It was an unauthorized, non-illustrated edition published in Toronto by Belford Brothers Publishers in July 1876, months before the authorized American edition came out. Conrad remembered how, like Tom Sawyer, he wanted to be a pirate as a child. And this edition was the "pirate" version that a furious Mark Twain claimed was stolen from the typesetters.

He glanced at the string of numbers he had copied down and flipped through the pages of the book. The first of the five strings—155.1.6—directed Conrad to page 155, line 1, word 6.

Conrad flipped to page 155 and deciphered the first number:

SUN

He quickly deciphered the next two numbers and stared at the note:

SUN SHINES OVER

The sun was probably a final, invisible celestial marker, and what it was shining over was the final terrestrial landmark—the location of something his father thought was so important.

He flipped to page 111. The next word was SAVAGE.

SUN SHINES OVER SAVAGE

He was about to flip to page 54 and the last word when he heard the bathroom door creak upstairs and he froze.

"Conrad?" a voice called out. "Is that you?"

Brooke! She had been home the whole time. He didn't expect her so early, but a glance at his watch told him she finished her show two hours ago.

Conrad slapped *Tom Sawyer* shut, slipped it under the sofa, picked up a remote and turned on the plasma television. Brooke TiVo'd her weekend sports show on Fox. He found it on the program guide and tuned in.

On the screen the logo for her show came up with the Wagnerian music score before the commercials. It mixed sports and politics. All of the sponsors, it seemed, were powerful, industrial global giants involved in "communications" and "energy" and "financial services." The average viewer was a white, middle-aged man with a bulging stock portfolio and golf pants to match as he ogled Ms. Scarborough and sipped his Arnold Palmer in the clubhouse.

"Why don't we declare war on Muslim terrorists?" she chirped to baseball's A-Rod, shown on the field. The New York Yankee looked at her like he had woken up in an alternative universe. "They've declared war on us for years," she went on. "The Crusaders had it right: We need to sack them or put them in our jerseys."

Conrad had fought his own battles with Islamofascists and was all for winning the war on terror. But he couldn't believe they let her say this stuff on the air. Yet hers was one of their highest-rated political talk shows. It was better watching her with the TV muted, but instead he turned up the volume for the benefit of anybody listening.

The real show involved gratuitous, low-angle full shots of her legs and her flipping her long blonde hair while she blathered conservative social commentary— lower taxes, no more affirmative action, and guns for everybody. He knew she kept a loaded .357 Magnum in a Manolo Blahnik shoebox at the top of her bedroom closet upstairs. Of course, since she had about 200 shoeboxes, he could never be sure which one it was.

He craned his neck and looked up the stairs as a pair of long legs stepped into view. It was Brooke in a pair of strappy Jimmy Choos and a green Elie Saab evening gown that showed off her faultless figure to full effect.

"There you are," she said, eyeing the pasta bowl and Sam Adams on the coffee table. "Where were you?"

"The graveyard," Conrad said.

"I know, sweetie, I'm sorry I wasn't there." Brooke walked over and kissed him on the lips. "But that's why we planned to go out tonight, remember? To put the past behind you and to celebrate us and the future. The Olympics reception at the Chinese Embassy is tonight. Everybody from the network is going to be there."

Conrad stared. He had completely forgotten.

"I just buried my father, Brooke," Conrad said, his thoughts on the book under the sofa. "I'm not in a party mood."

She frowned and her crystal blue eyes, which at times could look vacant, seemed to come into sharp focus like the automatic lens of a camera.

He expected her to say, "You hated your father," but what came out was sugary sweet. She was great that way.

"I know it must be hard, Conrad," she cooed. "But at least yours went out with a bang. My grandfather was a veteran who died in a retirement condo in Florida while he nodded off watching Errol Flynn in *Night of the Dawn Patrol*."

"So you think I'm going to kick off watching *Top Gun* while you're out?"

"No, you're going to kick off being my Top Gun tonight," she said with shining eyes. "If you're lucky."

Conrad smiled as he looked at her. Although she had quite a killer body now, with a kick-ass personality, Conrad had met her and dated her when they were but gawky teenagers at Sidwell Friends School after his father had dragged him to live in D.C. for two years. Now she was poised, confident, sexy, having filled out her curves and buffed her body to perfection. She seemed to have all the answers.

"Wake me up when you get back," he told her.

Brooke sighed, picked up his raincoat from the bench and put it in the closet. She turned to the foyer mirror and started to apply more lipstick. "I might bring somebody home with me."

"More the merrier." Conrad turned the sound back on the TV. "Make sure she's a brunette."

"I hate you," she said.

"Everybody does in time."

She marched over and took the remote from him.

"Hey, I was looking for *Top Gun*."

"The only thing you're watching tonight is me."

"But I was watching you."

"In the flesh, Con. We're staying home together."

She leaned over, her cleavage practically enveloping his head, and kissed him full on the lips with passion. That she would stay home for him spoke volumes about her devotion, and her soft lips lifted his mood in spite of himself.

"What about the Chinese?" he asked.

She smiled. "We'll order take-out."

She took him by the hand and led him upstairs. Only once did he glance back at the book under the corner of the sofa.

4

CONRAD LAY on his back in bed, staring at the ceiling, thinking of Serena. Sex with Brooke had certainly released his pent-up energy, but he felt guilty as hell.

He looked over at Brooke. They had gone out together in high school, and she was the first girl he'd ever made love to. Now that his father was gone, she was the only connection to his past. After school, he had left her behind to go off on his digs and to other women, catching clips of her colorful commentaries now and then on NBC and later Fox.

Then Serena had made him forget his previous life entirely, made him forget everything the moment he first met her in South America.

It was only after Serena had deserted him after the disaster in Antarctica and he had come back to D.C. that he and Brooke reconnected. He had been jogging through Montrose Park just a few blocks away, as he did almost every morning. She was walking her dog. They practically collided in front of the park's sphere-like sun dial. It was fate. Almost instantly, it seemed, she had brought him home with her. The dog must have known it had lost its place in Brooke's heart to Conrad, because it ran away the day before he moved in. Ever since it was like they had never been apart.

Until now. Until Serena had shown up at Arlington.

Conrad's thoughts turned to *Tom Sawyer* downstairs and the incomplete message he had deciphered. Just one more word to finish it.

He looked at Brooke, watched her full breasts rise and fall rhythmically and was convinced she was asleep. He slipped out of bed and glanced out the bedroom window. The black SUV was gone, but that didn't mean someone or something out there wasn't watching or listening.

He quietly walked downstairs, where he headed for the living room and retrieved the book from under the sofa. He didn't like hiding things from Brooke, mostly because he knew how much she hated it when he did. But he doubted he could bring up the book code without bringing up Serena—or looking like a liar if he failed to mention their encounter and she found out. And Brooke would. She always did.

He walked into the hallway bathroom, put the toilet lid down and sat with the book in the soft glow of the nightlight over the sink.

He looked up the last word from the book on Page 54: It was the word "land." When he finished writing it down, Conrad stared down at the note in his hand and the complete message his father left him:

SUN SHINES OVER SAVAGE LAND

What the hell did that mean? Was it simply the misguided musing of an old, disillusioned former Apollo astronaut and much despised Air Force general? Or did it mean something more? It had to mean something more, because it was intended only for Conrad—just like the astrological symbols on the obelisk. But why? And what was with the stand-alone numeric code 763 from the back of the obelisk? It had no correlation to the book code.

Conrad stared at the binding of *Tom Sawyer*, which lay open on the last page he had looked up. Something about it bothered him.

Conrad noted a slit where the binding separated. He opened it wider and realized there was a hidden pocket of some sort inside the cover of the book. He flipped through the rest of the book. All the other pages were fine and there was no other break in the binding. This secret slot was meant to hide something.

He carried the book into Brooke's study and found a letter opener in the drawer of her colonial rolltop desk. He folded the book back at page 54 and reached in with the letter opener to drag out an envelope.

It was yellowed with age. The word STARGAZER was written in faded bold script across it.

Conrad opened the envelope carefully and removed a folded document from inside. Unfolding it, he realized there was text on one side and some kind of map on the other.

Conrad instantly recognized the topography of the Potomac. He also recognized the layout. It was a terrestrial blueprint for Washington, D.C. In the upper left corner was the moniker WASHINGTONOPLE. In another corner was a watermark: TB.

Serena had to see this.

More fascinating still was the text on the other side of the map. It was a coded letter of some kind, and someone—his father, he assumed, based on the handwriting—had deciphered the salutation and signature. It was dated September 25, 1793.

The body of the letter was written in an alphanumeric code he didn't recognize. Probably a Revolutionary War–era military code. But the translated salutation was plain to see, and his hand trembled when he saw the signature. It was from General George Washington, and it began:

To Robert Yates and his chosen descendent in the Year of Our Lord 2008. . . .

5

THAT MORNING Conrad found Brooke downstairs at the breakfast table scanning five newspapers while the morning news shows blared on the TV, which she had split into six screens to follow the major broadcast and cable networks simultaneously. She was having her usual half grapefruit and Wasa cracker along with her coffee—some diet that she religiously followed from a Beverly Hills doctor to the stars. It required her to take a tiny scale with her wherever she went to weigh her food—no more than three ounces of anything at a time, no less than four hours apart.

"You're up early," she said as she poured him some coffee. "The *Post* ran a nice obit on your dad."

She showed him the picture and headline: *Body of Former Air Force General Found in Antarctica Laid to Rest*.

Conrad glanced at the photo of his dad, circa 1968, back in his "Right Stuff" days with NASA, a genuine American icon.

"I figured I might as well get a jump on the documentary for the Discovery Channel," he told Brooke. "You know, put the past behind and look ahead. So I'm going in early this morning to the offices in Maryland. See if Mercedes goes for it."

"Just see that she doesn't go for you, Con," Brooke said without looking up from her newspapers. "That one, unfortunately, isn't a nun."

Conrad paused, wondering if he had talked about Serena in his sleep. But then he noticed Serena on four channels of the TV screen. She was talking about the state of human rights in China on the eve of the Olympics, as well as China's status as the world's biggest polluter because of its high carbon emissions. The two other channels had segments about the bird flu, which had landed in North America and caused some poultry deaths but had not yet jumped to human-to-human contagion. That, of course, the expert with the mask on TV droned, was only a matter of time.

"I'll be careful," he laughed and kissed her goodbye.

Outside on the front steps, he looked out and noticed no suspicious vehicles. No spy types lurking in the shadows. He hurried down the sidewalk toward 31st Street and hailed a cab. He climbed inside and said, "Union Station."

Brooke watched Conrad disappear around the corner, then went into her study and stopped. Something was off. She scanned the shelves and noted a gap on the third shelf that caused some books to slant. Conrad had removed and replaced a book. *The* book, she suddenly realized, the one everybody had been looking for.

So he cracked the book code.

She walked over to the bookcase, removed *Tom Sawyer,* and flipped through the pages. She was about to put the book back and call it in when she noticed a break in the binding. There was a slit, revealing some sort of hidden pocket. She swore.

Hands shaking, she went to the kitchen and returned with a razor blade. Carefully she traced the inside cover until she formed a kind of flap. Ever so gently she peeled it back to reveal the empty pocket and, inside the flap, a smudge trace of writing. An imprint of some kind.

In a fog of dread she marched into the foyer and held up the book to the mirror, barely able to force herself to look. There in the mirror the word shone clear: STARGAZER.

"Holy shit," she gasped.

The map had been in her house all along, inside the book, right under her nose, and she had missed it.

She speed-dialed a local number in Georgetown on her coded cell phone. She identified herself to the agent who answered.

"This is SCARLETT," she said. "I've got a Priority One message for OSIRIS."

6

Conrad didn't recognize the tail until the young male attendant in the first-class compartment of the Acela Express came by to present a choice of hot or cold breakfasts. Conrad chose the bran flakes. The only other passenger in the compartment, a man who looked like an NFL linebacker crammed into a suit, ordered the Big Bob Egg Scramble.

That's how Conrad knew he was a federal agent. Only a fed on the taxpayer's dime would go first-class and order the Big Bob Egg Scramble, which sounded like Amtrak's version of a shrimp cocktail.

So much for the privacy he had sought by upgrading from business class after the attendant told him the first-class car was empty: Apparently none of the other passengers thought the Egg Scramble was worth the extra $80.

Except Big Bob a few seats back.

Conrad swore to himself and looked out the giant picture window at the barren pastures of Pennsylvania flashing by. The Acela Express was the fastest train on the continent, racing at speeds up to 150 miles an hour between Washington, D.C., and New York City. Conrad had hoped to reach Serena before lunch and make it back to Brooke by dinner without anybody knowing. Obviously, he wasn't moving fast enough.

Because there sat Big Bob, smiling at the attendant as he took a couple of tubs of cream and three blue packets of artificial sweetener with his coffee and pretended to peruse the *Wall Street Journal* until his Egg Scramble arrived.

Conrad got up from his seat and, without looking back, walked down the aisle to one of two bathrooms at the end of the car closest to the locomotive.

Conrad closed the door and braced himself. "Acela" was one of those names made up by some New York branding company that combined the words "acceleration" and "excellence." The secret to the Acela's speed was its ability to tilt in curves without slowing down or spooking passengers. Conrad could feel a slight tilt coming on now as he looked at himself in the mirror and thought about what he was doing.

He couldn't involve Brooke in any of this, for her own sake. At least that's what he told himself. Maybe he just didn't want her to know he was involved at all with Serena. But Brooke was a big girl. She knew he had never made her any promises. She probably also knew, better than he perhaps, just how slim the odds were of his ever getting together with Serena.

Facing the mirror, he slowly unbuttoned his shirt to reveal the envelope he had taped to himself. He removed the map from inside and flipped it over to look at the text:

763.618.1793

634.625. ghquip hiugiphipv 431. Lqfilv Seviu 282.625. siel 43. qwl 351. FUUO.

179 ucpgiliuv erqmqaciu jgl 26. recq 280.249. gewuih 707.5.708. jemcms. 282.682.123.414.144. qwl qyp nip 682.683.416.144.625.178. Jecmwli ncabv rlqxi 625.549.431. qwl gewui. 630. gep 48. ugelgims 26. piih 431. ligqnniphcpa 625.217.101.5. uigligs 2821.69. uq glcvcgem 5. hepailqwu eu 625. iuvefmcubnipv 431. qwl lirwfmcg.

280. qyi 707.625. yqlmh 5.708.568.283.282. biexip. 625. uexeqi 683. ubqy 707.625. yes.

711

All his father had translated was the alphanumeric salutation—*To the chosen descendent of Robert Yates in the Year of Our Lord 2008*—and the numeric signature—*General George Washington*. Perhaps his father thought that was enough information for him to crack the rest of the cipher. Or perhaps his father could never figure it out.

All Conrad really knew about Robert Yates was that his father's side of the family had adopted the "Yeats" spelling to distance themselves from Robert Yates, who was one of America's more controversial Founding Fathers. Besides helping to draft the first Constitution for the State of New York, he represented New York as a key delegate at the convention in Philadelphia to draft the U.S. Constitution.

That's where things got ugly.

For it soon became clear to all that the Constitutional Convention, under the leadership of George Washington, wasn't tweaking the Articles of Confederation among the thirteen states as advertised. It was creating a new, centralized power: the federal government. A new sovereignty with the power to levy taxes and maintain an army.

That's when Robert Yates berated Washington, stormed out of the proceedings, and did everything in his power to defeat ratification of the U.S. Constitution, going so far as to run for New York governor in 1789. He failed. But in 1790 he became Chief Justice of the New York Supreme Court, and for the rest of his life was one of America's fiercest and most outspoken defenders of state rights and critics of federal authority.

Even the grave couldn't silence Yates. In 1821, twenty years after his death, his notes from the Constitutional Convention were published under the title *Secret Proceedings and Debates of the Convention Assembled . . . for the Purpose of Forming the Constitution of the United States.* By then, of course, the Louisiana Purchase had doubled the number of states in America, and the notion of still questioning the constitutionality of the federal government became, well, embarrassing for the family.

That's about the time, Conrad recalled, that his father's branch of the family stopped calling itself "Yates" and joined their cousins by spelling their surname "Yeats."

At least that's what Conrad could recall. He never paid much attention to the Yeats family tree growing up because he was adopted.

Conrad felt another tilt and acceleration as the Acela took a curve. He taped the map with the text under the phone shelf and buttoned up his shirt. Somehow he had to elude Big Bob and reach Serena.

He pulled out his Vertu cell phone and was tempted to dial Serena's private number to arrange a pickup at Penn Station. But he slipped it back into his pocket, figuring that somehow Big Bob's friends would be listening. Ditto for any text messages.

Instead he would have to use one of the train's onboard phone booths in the dining car. And for that, he'd need a credit or debit card, and it would have to belong to somebody else.

When Conrad emerged from the lavatory, breakfast had been served on the extra large tray tables. He walked past his seat, which still said OCCUPIED on the LED readout in the overhead bin console, picked up his coffee, and went straight up to Big Bob, who had already scarfed down half his Egg Scramble.

Conrad said, "Looks like you overdid it with the Tabasco sauce."

Big Bob glanced down at the orange smudge on his tie and swore. He dabbed it with his napkin as the train took another curve.

Conrad went with it, swaying enough to spill his coffee on Big Bob. The guy bolted in his seat, knocking the tray table up and hitting his head on the overhead bin.

"Gosh, I'm sorry," said Conrad, steadying Big Bob as he slipped his hand inside the guy's suit and lifted his wallet.

Big Bob said, "What's the matter with you?"

"Let me get something from the snack car for you," Conrad said, slipping the wallet into his own pocket and walking away. "My apologies."

Conrad approached two pneumatically operated sliding glass doors. They whooshed aside like the deck of the *Starship Enterprise*, and he passed through the spacious and quiet intercar passageway into business class.

Both business cars were half full, maybe forty passengers each, most busying themselves with their newspapers, laptops, and iPods when they weren't cursing at their BlackBerries and mobile phones for cutting out in the middle of conversations.

He passed through two more sliding doors to reach the snack car. About a dozen patrons were in the lounge area, perched uncomfortably on the high and low stool seating. A plasma TV on the wall flashed highlights of the weekend in sports.

At the far end of the snack car was a business center with a fax machine, copier, and two onboard Railfones, one of them in an enclosed booth. Conrad stepped inside. The Railfone didn't accept coins or bills and required payment by a major credit card. Fortunately, Conrad had a Visa card with the name Derrick Kopinski, Sergeant Major of the Marine Corps, aka "Big Bob."

Conrad dialed Serena's number and looked at Kopinski's ID card while the other end rang. The driver's li-

cense had him in Oceanside, CA. That meant Kopinski
had until recently been stationed out of Camp Pendle-
ton. Kopinski was a Marine. Probably green at the Pentagon. Definitely DOD, one of SecDef Packard's men.
An E-9 Special pay grade.

Besides forty dollars in cash, Kopinski's wallet included a picture of his wife and kids in a Sears portrait,
for sure. She looked like Goose's wife from *Top Gun*, a
young Meg Ryan. Very nice. Same with the kids, who
fortunately looked more like their mother. Even a little
baby baptism card. Eastern Orthodox. And coupons for
Starbucks coffee, McDonald's Extra Value meals, and
Dunkin' Donuts. Lots of Dunkin' Donuts coupons.
Jeez, they didn't pay this guy enough.

The call finally connected and Conrad got a voice-
mail from Serena speaking French that asked him to
leave a voice or text message. Before he could punch in
anything the signal cut out and the call was dropped.

Conrad hung up and paused for a moment. He removed the envelope from his body and taped it to the
underside of the shelf beneath the phone. Then he buttoned up and stepped out of the booth.

Back in first class, Sergeant Major Kopinski was waiting for him. As soon as the glass doors opened, Conrad
saw him standing there, jacket open to reveal a shoulder-
holstered gun. The stain on his tie looked even bigger.

"I want my wallet, Dr. Yeats."

"Yes, sir." Conrad handed it over and looked back to
make sure they were out of view of the business car and
alone in first class. They were.

"This mission can't be what you intended for your

life when you enlisted in the Marines, Sergeant Major," Conrad said. "You tell Packard to give you a real assignment."

Kopinski nodded, then to Conrad's dismay started convulsing. Kopinski's eyes rolled back in their sockets and something green began to leak out his nostrils.

Then he saw a tiny dart in the Marine's neck as the head tilted to the side unnaturally and the heavy body crumpled to the floor with a thud. He was dead. Conrad spun around to see the glass doors into first class wide open and the attendant pointing some sort of dart gun at him.

"You just killed a federal agent," Conrad said.

"Hand it over," the assassin said. "Slowly."

Conrad reached into his pocket and pulled out Kopinski's wallet.

"Forget the wallet." The assassin stepped forward, still pointing the gun.

"Who are you?" Conrad asked.

"The Grim Reaper, as far as you're concerned." The assassin waved the dart gun at him. "Turn around."

Conrad turned to face the picture window. More bland pastures passing by. He felt the assassin pat him down.

"Take off your boots."

Conrad removed his boots.

The assassin looked at them and then back at him. "Unbutton your shirt."

"I'm not that kind of guy."

The assassin tapped the point of his dart gun on Conrad's chest. "Open your damn shirt."

Conrad could see the guy's eyes were on fire, meaning business. He unbuttoned his shirt and pulled it open to show nothing but his chest. "I work out, as you can see."

"Where is it?"

"Where is what?"

"Whatever you took from that little book of yours."

Conrad said, "If you people did anything to hurt Brooke, I'll kill you."

"You should be worried about what we're going to do to you."

The assassin whipped the butt of the gun against the side of Conrad's head, and lightning flashed across Conrad's field of vision. The searing pain made it a struggle for him to stay standing.

"Give it to me," the assassin ordered, "or I'll open your ass to look for it."

"You know, that's just where I've got it." Conrad, his head throbbing, began to unbuckle his belt. "You look like the kind of guy who'd like to search for it there."

Conrad bent over, his butt up to the assassin's face, his own face inches over poor Kopinski on the floor, the guy's Egg Scramble and Tabasco sauce all over his shirt. He thought of the guy's wife and kids. A *Marine*, for Christ's sake. And this little shit behind him killed him.

"Now take a good, hard look," Conrad said. "You don't want to miss anything."

Conrad dropped his pants with one hand and reached into Kopinski's jacket with the other. He suddenly straightened up and turned around, his pants around his ankles. The assassin's eyes were looking down where they shouldn't, missing Conrad's arm swinging up with Kopinski's gun.

"Surprise," said Conrad and shot him in the stomach.

The bullet blew the assassin against the wall, and he crumpled to the floor in a fetal position.

Conrad looked back through both sets of glass doors into the other car to make sure nobody heard the shot, then leaned over and dug the pistol into the guy's neck. "Who are you people?"

The assassin's mouth broke into a wide, wicked grin. Conrad saw the cyanide capsule between his teeth. But before he could bite down on the suicide pill, Conrad smashed his front teeth with the butt of the pistol. The assassin started choking on his teeth and swallowed the capsule.

"Gonna take you a little longer to die now," Conrad told him. "And you don't have to. You can still get some medical help. But only if you tell me who you people are."

The assassin only glared at him.

"I see you still have a few teeth left." Conrad held up the pistol for another blow. "I think I can fix that."

The assassin didn't flinch, even as he coughed up some blood. "You'll be dead by sunset."

Conrad bent closer. "Says who?"

"The Alignment," the assassin gasped through his bloody teeth, and then slumped over, dead.

Conrad ripped open the man's uniform and found a BlackBerry device. There was nothing else on him except the strange dart gun on the floor. Conrad took the BlackBerry and tucked Kopinski's gun behind his back.

He dragged both corpses to the port galley in the first-class car, where he found the body of the real attendant. He stood and looked at all three bodies and shook his head. He'd have all of twenty minutes tops before they were found after they pulled into New York. He looked at his watch. It was 10:30. They were due in Penn Station in a half hour.

Back in the snack car, he had to wait five minutes to use the Railfone booth. He slid inside, felt beneath the metal shelf counter and pulled out the envelope with the map inside that he had taped to the underside. Then he called Serena.

7

UNITED NATIONS HEADQUARTERS
NEW YORK CITY

IN THE PANTHEON of modern megalithic architecture, China's new 25-kilometer-long venue for the 2008 Olympic Games—humbly dubbed the "Axis of Human Civilization"—was a sure bet to join America's interstate highway system, Central America's Panama Canal, and Europe's Chunnel as one of the great wonders of the modern world.

But to Serena Serghetti, now standing before the General Assembly, it was an environmental disaster, a state-run catastrophe that was endangering animals, destroying ancient temples, and driving more than a million people from their homes. All because China wanted to show the world that it had come of age.

"Now we have reports of avian influenza—or 'bird flu'—spreading in the squalor of the countryside where the homeless have been exiled," she said. "But the government has refused to even acknowledge the threat of a global health pandemic, let alone help the poorest of its own people."

Naturally, the Chinese ambassador to the United Nations didn't see it that way and seemed visibly annoyed.

This morning alone he had been forced to deny accusations that his country actively suppressed free speech and systematically imprisoned and executed people to harvest their organs. Now he had to contend with reports of avian flu just weeks before the Olympic Games in Beijing.

"We beg to differ," was all he said through a translator. "The industrialization and development of Beijing has created a rising standard of living for our people and better health care."

"At least allow us to help your needy, Mr. Ambassador."

Serena cited a report on relief efforts following the 2004 tsunami in Indonesia and the 2005 hurricane that wiped out New Orleans, events that also displaced more than a million people.

"As the head of FEMA has stated, some of the world's problems are just too big for governments," she said. "But the global church—Catholics, Protestants, and Orthodox together—is present in more than a million distribution plants worldwide. For food, shelter, vaccines, relief supplies, and helping hands, there's a local church on the ground wherever disaster strikes. And we're ready to help you."

"I am sure you are, Sister Serghetti, but we can take care of our own people," said the Chinese ambassador, and further discussion was tabled.

As Serena returned to her seat, she could think of at least one other person who would beg to differ: Conrad Yeats. She had left him for the work of the Church, the very hope of the world she was proclaiming in this chamber. But in Conrad's mind it was the Church that had denied him her love.

She picked up her bulky but lightweight white earpiece and sat down. Most delegates needed translators from the interpreter booths overhead to follow along. But not Serena, who was fluent in many of the world's languages. She used the earpiece to pick up messages unobtrusively and write them down. Now a voice in Italian told her that the media room said that "Carlton Yardley" from *The New Atlantis* magazine was there for his scheduled interview with her.

Her heart skipped a beat.

He must have found something, she thought, although she was embarrassed to realize she didn't care if he had nothing to show her but his face. His unshaven, stubbled face.

As soon as she could step outside the chamber and into the crowded visitors' lobby, Serena pulled out her iPhone and called Benito to bring the car out from the private garage. She scanned the cavernous glass atrium. The media line was at the entrance, behind the blue velvet rope. She started walking in that direction when Max Seavers stepped into view, blocking her path to Conrad.

"Serena!" Max said, smiling.

Serena stopped in her tracks.

Before he was tapped by the American president to help with the Department of Defense, Max Seavers had helped her humanitarian efforts in Africa and Asia on a number of occasions by donating vaccines. She couldn't just blow him off now.

"*Déjà vu,* Max. Weren't we standing here just a few

days ago with you showing me some rather unusual photographs? What brings you back?"

"Sounding the alarm here and on Capitol Hill about the coming flu pandemic. What about you? I hear you were telling the Chinese where to stick their new dam."

Serena couldn't help glancing over his shoulder toward the media line, where various cameras were set up to catch the comings and goings of dignitaries. She spotted Conrad, and he saw her and motioned.

"I suppose you have an opinion on the new Beijing?" she said as she started walking away from the entrance and toward the delegates lounge.

"A technological marvel," Max said, keeping pace with her. "You've got to give the Chinese credit for that. They've left nothing to chance. Even the date of the opening ceremonies on August eighth was chosen because the number 8 represents good fortune to the Chinese."

"I see. That's the eighth day of the eighth month of the eighth year of the new millennium," Serena said, pretending to marvel. "And I used to think three sixes in a row was the devil's number. Tell me, Max, what about the million souls the Olympics are displacing?"

"You mean driving from their homes which had no running water or electricity in the first place?" he said. "Sounds like progress to me."

Serena glanced sideways at him as she walked. "And the destruction of the ancient temples, their history?"

"Obviously the Chinese don't care about their ancient temples as much as you do, Serena. That's because the Chinese are looking to the future. They know that in time some other civilization is going to do the same thing to their Olympic Park that they're doing to those ancient temples."

She came to a halt. "I wonder if you'd feel the same way if these temples were the ones about to be destroyed?" She pointed out toward the Manhattan skyline—away from Conrad in the media area.

Max Seavers followed her finger and smiled. "If it was some act of God—like the tsunami, I'd be devastated. But if it was our government doing the submerging, for the betterment of the country, like the Chinese, then yes. Have you seen this?"

Serena realized he was referring to the nearby display of a model city in the lobby. It was the official Olympic Venue Construction Plan for Beijing. A nameplate read "Axis of Human Civilization." More PR.

"Impressive, Serena, isn't it?"

Serena looked at the model of the city's new Central Axis. The Chinese had successfully constructed a 25-kilometer-long boulevard connecting the new Olympic Park in the north with the Imperial Forbidden City and Tiananmen Square in the city center. She noted a stretch of avenue labeled "thousand-year path."

"It's certainly audacious, Max," she said. "This Beijing axis looks like the New Berlin that Hitler never got to build."

Max chuckled. "Funny you should say that. Because it was designed by Albert Speer Jr., the son of the architect who designed the New Berlin for Hitler's grandiose empire, the 'world capital Germania,' the capital of the so-called Thousand Year Reich."

Serena said, "You're joking."

"No." Max shook his head. "Charming old man, incredibly gifted. Tried to hire him myself for SeaGen's corporate headquarters in La Jolla, but the Chinese outbid me."

Serena stared at the model city. "Is Speer trying to copy his father or outdo him?"

"That's what the German news magazine *Die Welt* asked when the plan was unveiled," he said. "But it's all nonsense, of course. The Chinese insist Speer's design simply fulfills their own intentions of creating a central axis, and that the idea was laid out in the planning of the imperial capital centuries ago. I think the real point of interest is where the elder Speer found his inspiration for the New Berlin in the first place."

Serena shrugged. "You've got me, Max."

"Pierre L'Enfant's design for the National Mall in Washington, D.C.," he said. "What's more, Speer maintained that L'Enfant's plan was itself based on earlier source maps going back to ancient Egypt and Atlantis. That's Doctor Yeats's specialty, isn't it?"

Serena wasn't going to bite. Nothing good could come out of lingering here even a moment longer.

"Atlantis?" she asked, giving him a dubious look. "Now don't get all mystic on me, Max. We need you to keep those vaccines coming."

With that she turned and briskly walked away, exhaling slowly. As she approached the media line by the entrance, she was aware of Conrad in the pack. She walked right past him without a glance to the waiting limousine and got in. Benito closed the door, slid behind the wheel and drove away.

8

FURIOUS TO SEE Serena pressing the flesh with none other than that pseudo-philanthropist-billionaire Max Seavers, and feeling helpless because he couldn't risk being seen, Conrad walked out of the U.N., weaving between the flagpoles in front until he was far enough away to hail a cab and climb inside.

"Christie's," he said as the driver pulled away from the curb and into the lunch hour traffic. The driver glanced at him in the mirror and asked where Christie lived. "Rockefeller Center. She's an auction house."

Conrad didn't know where else to go until he could reach Serena, and he didn't want to tell the driver to just "drive." Worst case, there was a cute assistant curator at Christie's that he had seen off and on whenever he was in New York. Ironically enough, her name was Kristy. Maybe she could make some sense of the map, or at least its monetary value, and refer him to somebody outside the federal government who could help him decode the text.

Conrad took out the cell phone he had lifted off the body of the assassin aboard the Acela. He had tossed his own phone under the tracks before leaving the platform at Penn Station. The question was whether anybody had found the bodies yet and been sharp enough to start tracking this phone. Probably not. Hopefully not.

He keyed in Serena's number from memory and listened to it ring on the other end.

The driver's phone beeped at the same time. "Yeah?" he said.

Conrad heard the cabbie loud and clear—on his phone.

"Yeah?" the cabbie repeated.

A cold shudder passed through Conrad's body. He stared at the phone's display and realized he had redialed the last number the assassin called. Conrad looked up at the rearview mirror in time to see the slits of the driver's eyes widen.

"You're one of them," Conrad said and pointed the gun he lifted from the dead Marine at the driver's head.

Too late Conrad noticed the driver had only one hand on the wheel and ducked as a bullet burst from the front seat and shattered the rear window.

Conrad pumped a bullet into the back of the driver's seat. The bullet shattered the driver's spine and he slumped forward onto the steering wheel, his arms loose at his side.

Conrad felt sick to his stomach. He tapped the driver on the back of the head. The man's head rolled to the side, revealing a trickle of blood running down his neck.

The cab suddenly accelerated wildly.

Conrad lunged over the seat and put his arms over the corpse to reach the steering wheel, but the car was careening out of control.

A flash in the rearview mirror caught his eye and he looked back through the blown-out rear windshield to see an unmarked Ford Explorer with federal plates and red lights coming up from behind. Suddenly Conrad's shock turned to rage. He wrenched the steering wheel toward the road and the cab shot off.

The federal car gave chase, but Conrad quickly turned the wheel while pulling the brake lever, sliding the cab sideways with a long skid. Then he turned it against the street direction, driving straight toward the Explorer.

The driver of the Explorer didn't have a chance to remove his seat belt and pull out a gun. And he couldn't swerve in time before Conrad drove the cab head-on into the black SUV. Conrad's face slammed into the corpse on impact and bounced back in time for him to see the airbags inflate in the federal car.

He heard sirens closing in a minute later. He staggered out of the cab, his ears still ringing from the crash. Or was that the sound of police sirens growing louder? There was a squeal of brakes. A voice called, "Hey!"

It was Serena calling from the open window of a Mercedes limousine. She kicked open the rear door with the Vatican emblem on it and motioned him inside.

Conrad paused for a second, thunderstruck. She was a vision from heaven. Her lips were moving but he couldn't hear anything. He dove into the back, the door slamming shut behind him as the limousine peeled away.

"Anything else you want to destroy, Conrad, or are we finished for now?" said Serena as Benito swung them into traffic on First Avenue.

He stared at her, incredulous. In her black Armani suit and white silk blouse, she looked completely unruffled.

"I'm fine, thanks."

"Too bad I can't say the same for that poor Amtrak attendant and Marine the police band says you killed," she said softly. "Please tell me the Alignment was responsible."

He stared at her. "You know about the Alignment?"

"If you're referring to the secret, centuries-old organization of military imperialists, then yes," she said. "What an amateur you are, Conrad. The Church has been at war with the New World Order for eons. From the way you talk, you'd think you discovered it. Now hand it over so I can at least make sure you found the proper document."

He produced the map and Serena took it from his hands.

Conrad watched as Serena slowly scanned the map and then flipped it over to study the text. Her hands began to tremble, and Conrad swore he saw what looked like the tiniest pearl of perspiration on her smooth forehead long before she had reached the last paragraph. Conrad had never seen Sister Serena Serghetti, the Vatican's top linguist, ever break a sweat.

She looked up at Conrad in wonder. "You're Star-gazer."

"What?"

She pushed a button on the partition to reveal Benito in front. "Benito," she said. "The jet."

"*Si, signorina.*"

Conrad recalled that Benito was a former Swiss Special Forces soldier, a crack marksman, and the only Vatican bodyguard who could keep up with Serena on the slopes at Davos during World Economic Forums. He hoped the same was true for the streets of New York City.

"What's going on, Serena?" Conrad asked. "Less than twenty-four hours after you show up on the scene, people die, and my life goes into the crapper."

"That's why we have to get you out of here. You're in grave danger, and so is America and the whole world."

Suddenly a phone started ringing up front and Conrad jumped. The ringtone sounded familiar. It was an old Elton John song, "Benny and the Jets." Benito the driver didn't bother to pick up.

"The jet is fueling up at the airstrip, *signorina*," Benito said. "If we can reach it."

They turned a corner and Conrad saw the flashing lights of several blue-and-white police cars blocking the road. A young cop approached the limo, hand on his weapon.

"Alignment?" Conrad asked.

"God knows these days. Say your prayers."

Conrad looked at Serena, who crossed one leg over

the other and then pulled out a flap revealing a space beneath the rear seat of the limo.

"You're kidding me, right?" he asked.

"Get under and shut up," she told him.

"Whatever happened to the missionary position?"

"May God have mercy on your soul, you wanker." She gave him a final kick inside and pushed the flap back into position behind him.

"Easy does it, Benito." Her voice sounded muffled to Conrad in the dark. He could feel the car slow to a halt. The squeak of a window lowering came next, then Serena's voice. "Yes, officer?"

There was a long pause, and Conrad crouched very still in the darkness. Then he heard the young cop clearing his throat. "Sister Serghetti," he said. "It's an honor."

"Is there a problem, Officer O'Donnell?" she said, reading his badge.

Thank God, thought Conrad. An Irish Catholic cop.

"Nothing concerning you, Sister. Looks like terrorists failed at both Penn Station and the United Nations."

"Is everything OK?"

"Nothing was stolen or destroyed," the officer told her. "But two federal agents, an Amtrak employee, and a cabbie were killed."

"I'm so sorry. Is there anything I can do to help? Do you need to search my car?"

Beneath the seat Conrad punched her in the rear.

"No, ma'am. That won't be necessary. To begin with, you've got diplomatic plates and a search would be illegal."

Conrad heard a shout and then a screech as one of the squad cars reversed and the Mercedes lurched forward as they were waved on through.

"God's angels watch over you, *signorina*," said Benito.

No, Benito, Conrad thought. *She's the angel.*

9

ROME
JUNE 24

THE NEXT MORNING Serena stared out through the tinted glass of another limo at the towering ancient obelisk in St. Peter's Square as Benito drove through the gates of Vatican City. She thought of Conrad and wondered if it was wise to have left him back at the secret safe house outside New York City before flying here to press their case.

There were a few police outside on the plaza, but no tourists or *paparazzi* this early in the day. More pigeons than people, really.

"Not like the old days, *signorina*," said Benito, referring to the protestors and media circus that once surrounded her arrivals at the Vatican.

Back then she was only in her 20s but had already made a lifetime's worth of enemies as "Mother Earth" in the petroleum, timber, and biomedical industries— anyone who put profit ahead of people, animals, or the environment. Today she was an older and wiser 31, but the damage was done: Those inside the Vatican who had ties to these outside governments, corporate CEOs, and other "deep pockets" still didn't trust her and never would.

Which was why she had decided Conrad was better off back at the safe house.

"That was another era, Benito."

"Another pope, *signorina*."

They curved along a winding drive and arrived at the entrance of the *Governorate*. The Swiss Guards in their crimson uniforms snapped to attention as Serena walked in.

The old pope, by favoring her with his friendship, had protected her within these walls. In one significant way he still did. Before he died, he shared with her a vision he believed God had revealed to him about the end of the world. And he let others know as much. The halo effect ensured that at least some door would always be open to her here.

The new pope she hardly knew. He was a good man, although she had heard that he had voiced his displeasure at the special favor his predecessor had shown her. Which was reasonable, she concluded, given that the new pope knew her only by her nickname among his former peers in the College of Cardinals: "Sister Pain-in-the-Ass."

That included Cardinal Tucci, gatekeeper of the secret maps collections. She had called Tucci from somewhere over the Atlantic to demand access to the Vatican archives, an extraordinary privilege she had enjoyed under the old pope but which Tucci had revoked with the new pope.

"Sister Serghetti," Tucci said flatly when she entered his office, which was tucked away at the end of an obscure hallway, reached only by an old service elevator. "Welcome back."

Tucci rose from his high-back leather chair, a pair of seventeenth-century Bleau globes on either side, and extended his hand. Only in his late 40s, Tucci was a "secret cardinal." That is, he was appointed by the pope to the position and nobody else was informed of it, although Serena was aware of two others besides herself who also knew.

A secret cardinal to hide the secrets of the Church.

Every Christian, Serena knew all too well, must wrestle with the tension of living in this world without becoming a product of it. But she suspected that Cardinal Tucci had lost that battle a long time ago.

"Your Eminence," she said, and kissed his ring with the Dominus Dei insignia. *Dominus Dei* meant "Rule of God" and was an order within the Church that predated the Jesuits and traced itself back to the first Christians who served in the palace of Caesar in the first century. Secrecy was their highest value, as it meant survival in the early days of Christianity. Serena didn't like secrecy. It had become an excuse over the centuries for a host of crimes, crimes that made the fictionalized evils of Dominus Dei's upstart cousins in Opus Dei look like acts of charity.

"To what do I owe this pleasure?" he asked suspiciously as they sat down.

"I want to see the L'Enfant Confession," she said, just like that.

Tucci looked at her with undisguised disdain. He seemed tired of her already, and perturbed. Perturbed because she had pressed his aides to wake him up in the wee hours of the morning to take her call. Perturbed by her very existence.

If Tucci wondered how she got as far as she had within the Church, the feeling was mutual. He was boyish by Vatican standards and yet mature enough to sport the smile of a man who experienced enough of life to find it a bad joke. Even his name was ironic, implying he was some indigenous Italian bureaucrat when, in fact, his mother's side of the family came to America on the Mayflower and was Yankee through and through. He came to the Vatican by way of Boston, where he was known as a raucous but brilliant student at Harvard and an even more brilliant priest and professor of American history at Boston College. He had risen very far in Rome, very fast.

Even now, as she awaited a response, Serena couldn't help noticing, with some envy, the medallion that Tucci wore around his neck. In its center was an ancient Roman coin, a silver denarius with the image of the emperor Tiberius. Legend had it that this coin was the very "Tribute Penny" Jesus held up when he told his followers that they should "render unto Caesar what is Caesar's and unto God what is God's." It had been passed down through the ages, from one leader of the Dei to the next. Some argued it represented power greater than the papacy.

"The L'Enfant Confession?" Tucci repeated, as if he had never heard of it.

Serena said, "The deathbed confession of Pierre L'Enfant, the original architect of Washington, D.C., to John Carroll, the first Catholic bishop of North America."

Tucci looked mystified. "What exactly did Pierre L'Enfant confess?"

"Something to the effect that the major terrestrial monuments of America's capital city are aligned like a map to the stars, as are Egypt's pyramids and South America's Way of the Dead," she said.

"What do you mean the monuments are aligned like a map?"

She showed him a digital photo of General Yeats's tombstone at Arlington, of the side with the four astrological symbols. "These are the zodiac signs for the sun and the constellations Boötes, Virgo, and Leo. Each celestial coordinate has a terrestrial counterpart in the city of Washington, D.C."

"And you're telling me that George Washington had L'Enfant use these constellations to anchor America's capital city?" He inflected his voice in a tone to hint at just how ridiculous and a waste of time the idea was. He glanced at the antique clock on the wall to underscore his displeasure.

"Yes," she said without flinching. "And we can follow those monuments that correspond to the stars like a treasure map."

"And where does this heavenly treasure trail lead?"

"To a specific place beneath the National Mall, or perhaps even a specific date in America's future," she said. "I was hoping you could tell me."

"My forte is American history and cartography, Sister Serghetti, not eschatology," Tucci said, amused. "But, as a historian, I know that Pierre L'Enfant was a Freemason. And I don't have to refer to my *Freemasons for Dummies* book to tell you that his secret society—like all those who seek the light of God outside of the Holy Church—has had a long and tortured history with us. So you'll have to forgive my skepticism when I ask you why on earth would L'Enfant confess anything to a Catholic priest, let alone Archbishop John Carroll, about this alleged secret geography of the American capital?"

"You mean why under the earth," Serena said, confident that Tucci knew full well what she was about to say. That's why she had come to him in the first place. "It was Daniel Carroll, the Archbishop's brother, who owned Capitol Hill and sold it to Washington. All that land, by the way, once belonged to a Catholic named Francis Pope who called it Rome."

Tucci tapped two fingers to his lips as he looked at her thoughtfully. Finally, he cleared his throat and sat back in his chair.

"There is no L'Enfant Confession, Sister Serghetti," he said. "Never was."

"Like the Alignment?" she asked.

Tucci frowned, aware that she had him there. After all, the sole reason his own group Dominus Dei still existed was allegedly to fight the Alignment threat to the Church. Without the Alignment—fact or fiction—there could be no funding, no foot soldiers for Tucci's order coming from the pope.

"The Alignment is simply an umbrella term for all

secret societies aligned against the Church and operating in the shadows of power around the world," Tucci said. "Don't tell me you sincerely believe it's an actual group of warriors who trace their ancient knowledge to the survivors of Atlantis and use the stars to control world events to their own ultimate agenda? Please."

"I didn't until now," she said. "But George Washington was a Mason. As was his chief architect, Pierre L'Enfant. As were fifty of the fifty-six signers of the American Declaration of Independence. Perhaps you could humor me and tell me what link the Masons have to the Alignment—if the Alignment were, in fact, an actual group."

"Why, the Knights Templar, of course," Tucci said, obliging her with a conspiratorial smile.

Tucci was referring to a tiny band of nine French Crusaders at the end of the first millennium who for nine years protected pilgrims visiting Jerusalem. Legend, Serena knew, suggested they were really searching for some priceless relic like the Holy Grail or a piece of the cross on which Jesus was crucified. Whatever it was, they apparently found it, because the Knights Templar over the next two centuries exploded in membership and money among Europe's nobility. The Church, threatened by the power and influence of its holy defenders, suddenly and expediently decided that the Knights Templar were conspiring to destroy it, and in 1307 launched a seven-year war that ended with the Grand Master of the Knights Templar being burned at the stake.

It was only last year, seven hundred years too late,

that the Vatican issued a formal apology for its persecution, and Serena knew that Tucci was that apology's key architect.

Serena said, "I thought the Church, through Dominus Dei, took care of the Knights Templar centuries ago."

"Not quite," said Tucci. "A few Knights escaped to Britain and formed a new network called Freemasonry, once again hijacking another society, this one formed of the builders and bricklayers of the great cathedrals and palaces of Europe. It was only a matter of time before the Masons came to America, penetrated its elites like George Washington, and used their influence to establish a new country and, they hoped, a new world order."

"So do you still consider the Masons to be a threat to the Church?"

"Hardly," Tucci said. "The Alignment long ago left the Masons, having moved on to controlling U.S. policy through the Council on Foreign Relations, the Trilateral Commission, and your friends at the United Nations."

There was a twinkle in Tucci's eyes, a glimmer of triumph that he had succeeded in utterly humiliating her for her gullibility and in drawing their little meeting to a resounding close.

"We could go on all day about this, Sister Serghetti," Tucci said. "But like I told you, there is no such thing as the L'Enfant Confession. It's a myth."

"So is this," she said and produced the map Conrad gave her.

Tucci bolted upright as she unfolded it on his desk. "Where did you get this?"

"From Stargazer," she said, and watched a flicker of recognition at the code name registered in Tucci's horrified eyes.

"Conrad Yeats," he muttered, putting his knowledge of her long-standing and controversial relationship with Conrad together with his knowledge of the Yeats family's long-standing history in American politics and the Masons. "Yeats is Stargazer. But, of course. I should have known."

"What matters is that it's the genuine article," Serena said, sensing she was on the verge of getting more out of this meeting with Tucci than she ever imagined.

Tucci grabbed a magnifier and leaned over the map. The upper left corner had the word WASHINGTON-OPLE, the original name for George Washington's namesake city.

"Mother of God!" Tucci exclaimed, truly awed.

He then passed the magnifier over the city radiants. The ornate, crown-like seal with the initials TB must have jumped into view, because he snapped his head back in wonder.

"That's the seal used by the English papermaker Thomas Budgen for paper he manufactured from 1770 until 1785," Serena told him, letting him know she had done her own analysis on the map.

"I know what it is," he said sharply.

Serena said, "I always thought L'Enfant's original blueprint for Washington, D.C., was either on display or in preservation at the Library of Congress."

"That one is a later draft that Washington submitted to Congress in 1791," Tucci said automatically. "What you have brought me is the original terrestrial blueprint for America's capital city, which L'Enfant's own handwriting here says is based on an earlier star map drawn by Washington's chief astronomer, Benjamin Banneker."

Tucci sank back in his chair and stared at her, his eyes sizing her up for the first time. It was obvious that he had underestimated her, and she could actually see the wheels turning in his head as he contemplated just how much she knew that she wasn't telling him, and just how much she knew that *he* knew.

"What else did the pontiff tell you before he died, Sister Serghetti?" Tucci asked. "I've heard the rumors. A fifth Fatima? A revelation of the Apocalypse?"

"Many things, Your Eminence," she said. "But today I come to discuss only one."

She could see the white flag of surrender waving in his eyes. "And so he still protects you."

"God alone is my refuge and strength," she demurred.

Tucci removed a leather binder from the center drawer of his desk, and out of the binder withdrew a single sheet of parchment that looked very much of the same stock as the map she had shown him. He passed it across the desk to her.

"This is what you wanted to see, Sister Serghetti."

Serena Serghetti slowly read the handwritten testimony of Pierre L'Enfant that had been signed by John Carroll. Her heart began to race long before she reached the last paragraph.

"L'Enfant claims that the relic that the Alignment found in Jerusalem through its proxies, the Knights Templar, was a celestial globe," she said, translating from the French as she studied the confession.

"Yes," said Tucci. "The globe once stood upon one of two pillars in King Solomon's temple. Masonic lore says that this globe was hollow and contained ancient scrolls detailing the history of human civilization and its sciences before the Great Flood, and thus before the Book of Genesis."

Serena read on.

L'Enfant claimed that the Alignment brought the globe to America through the Masons in order to use the ancient knowledge it contained to establish a new world order. By no coincidence, the globe came into the direct possession of General George Washington, perhaps America's most visibly prominent Mason and a Grand Master in the order.

But then Washington discovered that his Masons, and perhaps even his armies, were in fact controlled by the Alignment, whose vision of a new world order had little in common with the cause of freedom. Rather, they saw the United States as a blunt weapon they could use to smash the world's dynasties and pave the way for resurrecting Atlantis and its ancient faith in the stars and fate.

Washington knew he couldn't expose and destroy the Alignment without criminalizing the Masons and jeopardizing the fledgling United States itself. So immediately upon becoming America's first president in 1789, Washington secretly instructed L'Enfant to use astronomical charts drawn by his chief astronomer, Benjamin Banneker, to align the proposed capital city of Washington, D.C., to the constellation Virgo—as a warning sign for future Americans. His hope was that in time the American people would be free enough and strong enough to reject the Alignment's agenda.

L'Enfant concluded his confession by saying that he did not know the significance of the specific date in the distant future that Washington chose for the conjunction of monuments and stars, only that Washington buried the celestial globe containing the horrible secret he had discovered somewhere under the Federal Triangle.

Serena looked up from the text at Cardinal Tucci, seated in his massive throne-like chair with a Bleau globe on either side, one terrestrial and the other celestial. She stared at the celestial globe.

"Impossible," Serena said in disbelief. "Washington's celestial globe has been on display in his study at Mount Vernon for more than 200 years."

But Tucci looked sure as ever. "That globe is an inferior replacement made in England during the 1790s. Its surface, which is only papier-mâché, has been flaking so badly in recent years that it's been moved to the new museum at the estate for preservation. The original globe, according to L'Enfant, was made of bronze or copper and etched with the constellations. Washington buried it someplace under the American capitol sometime before he died."

Serena shifted uncomfortably in her seat as she glanced again at L'Enfant's confession.

"The handwriting holds up to analysis," Tucci said.

"Whether it's true or the blatherings of a madman is another thing entirely."

Tucci was known for playing things very close to his vestments. He was *not* known for wild speculation or outright disinformation. If he was sharing this information with her, it was because he believed it to be accurate.

"So L'Enfant says he followed Washington's instructions to lay out the city of Washington, D.C., so that key monuments would lock with key stars at a specific date in the future," Serena said. "A doomsday warning, if you will. And what's going to happen on that date is revealed by the celestial globe Washington buried."

"Or by what's inside the globe," Tucci said. "Not since the War of 1812 has anyone in Rome believed L'Enfant's confession. But if this map you've shown me is real and Stargazer is real, there can be little doubt that L'Enfant's confession is true. Which means America is in grave peril. Look at the end date."

She stared down at the date: July 4, 2008.

"So you see, Sister Serghetti, Stargazer has six days to stop the alignment of the monuments with the stars or the United States of America will cease to exist."

Serena said, "You mean stop the organization we call the Alignment."

"They are one and the same, Sister Serghetti," Tucci said. "If anything is going to happen in heaven and on earth in six days, you can be sure the Alignment will make it happen. They have been gathering strength for centuries. This conjunction of landmarks and stars—this metamorphosis of America into something its founders

never intended—is their *raison d'état*. Their twisted
sense of destiny is searching for any moral or legal justification to use the United States to unleash their will on
this world and wipe out their enemies *en masse*."

Serena couldn't hide her shock or skepticism. "By
what power, Your Eminence?"

"Perhaps by some new technology or weapon of mass
destruction or some natural wonder that can be ex-
ploited," Tucci said. "I don't know. Like I told you, I'm a
historian and not an eschatologist. But there is one thing
that I do know about America in Bible prophecy."

"What's that?" Serena asked.

"It isn't there," he said. "It's as if America never existed."

Serena grew very still, the utter insanity of everything
sinking in still deeper.

"So Washington set up the alignment of monuments
as a warning to Americans in the future," she said
slowly. "And Stargazer—Dr. Yeats—is a kind of ultimate
'sleeper' that Washington essentially sent into the future
to stop the Alignment."

"Crazy, I know," Tucci said. "And all from the lips of
Pierre L'Enfant, the pompous architect of the American
capital who spent his last penniless days wandering the
boulevards he laid out and bemoaning the changes from
his grand designs."

"So you think L'Enfant was a delusional *l'enfant*."

"I did until you gave me the original L'Enfant map
along with Washington's orders for Stargazer."

Serena looked Tucci in the eye, to avoid any doubt.
"You want me and Dr. Yeats to go under the capitol of

the New World Order to dig up this globe and save America from the Alignment."

"No," he said firmly. "I want you to bring the globe back to Rome."

Serena stared at him, feeling a tingle of fear creep up the back of her neck.

"The world is a better place because of the United States of America," Tucci said. "But world civilizations come and go. The Church is forever. If America should collapse as an imperial power or morph into something else, we must be prepared to confront a new New World Order."

"But Conrad . . . Dr. Yeats."

"Is never to see the inside of that globe should you come upon it," Tucci said. "Not if you want to save America, or him."

10

ABBEY OF OUR LADY OF LETTERS
WESTCHESTER COUNTY, NEW YORK

WHILE SERENA had run off to Rome with his map, Conrad was in hiding at her safe house way out in the hills of Westchester County, two hours north of New York City. Here at the Cistercian Abbey of Our Lady of Letters, the brethren wore robes, sang Gregorian chants, and ran an Internet retailer called Toned-Monks.com, which sold discounted printer cartridges and other office supplies to churches and charities.

According to the literature picked up by the school groups and tourists that visited the abbey by day, Toned-Monks.com was the brainchild of the honorary abbot, "Father McConnell," a member of the Catholic lay leadership organization known as the Knights of Columbus. In his former life McConnell had been a billionaire Wall Street hedge fund manager who decided it was far better to have something to live for than enough to live on.

The real story, however, was in a dimly lit, dank crypt beneath the abbey, where Conrad was working around the clock with a team of researchers to crack the codes from his father's tombstone and Washington's letter to Robert Yates.

The abbey and its front, TonedMonks.com, apparently did for Serena and the Vatican what venture capital fund In-Q-Tel did for the CIA: fund new technology to advance the kingdom, in this case the Kingdom of God. The abbey's specialty was document analysis. Serena ran the nuns and a secret archive of historical documents out of nearby Mount Saint Mary's, a local Dominican college on the Hudson where she taught on occasion, while McConnell ran the brothers and analysis in these crypts beneath this abbey.

The monks also made a mean espresso, and by his third day code-cracking Conrad was sleepless, fatigued, and jittery as he reviewed his progress on the screen before him.

He clicked on his digital chart table and reviewed the three constellations of Boötes, Leo, and Virgo. Using a digital pen he connected the alpha stars from each constellation—Arcturus, Regulus, and Spica—to draw a triangle.

He then called up a second window on his desktop, a scan of the terrestrial L'Enfant map, and placed it next to the celestial map. He used his digital pen to connect the three key markers on the terrestrial map labeled "Presidential Palace," "Congressional House," and "equestrian statue to honor Washington." Those were the early monikers for the White House, U.S. Capitol, and Washington Monument.

These, too, formed a triangle.

As he suspected all along, the star map mirrored key landmarks on the ground. The White House was aligned to the star Arcturus in the constellation Boötes, the U.S.

Capitol to the star Regulus in the constellation Leo, and the Washington Monument to the star Spica in the constellation Virgo.

But a triangle pointed nowhere.

That's what had stumped Conrad at the beginning. In the past he had used star maps to help find a specific location on earth—a secret chamber under the left paw of the Sphinx in Egypt, for example, or the Shrine of the First Sun in Atlantis. But this star map might as well be a circle, an endless loop. A star map was supposed to point to a specific location on earth.

Or a date in history.

That's when it all clicked for Conrad: These three key monuments along the Mall were not only each aligned to certain stars, but collectively to a celestial clock, to a single moment in time and space that any astronomer—or astro-archaeologist—conversant with the precession of equinoxes would know comes along only once every twenty-six thousand years.

It took him a few hours to work the astronomical calculations and correlate them with the astrology of L'Enfant's day, always a tedious task. That was because astrology was a bogus science, based on discredited beliefs. But it was upon those beliefs that ancient pyramids and monuments were once built. So not only did Conrad need to know some hard science, he had to reconcile it with the flawed worldview of a structure's builders during a particular era in history.

Finally, he was done.

Conrad typed in the password to launch his program and watched the screen. The triangles of the celestial and terrestrial maps slowly began to merge, the former on top of the latter. As they did, a digital calendar at the top of the desktop screen flashed like a cosmic odometer.

"Behold, the secret design of Washington, D.C.," he announced to himself.

He stared intently as the terrestrial and celestial triangles became one and the calendar clock froze at 07.04.2008.

July 4, 2008.

Conrad let out a breath. That was only five days away.

What's going to happen in five days?

"I'm wondering the same thing," said a voice from behind.

Conrad turned to see the abbot, Father McConnell, looking over his shoulder. Conrad must have spoken aloud. That or he was going crazy, which by the looks of his surroundings was becoming more plausible by the day.

"So you broke the astrological code, Dr. Yeats."

"The first level," Conrad said. "There's more to everything than meets the eye."

"There always is, son."

Conrad asked, "When is Serena coming back to return my terrestrial L'Enfant map with the Stargazer text on the back?"

"Tomorrow. Meanwhile, I found something for you from the archives at Mount Saint Mary's."

McConnell showed him a text written by Pierre L'Enfant in March of 1791, just after arriving to begin his preliminary survey. His work, L'Enfant wrote, would be like "turning a savage wilderness into a garden of Eden."

Conrad said, "So you think Washington's use of the term *savage* is referring to the original L'Enfant map Serena took, and that the map will show us the way to whatever we're supposed to find?"

"That's my bet," McConnell said. "But you don't look so sure."

"I think that's partly right. I get the impression that this savage is a person, but we'll need more to go on."

"Then we'll keep looking and leave you alone." McConnell walked away.

Conrad felt like he was getting his second wind after his breakthrough with the star map code. He was afraid he'd lose momentum if he stopped.

He turned his attention to the coded letter to Stargazer. The digital scan he had taken of the text remained a jumble of numbers.

763.618.1793

634.625. ghquip hiugiphipv 431. Lqfilv Seviu 282.625. siel 43. qwl 351. FUUO.

179 ucpgiliuv erqmqaciu jgl 26. recq 280.249. gewuih 707.5.708. jemcms. 282.682.123. 414.144. qwl qyp nip 682.683.416.144.625. 178. Jecmwli ncabv rlqxi 625.549.431. qwl gewui. 630. gep 48. ugelgims 26. piih

*431. ligqnniphcpa 625.217.101.5. uigligs
2821.69. uq glcvcgem 5. hepailqwu eu 625
iuvefmcubnipv 431. qwl lirwfmcg.*

*280. qyi 707.625. yqlmh 5.708.568.283.282.
biexip. 625. uexeqi 683. ubqy 707.625. yes.*

711

He tried to use what little translation his father had
given him to figure out the rest, but didn't have enough
to go on. He ran the message through every old military code Washington used as president and then
commander-in-chief, all to no avail.

Finally, he tried something else: an obscure
Revolutionary-era military code. It was a secret nu-
merical substitution code invented in 1783 by Colonel
Benjamin Tallmadge, America's first spy chief. Tall-
madge substituted strings of numbers for words that
Washington would insert into secret communiqués.
"New York," for example, became the number 727 in
Tallmadge code.

I wonder if there's a word for the number 763.

According to his database, there was: "Headquarters."

Suddenly the dateline at the top of the Stargazer letter made more sense:

Headquarters September 18 1793

But many words in the rest of the text didn't have a
number code. For those words, he would have to use
Tallmadge's letter-substitution cipher:

a b c d e f g h i j k l m n o p q r s t u v w x y z
e f g h i j a b c d o m n p q r k l u v w x y z s t

Conrad thought it a long shot since Washington was not the kind of spymaster to resort to sixteen-year-old codes on his deathbed. But he applied the letter-substitution cipher, and when he looked at the display of his digital chart table, the translation, clear as day, read:

Headquarters September 18 1793

To Robert Yates and his chosen descendent in the Year of Our Lord 2008:

My sincerest apologies for any pain I have caused you and your family. If we do not deceive our own men we will never deceive the enemy. Failure might prove the ruin of our cause. There can be scarcely any need of recommending the greatest caution and secrecy in a business so critical and dangerous as the establishment of our republic.

The fate of the world is in your hands, and your reward is in Heaven. The savage will show you the way.

General Washington

Conrad was so excited he accidentally knocked his coffee mug off the table and it shattered on the floor. He didn't bother to pick up the pieces. He was too busy staring at the translation, pondering its implications.

He quickly got back to work. The word *Headquarters*

appeared to be the Tallmadge translation for the mysterious number 763 engraved on his father's tombstone. That solved that mystery, only to raise another: What did *Headquarters* actually mean?

Then there was the date: September 18, 1793. That was a good six years before December 14, 1799, the night Washington died, and the night that Robert Yates first received Stargazer's orders. Had Washington written the letter years earlier and only released it on his deathbed? Or had he written the letter the night he died and the date carried some significance for Robert Yates?

The phrase "the fate of the world," meanwhile, looked like a double entendre to Conrad. He didn't know what "the world" meant but sensed it was important, and that the key to unlocking both it and the "reward in Heaven" was the "savage" Washington mentioned.

Sun sets over savage land.

He remembered the message his father left him from the tombstone along with the number 763 and the astrological symbols. It was almost as if his father wanted to draw special attention to the word "savage" in case Conrad never found the L'Enfant map.

So who is the savage? he was wondering when McConnell breathlessly walked up to him with a document.

"We pulled this from the archives," he said. "It's dated the night of Washington's death on December 14, 1799."

Conrad took the letter and looked at it closely. It was a letter addressed to Bishop John Carroll and purported to be an eyewitness account of George Washington's last hours at Mount Vernon as seen by Father Leonard Neale, a Jesuit from St. Mary's Mission across the Piscatawney River.

From what Conrad could tell from the report, Father Neale was distraught that he wasn't allowed to perform last rites or baptize Washington before he died. Neither were the Episcopalians, Presbyterians, or Baptists. Only the Masons would be allowed to bury the body, Neale noted, even though Washington hadn't set foot in a Masonic Lodge more than a couple of times in the last thirty years of his life, nor practiced Masonry outside of a few public cornerstone-laying ceremonies.

The reason, according to Tobias Lear, Washington's chief of staff, was that while Washington believed the republic owed its freedom to men and women of faith, he had seen the sectarian strife in Europe and wanted no part of it for America. As a result, he would not allow himself to be allied to any particular sect or denomination.

But it was what followed in Neale's account that riveted Conrad:

> *Lear told me that it was Washington's duty to the unity of the republic that he be complimentary to all groups and to favor none, in death as in life. When I protested and asked if such duty meant a death of civility without Christian hope, he said, "Aye, even so." As I took my leave and wept, I saw Lear escort to Washington's bed chamber a runaway slave, Hercules, whose food I*

had occasion to taste. I had little chance to ponder this strange sight as the cries of the servants rang out in the courtyard, "Massa Washington is dead!" I was nearly run over by three horsemen—the slave Hercules with two military escorts.

Conrad reread the text to be sure he got everything right. Then he looked at McConnell. "So you believe that Hercules delivered the Stargazer text with the L'Enfant map on the back to my ancestor Robert Yates. You think Hercules is the savage?"

"Maybe." McConnell called up a portrait of Hercules.

Conrad looked at the picture of the slave with a proud look and fine clothing. There probably weren't too many slaves in those days who merited a portrait.

"Hercules may have delivered the Stargazer letter to my ancestor Robert Yates," Conrad said, excitedly. "But he's not the savage we're looking for."

Conrad called up another portrait, and McConnell did a double take.

The Washington Family was a gigantic life-size portrait of President Washington and his wife seated around a table at Mount Vernon with Mrs. Washington's adopted grandchildren. Spread across the table was a map of the proposed federal city. To the left of the family stood a celestial globe and to the right a black servant. In the background, open drapes between two columns framed a magnificent view of the mighty Potomac flowing to a distant, fiery sunset.

"This is hanging in the National Gallery of Art?" McConnell asked.

Conrad nodded. The map on the table was practically a live-scale model of the L'Enfant map to Stargazer. And the celestial globe and servant completed the picture.

"That slave isn't Hercules," McConnell said. "That's Washington's valet, William Lee. He's not the savage."

"No, he's not," Conrad said. "The painting is the savage."

McConnell looked confused. "Say what?"

Conrad clicked on the link with information about the painting and up popped the window:

Edward Savage
American, 1761–1817
The Washington Family, 1789–1796
oil on canvas, 213.6 x 284.2 cm (84 3/4 x 111 7/8 in.)
Andrew W. Mellon Collection
1940.1.2

"The savage is the artist Edward Savage," Conrad said triumphantly. "And this painting is Washington's way of pointing us to whatever it is he wants us to find."

11

THE WASHINGTON FAMILY.

As the Gulfstream 550 began its descent over the Atlantic toward the northeastern tip of Long Island, Serena rubbed her tired eyes, opened her window shade, and took another look at the high-resolution printout of the Edward Savage portrait from the image that McConnell had e-mailed her. The original oil, which she had seen herself in the National Gallery of Art in Washington, D.C., was larger-than-life, like America itself. Seven feet tall and nine feet wide, the picture was the only group portrait of the Washington family developed from live sittings.

"The savage will show you the way," she muttered to herself. "How could I have missed it?"

There was the celestial globe, plain as day, along with a map and clues to its final resting place. The answer was right in front of her, if she could just crack the portrait's secret. If the L'Enfant confession was to be believed, she and Conrad had four days to unravel this prophecy before America would go the way of Atlantis.

She looked closely at the Washington family sitting around a map of the federal city. According to Savage's catalogue, Washington's uniform and the papers beneath his hand were allusions to his "Military Character" and "Presidentship." With the L'Enfant map in front of her, Martha was "pointing with her fan to the grand avenue"—Pennsylvania Avenue. Their two adopted grandchildren, George Washington Parke Custis and Eleanor Parke Custis, along with a black servant, filled out the scene.

Well, it's no Mona Lisa.

However iconic today, *The Washington Family* was hardly accurate in its details, let alone any sort of masterpiece. In the seven long years it took to complete the portrait, Savage had never even seen Mount Vernon. That explained the two columns in the background. They didn't exist. As for members of the Washington family, Savage apparently took individual portraits of each family member in his studios in New York City in late 1789 and early 1790 after Washington's first inaugural. He then threw them all together in his imagined scene at Mount Vernon.

That would explain the awkward grouping of the family and their stiff poses. Each one stared off into every direction but the map on the table.

Conrad, however, had another explanation.

According to the report McConnell had e-mailed her, Conrad insisted that this bland portrait contained a great secret, one that Washington needed to get just right to preserve for centuries. And Conrad had demonstrated a simple test at the abbey to prove to the monks that the firm hand of George Washington was behind Savage's seemingly slapdash composition.

Repeating Conrad's experiment, she laid the picture flat on her tray table and with a marker drew two diagonal lines across opposite corners—one giant "X." Smack dab in the center of the portrait where the lines intersected was Washington's left hand resting on the L'Enfant map.

The controlling hand of George Washington.

This "secret geometry," Conrad argued, was a sure sign that Washington wanted to show that nothing about this portrait was left to chance. Rather, he was communicating an important message.

And she had to agree.

Conrad Yeats, you clever wanker.

The question, of course, was what that message could be. And clever as Conrad was, she knew he would never guess that "the fate of the world" Washington referred to in his letter to Stargazer was the location of the mysterious globe that America's first president had buried somewhere under his eponymous capital city.

Or would he? She had underestimated Conrad before only to regret it later.

Impossible, she concluded. Not without knowledge of the L'Enfant confession. Which she possessed and Conrad did not.

Using Conrad's experiment with Washington's left hand as a clue, she decided to take a fresh look at the portrait and what he was doing with his right hand. It was resting on the shoulder of his adopted grandson, a symbol of the next generation, who in turn rested his hand on the globe.

Just as interesting was what the boy was holding in his hand: a pair of compasses, Masonic symbols of the sacred triangle. It was as if he was about to measure something on the L'Enfant map.

An unbroken chain from the globe to the map, she marveled, *with nobody to witness it save for the black servant.*

Truly, Washington intended this portrait to work with the original L'Enfant map to lead Stargazer to the final resting place of the celestial globe.

All of which made Serena wonder about the more important question that Cardinal Tucci had warned her neither she nor Conrad should ever try to answer:

What was *inside* the globe?

Serena stepped off the plane at the Montauk airstrip to find a sober McConnell waiting for her with a black Mercedes. Dressed in a dark business suit, he stood coolly in the late June heat and opened a door for her.

Serena rode in the back of the town car with McConnell while Benito drove them through the pristine woods and moorlands. The land had once belonged to the Montauk Indians until the federal government of the United States took it a century ago and built a now-abandoned military installation. All that was left of the base now were the ruins of an old, enormous SAGE radar dish and the airstrip. Private jets owned by wealthy men like McConnell could land without much attention.

"So how is our friend Dr. Yeats?" she asked.

"Popular."

He handed her a printout of an FBI alert to various law enforcement agencies about Conrad's exploits last week. "They're not accusing him of anything. He's only 'a person of interest' at this point. Meaning they don't want any cop shooting him, or even letting his name leak to the press. They just want their eyeballs peeled in case he pops back up on the grid."

She looked at the picture of Conrad the FBI used. Somehow his face always came out looking far more menacing in photos than in person.

"Well, I can't wait to see him as a monk."

"I'm afraid he won't give you that satisfaction. In the process of deciphering the letter to Stargazer, Dr. Yeats cracked the meaning of 763."

Serena felt a pit in her stomach. "Please tell me he's still at the abbey, Father."

"I'm sorry." McConnell shook his head.

Serena stared at him. "You let him disappear on us?"

It was bad enough that Conrad probably suspected she had known about the Savage painting all along, which wasn't true, and that he couldn't trust her, which unfortunately, thanks to Cardinal Tucci, was true: her counter-mission was to let Conrad figure out the location of Washington's globe but take it herself back to Rome. It was the only way to protect him from the Alignment, she rationalized, even at the risk of him hating her forever.

"You know our mission statement requires that we can't keep anyone against his will, Sister Serghetti. But

Dr. Yeats has little incentive to flee far from the only sanctuary he has right now. And a plainclothes security detail is following him."

She held up the FBI alert. "Others might be, too."

"Don't worry. Dr. Yeats is in disguise."

"Disguise?"

"You'll need one, too," he said. "It's in the bag on the floor."

Serena looked down at the black bag and pulled out a white bonnet, blue blouse, and white puffy skirt. She couldn't hide her reaction at this reversal and knew she would have to confess it later.

"And just where in bloody hell did Conrad go?"

12

HEADQUARTERS
NEWBURGH

DRESSED IN BOOTS, britches, and a blue Continental Army coat, Yeats circled the large 25-foot-tall obelisk. It was made of fieldstone, like the Washington Monument, and built more than a hundred years ago by the Masons of Newburgh, New York, to commemorate Washington's greatest yet least known military victory.

For it was here at Newburgh and not at Yorktown that the last battle of the American Revolution took place. On this very spot Washington was offered the chance to be America's first king by his officers. But Washington refused the crown, which he considered anathema to the cause of liberty to which he and his soldiers had dedicated themselves. His officers then attempted America's first and only military coup.

Washington quelled the coup at the eleventh hour by appealing to their better instincts with a speech that came to be known as the Newburgh Address. Moved to tears, his officers reaffirmed their support for their commander-in-chief.

It was the Revolution's darkest hour and Washington's greatest victory.

At least that's what the history books say.

Today, this last encampment of the Continental Army is known as the New Windsor Cantonment State Historic Site, a state park just off the New York Thruway. Here interpreters in period dress reenact military exercises and show what everyday life was like for the camp's 7,000 troops and 500 women and children. Nobody on the staff at the visitors center gave much thought to the lone "cast member" wandering about the 1,600-acre enclave and winding up in front of the obelisk memorial.

Except maybe one. A ruddy, middle-aged man dressed as a Redcoat had given Conrad a funny look inside the gracious Edmonston House when he asked for records of names of those who may have visited Washington at the encampment. There were none officially, but Conrad was allowed to peruse a few journals of the day kept by members of the military. It took hours, but he finally found an entry dated March 15, 1783, which mentioned Washington had a visitor, Robert Yates, in his base home shortly before addressing his mutinous troops.

But there was nothing about the nature of the visit that Conrad could find.

Now he stood outside, bending over to examine the inscription on the obelisk monument, trying to discern what business his nominal ancestor and George Washington had conducted under these extraordinary circumstances.

He found what he was looking for in an inscription on the granite tablet on the south face of the obelisk:

> On this ground was erected the "Temple"
> or new public building by the army of the
> Revolution 1782-83. The birthplace of the
> Republic.

The birthplace of the republic, he thought when a voice from behind said, "My, don't you look fetching in breeches."

He turned to see Serena dressed in a white bonnet, puffy white skirt, and busty blue blouse that simply could not safely contain her natural endowments.

"Don't you dare say a word," she warned him. "Or I'll introduce you to the pleasures of spending the rest of your life as a eunuch. Now, why are we here?"

Conrad walked her over to a long, rectangular log cabin with a line of small square windows, like a church without a steeple. Serena recognized it from her visitor's guide as a full-scale replica of the camp's original "Temple of Virtue," erected at Washington's command to serve as a chapel for the army and a lodge-room for the fraternity of Freemasons which existed among the officer corps. On the parade grounds beyond, a musket and artillery demonstration was underway. Every now and then she heard the boom of a canon.

"Picture the scene," he said. "The British are defeated at Yorktown. End of war, happy ending. All the same, things aren't looking so good in early 1783. The peace negotiations in Paris are dragging on and on. Congress is balking about the army's back pay, pensions, and land bounties. High-ranking officers led by Major General Horatio Gates, Washington's second-in-command and commandant of this Cantonment, threaten to ruin the cause of independence by mutiny."

"Right, so he confronts them in the Temple of Virtue with his famous Newburgh Address," she said, wishing right now she had Conrad's and Cardinal Tucci's encyclopedic knowledge of American history.

"Except the speech doesn't work and his words fall on deaf ears," Conrad said. "So with a sigh he removes from his pocket a letter from a member of Congress that he wants to read to them. But he has trouble reading it and reaches into another pocket and brings out a pair of new reading glasses, which he has never worn publicly. Then he says, 'Gentlemen, you will permit me to put on my spectacles, for I have not only grown gray but almost blind in the service of my country.'"

This much Serena knew from the visitors guide. "Yes, and moved to tears by the unaffected drama of their venerated commander's spectacles, the officers vote to affirm their loyalty to Washington and Congress. The Newburgh conspiracy collapses. A month later the Treaty of Paris is signed and the eight-year War of Independence comes to an end. Washington resigns his commission and retires to Mount Vernon. The army disbands. Everybody goes home. End of story. You have a point, mate? Because this blouse is itchy."

"What if old George's bit with the spectacles didn't work?" Conrad asked. "It's really hard to believe it did if you think about it. What if this wasn't the birthplace of the republic? What if this was the birth of the empire and this group called the Alignment?"

"You're reaching, Conrad," she said. "You haven't even told me how you came up with Newburgh in the first place."

"The number 763 on my father's tombstone. You know, the code you were going to give me if I helped you."

Serena felt the intended sting of Conrad's remark. "I thought the Tallmadge code you used on the Stargazer text translated 763 as 'Headquarters.' Washington had many headquarters throughout the Revolution."

"But Tallmadge invented the code for Washington in 1783, when Washington was encamped here at Newburgh," he said, looking about. Serena could tell he was oh, so close to putting his finger on it. "This is where the paths of my family and Washington intersected. That's why Robert Yates stormed out of the Constitutional Convention in Philadelphia six years later and then wrote a book called *Secret Proceedings and Debates* about the formation of the U.S. Constitution. Something happened here."

Obviously something happened, Serena thought. *Otherwise this historical state park wouldn't exist and we wouldn't be standing here dressed like fools.*

"Just think about it, Serena," he said. "Washington delivered everything the Newburgh conspirators demanded. The soldiers got their pay. The oldest military hereditary society in the United States was formed with the Society of Cincinnati. Then the U.S. Constitution was ratified, establishing a strong national government and military."

Which was all true, Serena realized.

According to her literature, Washington served as the first president general of the Society of Cincinnati from 1783 until his death in 1799. The Society was named after the Roman farmer-general Cincinnatus, who like Washington centuries later left his fields to lead his republic into battle. Its noble motto: "He gave up everything to serve the republic." These days Serena knew the Society of Cincinnati to be a decentralized and outstanding charitable organization, one that she had worked with on occasion. But she wondered if originally it had been something more. Perhaps the Alignment had forced Washington's hand into creating for them a new host so they would leave the Masons, much like the biblical account of the demon that Jesus cast out of a man and into a herd of pigs. By the time Washington died in 1799, the Alignment may well have abandoned the Society if they had succeeded, as Washington feared, in penetrating every level of the new federal government. Thus his warnings to future Americans.

Serena said, "You think Washington cut some kind of deal with the military, something that's coming home to roost now."

"In four days," he said, staring at her with his warm, intense hazel eyes. "But we won't know for sure until we find whatever Washington buried under the Mall in D.C."

Serena gasped. *He knows*. "What are you talking about?"

"We're looking for a celestial globe," he told her. "Just like the one in the Savage portrait. Washington buried it for his ultimate sleeper agent, Stargazer, to recover at the end of time. By some cosmic joke, it appears that I am Stargazer. And only when I find this celestial globe will I fulfill my mission."

Suddenly it hit her. Not only did Conrad figure out what they were looking for, he knew where it was! How did he know?

"You know where the globe is buried?" she asked, thunderstruck.

"You had the answer in your hands all along. Do you have my letter from Washington? I thought I saw something in there," he said playfully.

He was referring to the cleavage her blouse exposed. Embarrassed, she turned her back on him, retrieved the letter and handed it over.

"Father Neale told Bishop Carroll that he saw the slave Hercules leaving Washington's chamber just before Washington died on December 14, 1799." He unfolded the letter with the map on back, looking around to make sure nobody was watching. "But the letter itself is dated September 18, 1793. See? That's the date he buried the globe."

Serena nodded anxiously, berating herself for having missed the discrepancy in dates. "It's got some astrological significance, doesn't it?"

"Enough significance that Washington chose that date to lay the cornerstone for the U.S. Capitol—on the hill that Bishop John Carroll's brother Daniel sold him."

With that everything came together, wholly and horribly.

"The globe is in the cornerstone of the U.S. Capitol," she said.

Conrad nodded. "And I'm going to steal it."

An hour later they drove south out of the New York tri-state area in separate cars, Conrad in McConnell's black Mercedes making a list of everything he'd need for his operation, Serena in her limo with Benito calling ahead to make sure the new safe house would be ready.

As Conrad and Serena headed toward their designated rendezvous in Washington, D.C., the man in the Redcoat costume was sitting in Horatio Gates's old headquarters at Edmonston House, calling a number in Virginia as he looked at a picture of Conrad Yeats he had torn from his fax machine the day before.

"This is Vailsgate," he said. "I need to get a message to Osiris."

13

PENN QUARTER
WASHINGTON, D.C.

DRESSED IN A FRESH Armani suit that Serena had provided with his new cover, Conrad stood at the rail of the penthouse balcony and listened to the sounds of a summer jazz concert drifting up from the glowing fountains of the Navy Memorial plaza. He looked out at the lit-up dome of the U.S. Capitol, rising above the National Archives like a glowing moon.

It would have been a perfect evening, Conrad thought as he swirled his wine. If only Serena wasn't a nun and true romance between them hopeless. If only big Benito wasn't standing guard by the door.

"We should have more dates like this," he told Serena as he walked back inside. "Definitely a step up from the abbey."

The penthouse atop the Market Square West Tower overlooked Pennsylvania Avenue, halfway between the White House and the U.S. Capitol. It once belonged to the late Senator Daniel Patrick Moynihan of New York. Now it belonged to yet another one of Serena's mysterious patrons. This one was an architect whose firm had a hand in the construction of the new underground Capitol Visitors Center and who had provided them with blueprints of the Capitol Building dating back to William Thornton's original 1792 design for the building.

"This is crazy, Conrad." Serena looked up from the pile of schematics spread across the large dining table. "The U.S. Capitol has to be one of the most heavily guarded structures on the planet. You're never going to pull this off. You may not even come out alive."

"I'll get the globe and whatever's inside it," he told her calmly. "All you have to do is get me inside the Capitol, and I think your friends at Abraxos have already done that."

He tapped the special identification pin on his lapel, made for him courtesy of an executive at a company of ex-CIA types who handled covers for the agency and were now handling Conrad's cover pro bono for Serena.

"As one of 435 relatively anonymous members of Congress, I get to bypass security. So for tonight, let's pretend I'm a powerful lawmaker and you're my sweet little intern who is going to get me into a lot of trouble."

She gave him her "not-a-chance" death stare. "I can get you in, Conrad. But how the bloody hell are you going to get out?"

He could tell where her intensity was coming from. She really didn't think he was coming back.

"I'm going to trigger a false positive result for chemical agents. Doesn't take much more than household Lysol to set off the alarms in the Capitol if you know where the sensors are. I'll clear out the whole building and escape in the process."

Serena raised an eyebrow. "With the globe under your arm?"

"I told you, I've taken care of my exit strategy."

"No, Conrad, you haven't told me bloody much of anything. You forgot to mention, for example, that the U.S. Capitol doesn't even have a cornerstone. Not one that anybody has been able to find after two hundred years of excavations."

"True." Conrad leaned over her shoulder and saw that she was studying the 1793 map of the U.S. Capitol foundations by Stephen Hallet. "You'd think that the most technically advanced nation in history would know where it laid its first cornerstone."

"So what makes you think you're going to find this cornerstone where everybody else has failed?"

"Because I'm not everyone else," he said. "But then you knew that since you measured this suit perfectly. Let's say I get rid of this and we go up to the roof. There's a pool if you want to take a dip."

He smiled and offered her some wine. But she wasn't biting, and his mock bravado did little to erase the furrow in her brow.

Serena returned to the Hallet map, all business. "History records that Washington laid the cornerstone at the southeast corner of the building in a Masonic ceremony. But nobody knows if that was the southeast corner of the original north wing that went up in the 1790s or the southeast corner of what would eventually become the entire Capitol Building."

"Neither," he told her. "The Masons typically lay the cornerstone in the northeast corner of their buildings."

"I've crossed all the records, Conrad. Washington definitely laid the cornerstone in the southeast corner."

"Look." Conrad guided her hand across the Hallet map. "Here's the original north wing of the Capitol, which was built first. And here right next to it is the proposed central section, which would ultimately support the dome and connect the north and south wings."

"I can see that, mate."

"Really?" He guided her finger to the southeast corner of the north wing, where Conrad was betting Washington laid the cornerstone. "What do you see now?"

"Holy Mother of God," she said, staring at her finger. "The southeast corner of the north wing is also the northeast corner of the central dome section."

"And the dome represents not only the heart of the U.S. Capitol, but of the entire city of Washington, D.C., as well," he said. "So my location for the cornerstone is both historically accurate and Masonically correct."

Still she refused to let go of her doubts. "Very clever," she said. "But a lot's changed since the cornerstone was laid. For starters, everything built on top of your cornerstone was razed to the ground by the British in the War of 1812. And the original turned out to be so heavy the entire East Front of the building had to be rebuilt—directly over your bloody cornerstone—just to hold the thing up. So how are you going to find it under all that modified rubble?"

"Come with me."

He took her hand and they walked out onto the balcony thirteen stories above Pennsylvania Avenue. The concert was still going on down in the plaza, and Serena looked positively radiant, the view marred only by the FBI building looming behind her.

"This is supposed to be the city's grand avenue, linking the White House to the U.S. Capitol," he said. "By design the buildings were supposed to be within each other's line of sight. And for years they were until the Treasury Building went up and obstructed the view."

"Money usually does," Serena said, still letting him hold her hand. "But the symbolism was that the executive and legislative branches of the American government could keep a watchful eye on each other. I get it. So what?"

"So this terrestrial arrangement is mirrored in the heavens," he said. "Look up at the stars. There's the star Boötes over the White House. And over there is Regulus over the U.S. Capitol. See?"

"Actually, Conrad, I can't."

"The city lights make them harder to see. But they're there, and there's an invisible radiant connecting them right over our heads."

She raised an eyebrow. "Stars I can't see? Connected by an invisible radiant? Does this work on other women?"

She was joking, but he could hear the tension in her voice. For all her spirituality, Serena Serghetti was the most practical, down-to-earth woman he had ever known. She was scared for him, and all his mumbo-jumbo wasn't going to change that.

"All I'm saying is that Pennsylvania Avenue by design extends to the center of the U.S. Capitol, somewhere under the basement crypt, which is directly below the rotunda, which is directly below the Capitol dome, which itself is a representation of the celestial dome."

Serena looked frustrated and upset. "I told you, Conrad, the shape of the hill beneath the Capitol has been altered over the centuries with all the terracing, let alone the structure above."

"But the stars haven't, Serena. Which is why you and the feds can't find the cornerstone. You're looking at blueprints. I'm looking for the *intended* center of the dome. And my cosmic radiant in the sky, with the assistance of the Pentagon's Global Positioning System, is going to lead me to the cornerstone and the celestial globe."

Serena took a deep breath and looked him in the eye. "Now how can I argue with a man who has the logic of Don Quixote. Or is it Don Juan? It's so hard to tell with you."

She wiped an eye, and Conrad couldn't tell if it was a tear or the wind.

"Maybe a nightcap would clear things up for you," he said. "After all, this could be my last night alive."

"I hate you," she said and punched him hard in the chest.

Laughing, he rubbed an aching rib. "So why save America?"

She looked conflicted. "Because the cliché is true: America is the world's last best hope."

"I thought you believed Jesus was."

"I meant right now, politically, America is the best we've got for the unencumbered work of the Church and freedom of religion, which isn't going over too well in other parts of the world like the Middle East and China."

"Is that you or Rome talking?" he asked, hoping to raise her ire and get her worries off him. "Because there are some people, mostly in Europe, the Middle East, and Asia, who feel that the Church *is* the problem and that the world would be better off without it."

His ploy seemed to be working.

"The Church, however corrupt an institution, is a symbol of the kingdom of heaven in a world that is passing away," she said. "As such it stewards the eternal, life-changing message of redemption."

"Oh, so the Church is the last best hope?"

She looked him in the eye, lost in some dark thought, and then glanced away.

"No, Conrad. Unfortunately, as things now stand, you are."

Scary thing was, Conrad felt she really believed it, because she started to cry softly. He held her tight in the dark and looked out at the dome of the Capitol glowing in the night, wondering if she was in his arms for the last time.

PART TWO

JULY 1

14

U.S. CAPITOL BUILDING
WASHINGTON, D.C.

INSIDE A SECRET ROOM in the Capitol, Max Seavers sat before congressional leaders with officials from the intelligence community and Health and Human Services. Three years ago, as the Chairman and CEO of SeaGen Labs, he had told this same group that a bird flu pandemic could one day kill millions of Americans. This morning, as the head of DARPA, he was there to announce that that day had come.

"This was taken yesterday from a village in the northeastern province of Liaoning in China," he said, wrapping up his confidential briefing with a slide stamped "top secret" across the bottom.

The slide showed Chinese health officials in protective gear burning the bodies of men, women, and children outside a poultry farm.

"As you can see, our intel raises serious questions about Chinese disclosure of the spread of bird flu among their population. They want nothing to cloud the upcoming Olympic Games next month. And they have already warned us that any attempt to publicize our concerns will be taken as a political act to undermine the Games and international relations. Unfortunately, by then it will be too late. Worse, the Games themselves, with people attending from all over the world, may prove to be the ultimate launching platform for a global pandemic when they go back home."

Seavers moved on to his next slide. It was a grainy black and white.

"The Spanish flu pandemic of 1918, which was a form of bird flu, killed fifty million people. The new H5N1 mutation is far more dangerous today, targeting adults in the prime of life, and killing more than half of those it infects. No one in the world is immune, putting all six billion of the planet's human population at risk."

Senator Joseph Scarborough, the chairman of the committee, turned red with anger. He peered down his glasses at the man seated next to Seavers, an official from the Centers for Disease Control and demanded, "And what the hell is the CDC going to do about this?"

"The messy medical reality is that people can spread flu a full day before they show symptoms," the official said, meekly tap-dancing around the fact that "nothing" was his real answer. "So even shutting U.S. borders against an outbreak at the Beijing Games offers no reassurance that a super-strain isn't already incubating here. Should an outbreak hit American shores, the best we can do is limit international flights, quarantine exposed travelers, and restrict movement around the country. That could slow the virus' spread and give us time to dispense our stockpiles of the SeaGen super-vaccine to limit the inevitable economic and social chaos."

The senator now fixed his gaze on Seavers. "I thought

the SeaGen vaccine wasn't designed to fight this new strain."

"On the contrary, we've always known that human-to-human contact of the virus would one day be widespread. But advance preparation is always iffy because a vaccine developed to combat today's bird flu may be ineffective against tomorrow's mutation. SeaGen's smart vaccine solves that problem with its ability to 'dial up' or 'dial down' certain genes, modulating the immune system to combat whatever mutation the virus assumes."

"And how exactly does your vaccine 'dial down' a person's immune system?"

"Through a microbiobot inside the vaccine that can receive instructions via wi-fi signals."

"You mean from outside the body?"

"Yes, sir."

"What if somebody doesn't have the flu, Dr. Seavers? Could signals from the outside instruct this 'biobot' to dial down targeted genes?"

"Theoretically, I suppose, yes, but the chance—"

"Goddamn it, Seavers. You people did it again. You took federal dollars to develop a vaccine to save lives and instead you weaponized it. Now you want to give it to every American."

"Not yet," Seavers said. "The first step is to inoculate first responders. To keep a country's basic infrastructure working in the event of a pandemic, an estimated 10 percent of the population must be inoculated—including all doctors, nurses, police, and other emergency personnel—as soon as the virus strain is identified and the first batch of vaccine becomes available."

"Is that all?"

"And I'd want mandatory vaccinations of armed personnel and elected officials as well, since a pandemic could disrupt government and render the Twenty-sixth Amendment useless. If need be, we can scale up to the general population once the bird flu lands in the U.S."

Max Seavers and Joseph Scarborough stared at each other, the silence in the chamber thick. Behind the tension was the complexity of a symbiotic relationship in which Scarborough held the purse strings for the Pentagon while the Pentagon's contractors underwrote Scarborough's reelection campaign and lifestyle. Seavers often found it hard to tell when Scarborough was posturing for effect or genuinely incensed.

"As a former Boy Scout, 'be prepared' was my motto growing up," the senator said, and Seavers felt he was on the verge of getting what he had come for today. "As a senator, that sentiment rings true even . . ."

Seavers's BlackBerry, on silence mode, vibrated.

He glanced down at the text message. It was an official alert from the Capitol Police. The subject line read:

> 10:45 a.m.: "Subject: An Emergency Exists
> for the Capitol Building—Evacuate Building
> Importance: High."

Seavers could see vibrating phones throughout the chamber jumping on tables. Almost simultaneously, the doors to the chamber opened and Capitol Police officers rushed in from the corridor to direct people toward the exits.

He looked at Scarborough. The Senator, who hated being cut off by anyone or anything, stood up with a scowl and left the chamber.

As Seavers and the rest were hustled down the corridor after the senators, he saw the incoming Haz-Mat teams in protective gear and clicked the message header on his BlackBerry for details:

> *This is a message from the U.S. Capitol Police. If you are in the Capitol Building, then evacuate. Chemical sensors detect a biotoxin threat. Haz-Mat teams are responding.*
>
> *If nearby, grab Go-Kits and personal belongings. Close doors behind you, but do not lock. Remain calm. Await further instructions outside. Do not remain in the building.*

Seavers heard a loud whine and a thud and looked up. They were shutting the ventilation system down to prevent the spread of any biotoxins.

He tugged at the multisensor badge on his lapel. Developed by the counter-bioterrorism group at DARPA, the badge could detect the presence of biotoxins in the atmosphere in real time. That's because DARPA was able to package dozens of photothermal micro-spectroscopy procedures onto a single microchip, including the electrokinetic focusing of bioparticles. Durable, lightweight, and with no external power requirement, this "lab in a badge" provided an immediate visual indication of the presence of any contaminants.

Except there were no contaminants, according to his sensor.

Outside on the east lawn of the Capitol, Senator Scarborough was waiting for him, his face red and puffy.

Scarborough said, "This sure as hell better not be some stunt you're pulling to convince us to go ahead with your program, Seavers."

"Absolutely not, Mr. Senator," Seavers replied hotly. As a billionaire he hated begging for federal funding or agency approval, especially from politicians. They were worse than his private equity investors. "And I don't think there's anything to worry about."

"Why the hell not?"

"My sensor says so." He handed the senator his biodetector.

Scarborough turned it over in his hands and glanced at Seavers with the faintest hint of respect. "Maybe I should have one."

"I think you should. I think all senators should, along with a shot of the SeaGen vaccine."

Scarborough grumbled something about waving the white flag and walked off toward a cluster of his staffers who were waiting for him by a police barricade.

Seavers looked at his badge detector again. There was nothing, absolutely nothing in the air that was deadly, not even in trace amounts.

He looked back at the building. False alarms happened all the time in Washington, D.C. But something felt wrong as he paced outside the Capitol's east entrance. Beyond the police barricades, rows of news vans crammed the street, and he could hear the reporters breathlessly blathering on about nothing. There was little to report so far. Everybody was standing around talking or watching the Haz-Mat teams enter the building and people coming out: senators, staffers, and Serena Serghetti.

An alarm went off in his head, the one that never gave false readings. What was *she* doing here?

Then it hit him: *Conrad Yeats*.

15

A FEW MINUTES before the alarms went off, the public tour of the U.S. Capitol was running behind schedule. So Conrad was still inside the original north wing, impatiently standing outside the Old Supreme Court chamber, staring at a plaque that read: *Beneath this tablet is the original cornerstone for this building*.

Like most things coming out of Washington, D.C., the plaque wasn't entirely true, as the pleasant docent explained to the group, which included a dozen Boy Scouts from Wyoming.

"The plaque on the wall refers to the tablet on the floor before you, and the tablet on the floor only marks the spot where a former Architect of the Capitol once believed the cornerstone resided."

Conrad looked down at the stone, which was about four feet wide and two feet tall and embedded into the floor, and read the engraving:

LAID MASONICALLY SEPT. 17, 1932
IN COMMEMORATION OF THE LAYING

OF THE ORIGINAL CORNERSTONE BY
GEORGE WASHINGTON

"So we've got plaques commemorating stones in commemoration of other stones," muttered the scoutmaster next to Conrad in the back as the group finally headed to the crypt. "Am I missing something?"

"Just your federal tax dollars," Conrad replied and looked at his watch. The Capitol Police were probably already sending text alerts to higher-ups and it was all going to trickle down in a very loud display of alarms any second now.

The tour ended at the crypt under the rotunda, where George Washington was supposed to be buried. It was a vast chamber with 40 massive Doric columns of Virginia sandstone, upon which rested the rotunda and dome above, much like America itself rested on Washington. In the center of the black marble floor was a white starburst.

"This crypt is the heart of Washington, D.C., and the end of our tour," the docent said. "Following Pierre L'Enfant's design, the city's four quadrants all originate at the U.S. Capitol. The starburst on the floor of this crypt is the center."

The starburst marked what was to be a window into the tomb of George Washington beneath the crypt. The idea was that Washington could look up from his tomb and ultimately see his glorified self in heaven as painted on the ceiling of the capitol dome. Only Washington wasn't in the tomb below—his widow Martha had insisted he be buried at the couple's Mount Vernon estate.

As the tourists took turns standing on the starburst, Conrad drifted off to the wide marble staircase nearby and walked down to the subbasement level of the Capitol, passing several glass-enclosed offices packed like mouse cages.

He took an immediate right back under the stairs and passed a sign that read "No visitors allowed," just as the public alarms went off.

Now he had to move fast. He had only minutes to find the cornerstone before the Haz-Mat teams reached the subbasement levels.

He glanced back at the small warren of offices behind him. Staffers, mostly scruffy middle-aged types with PDAs, were shaking their heads, gathering belongings and heading for the exits. Conrad proceeded up a few crumbling stone steps, passing a nuclear fallout shelter sign as he entered a long, yellow brick tunnel.

He pulled out his modified smartphone and looked at the screen with the schematics and GPS tracker. Conrad was the white flashing dot in the maze.

At the end of the tunnel was a black iron gate like something out of a medieval church, and beyond the gate the tomb intended for George and Martha Washington. The only thing inside the tomb was the catafalque, the structure on which the corpse of Abraham Lincoln, the first president to die in office, rested when he lay in state for public viewing in the rotunda after his assassination.

Conrad turned to his right and saw the rust-colored access door he was looking for. It was marked:

SBC4M
DANGER
Mechanical Equipment
Authorized Personnel Only

It had no handle or knob, but he thought he could pry it open. As he did, he heard the scrape of metal against stone behind him, and turned to see the metal door marked SB-21 on the opposite side of the tunnel open.

A technician emerged in a work outfit and a look of surprise when he saw Conrad. "There's an evacuation alert, sir."

"Yes, they're passing these out." Conrad pulled a surgical mask from his suit pocket. "Take it," he said and smothered it over the man's mouth.

Conrad pushed him back through the door, and the man crumpled to the floor next to some electrical machinery. Conrad closed the door behind him, picked up the chloroform-soaked mask and dragged the technician past a bank of equipment and exposed piping to a utility room.

Inside he found a single marble bathtub, a relic of the old Senate spa that offered members of Congress and their guests hot tubs, haircuts, and massages. He put the man inside the tub, closed the utility door and moved down to the old furnace area.

According to the GPS marker on his phone, he was

near enough to the northeast corner of the central portion of the Capitol to use his pocket sonar. He popped what looked like a memory card into the slot atop the handheld device. A thermal-like image of red and yellow splotches against a glowing green backdrop filled the small screen.

DARPA had developed the pocket sonar for Special Ops forces searching for small underground structures like caves that could serve as hiding places for weapons of mass destruction or tunnels for smuggling weapons and terrorist infiltrators across borders. Conrad had adapted the sonar for exploring megalithic pyramids and temples in order to find and map his own secret chambers and passageways. Today he was looking for a hollow space in a foundation stone—the cornerstone.

He had done it once before, under remarkably similar circumstances, when he helped historians in Hawaii find a long-lost time capsule buried by King Kamehameha V in the cornerstone of the landmark Aliiolani Hale building. They knew the cornerstone contained photos of royal families dating back to Kamehameha the Great and the constitution of the Hawaiian kingdom. What they didn't know was its exact location. Conrad helped them find it within ten minutes, using his pocket sonar to locate the hollow spot in the northeast corner of the building.

He had to beat that record now.

Conrad watched the screen of the sonar as he made his way toward the southeast corner beneath the original north wing. For a second he thought he had something, but it turned out to be an old grating in the stone that led to the massive steam pipes.

There are miles of underground utility pipes that provide heat and steam from the Capitol Power Plant to the Capitol campus and surrounding areas. And these miles and miles of pipes were maintained by a team of ten employees from the office of the Architect of the Capitol.

Ten men to maintain miles of underground pipes.

His GPS tracker beeped and then he saw it, the dirt trench he was looking for. It was about three feet wide and four feet deep, dug by a previous Architect of the Capitol along with members of the U.S. Geological Survey. They had used metal detectors to look for the silver cornerstone plate beneath the stone, but had never found it.

If only they had used sonar, he thought. *If only they had dug a few feet in the opposite direction.*

Conrad aimed the sonar at the wall of large foundation stones to his right. The metamorphic sandstone had been ferried here on boats from quarries in Aquia, Virginia. And on the other side should be the northeast corner of the central section.

He watched the screen . . .

Ping!

He found a hollow space within the rock and made a crooked X on the stone with a marker. His hand was shaking.

The cornerstone of the U.S. Capitol. This is it! The very stone that Washington laid on September 18, 1793.

Based on the way it was set in the bedrock, it was slightly bigger than he expected—about two feet high and four feet wide.

This was the good part, he thought, the part the Hawaiians wouldn't let him do with the cornerstone back at the Aliiolani Hale. They said digging it up would destroy the building above, which was also a historic treasure. But you didn't have to dig it up to dig out what was inside.

He pulled out his pocket microwave drill, an incredibly useful tool originally developed at Tel Aviv University. The drill bit was a needle-like antenna that emitted intense microwave radiation. The microwaves created a hot spot around the bit, melting or softening the material so that the bit could be pushed in.

Conrad had used it beneath the Great Pyramid in Giza to slip a fiber optic camera into a previously closed shaft, much to the dismay of the Director General of the Egyptian Supreme Council of Antiquities, who liked to stage live "opening the tomb" spectacles for the American television networks.

If only this were televised, he thought, *I'd be an American hero, maybe get "Ancient Riddles" back on the air. The feds could keep the damn globe so long as I got credit for the find. Then Serena and I* . . .

The dream always got fuzzy in the end, because it was never going to happen with him and Serena. Not in this life, which was about to come to an abrupt end if he didn't finish this job.

With steady hands now, he began to bore a hole a centimeter wide through the sandstone, watching the tip of the drill bit glow an intense purple. The beauty of the microwave was that it was silent and didn't create dust. The only downside was the intense microwave radiation the drill produced. The shielding plate in front of the drill bit seemed awfully small to Conrad, who began to drip with sweat.

It was done in less than sixty seconds. Conrad cut the heat and pulled out the drill wire. He then snaked the fiber optic line through the hole and looked at the screen on his handheld device. The hair-thin cable emitted its own light and would give him a view inside the cavity of the cornerstone.

A few seconds later he saw it: nothing. The cavity was there, but it was empty.

Damn.

He leaned back in the dark, dumbfounded. Why would the Masons drop a recessed cornerstone and not put anything inside? It made no sense.

There was a movement behind him. Conrad turned. A man in a Haz-Mat mask stepped forward into the dim light. He removed his mask and reached for a radio.

"This is Pierce," he called in. "Alert sublevel 2, old furnace area. Suspect cornered."

"You people got here sooner than I thought," Conrad said, clenching his right fist around his handheld. "That's some nifty gear you've got."

"Who are you?"

"I'm you," Conrad told him and delivered a right hook to the man's temple that took him down.

The radio of the unconscious Haz-Mat technician squawked. The signal was breaking up in the subbasement, but Conrad heard enough to know he needed to get out, and he had known from the beginning he'd never get out the way he got in. Now, he could use the technician's gear for where he was headed.

As Conrad zipped up his Haz-Mat suit, a Capitol Police officer entered the old furnace area and saw the body on the ground. The CP drew his weapon and ran over. Conrad stood very still, pointing to the man on the ground.

"He was down here doing God knows what," Conrad said in a muffled voice through his mask.

The CP was bent over the body when he noticed Conrad's dusty wingtip shoes protruding from his newly donned suit, and quickly drew his pistol.

Conrad blocked the officer's arm and the gun fired. The sound of the shot inside the old walls was deafening. Conrad stiff-armed him in the neck, knocking him back against an electrical box, then raced for the grating to the network of old gas pipes.

He heard shouts and looked back to see a team of CP officers, rifles at the ready, running toward him, attracted by the sound of gunfire.

Conrad gave the grating a good hard yank and it came free.

The police were firing now and his mask was fogging up in the dark. A bullet ricocheted by Conrad's ear, sending him to the floor. He popped up again and, on all fours, lunged forward. A moment later he plunged into the steam tunnels.

16

By the time Max Seavers arrived on the scene at the old boiler room in the subbasement, a dozen Capitol Police were crowded around the piping entrance.

"What are you waiting for?" Seavers screamed.

But the Capitol Police officer halted his men and pulled out his radio to speak: "Suspect is in a Haz-Mat uniform and has entered the steam tunnels. Repeat, suspect is in the tunnels."

Seavers stared at him: "You're not going after him?"

"We won't even let our dogs go after him," the officer said. "Not down there. Too dangerous. All that crumbling concrete and carcinogenic asbestos. And our phones and radios don't work in the tunnels."

"This is a national security issue! That terrorist could be planting a suitcase nuke to blow up Capitol Hill!"

"That doesn't seem to be the case, sir, based on what we're seeing down here."

"And what the hell do you know?" Seavers said. "It was a CP officer who staged one of the last false alarms here a couple of years back. You know how they knew it was a CP officer? He was so stupid he couldn't even correctly spell out his 'anonymous' warning note."

"Easy, sir," said the CP officer. "The R.A.T.S. are coming."

"Rats?"

"Recon and Tactics Squad," the officer said. "A select group of us have undergone special training to access the miles of utility tunnels underneath the Capitol complex. They're arriving now."

Seavers turned to see the elite unit march up with their navy blue baseball hats, flak jackets that said R.A.T.S., and special night-vision Haz-Mat masks. The laser-sighted automatic machine guns in particular impressed Seavers, as he instantly recognized them to be German-made G36s by their distinctive translucent magazines. Their short-stroke gas system enabled them to fire tens of thousands of rounds without cleaning, perfect for use in the tunnels. And he especially admired the commanding officer's AG36 40mm grenade launcher.

"Well, it's about time," he said.

The knife-thin commanding officer lowered her mask to reveal a young, dark-skinned face. "I'm Sergeant Randolph, sir."

"Have you ever done this before?" he demanded.

She ignored him as she unfolded her classified schematics of the steam tunnels and reviewed choke points with her team.

"We won't have any radio signals down there," Sergeant Randolph said. "We'll stick to light signals. Converge at point C."

Seavers said, "Where is point C?"

"I'm sorry, sir," she said, folding up her blueprints and slipping them inside a hidden vest pocket. "But the Capitol Police can't provide any further details about how we protect the tunnels. You know, national security."

Seavers watched her put on her mask. She motioned a man to widen the open grating and a blast of scalding steam came out. Seavers covered his face and watched Sergeant Randolph and her R.A.T.S. vanish into the pipes.

17

CONRAD RAN THROUGH the dilapidated network of steam tunnels beneath Capitol Hill, hands up to brush aside falling debris from the crumbling ceilings. He could hear his heavy breathing inside his mask and feel the sweat drench his body. He had found the cornerstone but no globe, and right now his only mission was survival.

He knew that all the buildings in the U.S. Capitol complex could be entered through the steam tunnels. But he never imagined their state of repair to be this poor. Not after the feds just spent a billion dollars on the underground Capitol Visitors Center. They must have just sealed off the new construction and said to hell with the steam tunnels.

He came to a cross tunnel. Something inside prompted him to stop and listen. Besides a continuous low rumble in the background, he couldn't hear a thing. But when he looked over his shoulder, he saw the green glow of night vision gear.

He started to run.

A shot rang out, and he ducked as a bullet ricocheted

off the tunnel wall. He froze as several chunks of the ceiling came down around him. Slowly he turned around and squinted in the dark.

A thin shadow was wafting toward him. He looked down and saw the glowing red dot on his chest.

Suddenly a beam of white light blinded him and a voice in a ringing alto shouted: "Hands up where I can see them!"

It was a woman's voice, and she was mad as hell.

Conrad put up his hands and heard a deafening crack. But he wasn't shot. It was the floor—it was beginning to crumble.

The policewoman yelled: "Stop!"

But Conrad stomped on the floor as hard as he could. His knees began to buckle. The tunnel floor gave way under him and he plunged into darkness.

Sergeant Wanda Randolph kept her G36 steady in spite of the tunnel collapse, both eyes peering through her electronic red dot sight. But when the smoke cleared, her man was gone.

Quickly but cautiously, she moved through the dust to the crater in the tunnel floor, coughing through her mask. Finger on her trigger, ready to unload a round, she pointed her G36 down and hit her high beams, bathing the rubble below in light. There was no suspect underneath the chunks of concrete.

There was, however, another tunnel, one not on her schematics.

"Sweet Jesus," she said, although she wasn't surprised.

Before she joined the Capitol Police, Sergeant Wanda Randolph spent two years in Tora Bora and Baghdad crawling through caves and bunkers and sewers ahead of American troops in search of Bin Laden and later Saddam Hussein. She was tall and lean, with narrow shoulders and hips that enabled her to slip through holes and places people just weren't created to go. And while dogs could sniff explosives with their noses, they couldn't see tripwires, so they sent her ahead of even the dogs.

It was a year later that ten employees who worked in the Capitol Power Plant tunnels sent a letter to four members of Congress to express their concern that there was no police presence in the underground tunnels. The tunnels provided steam to heat and cool the Capitol campus and ran from the Capitol Power Plant to the House and Senate office buildings, the Capitol and surrounding buildings.

Now she was "Queen Rat," chief of the Hill's special Recon and Tactics Squad. The mission of the R.A.T.S. was to police the crumbling, asbestos-lined tunnels that had become a giant health trap to federal employees and a gaping hole in national security. As dirty and humble as her life's work had turned out to be, she was the best at it and proud to serve the United States of America.

"All R.A.T.S., report," she called into her radio, but knew it was no use even before static filled her earpiece. She flashed her call sign twice into the dark. No response.

As usual, she was on her own.

She climbed down into the new tunnel, using the rubble like a staircase until she reached the bottom and straightened up with her G36 pointed ahead. She hit her high beam again and gasped.

The tunnel wasn't a steam tunnel at all, but something else, like something out of ancient Rome. With one arm still holding up her weapon, she ran her other hand along the stone wall, awed by the solid construction of the stonecutters. She had seen enough tunnels beneath centuries-old cities to know this tunnel was older than the steam tunnels above, which themselves were more than a hundred years old. For all she knew, this tunnel was older than the republic.

Either the government had forgotten this tunnel was here, or knowledge of its existence was way beyond her pay grade. In any case, she had an intruder to capture or kill, and she marched down the corridor.

About three minutes later she saw the perp in his yellow Haz-Mat gear standing before a fork in the tunnel, his back to her.

"Turn around, hands up, or I shoot in three," she shouted, her G36 up and locked on the perp. "One . . ."

His arms seemed to waver but he wasn't turning around.

She aimed the glowing red dot between his shoulder blades.

"Two . . ."

Now his right leg seemed to waver, but still he didn't turn around.

She took a breath and tightened her grip on the trigger.

"Three."

One of his arms came down and his body twisted toward her. She wasn't about to wait for him to get off a shot and pulled the trigger, letting loose a burst of fire.

The bullets hit her target in the chest, blowing him back into the tunnel.

She ran down the stone floor to the crumpled body, her G36 pointed at the mask. She lowered the barrel and lifted the mask to see that it was empty. The perp had shed the suit and strung it up.

She looked down one tunnel with her high beams and saw nothing, then down the other and saw a glint of metal. She gave a war cry and ran down the tunnel only to find a shiny vaultlike door at the end.

It was an emergency hatch. All the old sublevel hatches were replaced several years back with new ones. And like all the safety precautions in place in the tunnels, it was designed to keep people on the outside from getting in, not people on the inside from getting out.

She opened it and climbed out of the ancient tunnel and into a machinery room. A minute later she popped through a metal door into an underground passageway and startled a group of young Capitol pages. They were exiting the Capitol complex with their supervisors and heading back to their school on the top floor of the Jefferson Building at the Library of Congress.

At this point, Sergeant Randolph knew that even if she saw the perp she wouldn't know him now. She wanted to scream, but it would only scare the Hill staffers.

Her radio, now in range of the command post, squawked.

She picked it up and said, "Suspect's gone native. Time: 1304 hours."

The Jefferson Building at the Library of Congress was the most ornate building in Washington, D.C., the greatest library in history since the Library of Alexandria burned to the ground two thousand years ago. Besides a fifteenth-century Gutenberg Bible, there were ancient maps of Antarctica that showed the subglacial topography of the continent before it was covered with ice, complete with curious addenda by the U.S. Air Force. Then there was a nineteenth-century manuscript copy of U.S. Senator Ignatius Donnelly's worldwide bestseller *Atlantis: The Antediluvian World*. Most prophetic, perhaps, was a sixteenth-century essay of Francis Bacon's on "The New Atlantis," all about the New World and the land that would become America.

Not that any of that interested Conrad right now as he split from the procession of Capitol pages and passed through a deep arch into the library's central atrium a few minutes later.

The ornate Great Hall was flanked by two grand staircases and constructed almost entirely of white Italian marble. Floating 75 feet overhead was a spectacular ceiling with stained glass skylights, paneled beams, and 23-karat gold leaf accents.

The street exit was just a stone's throw away. He

started for it when he saw several Capitol Police officers coming in, talking on their radios.

He turned around and ducked into a public restroom, where he removed his dirty suit jacket and jammed it into a trash can. Then he ripped off his fake goatee and threw cold water on his face. He rolled up the sleeves of his blue dress shirt and looked at himself in the mirror, a relatively new man. After he wiped the dust off his shoes, he walked back out into the Great Hall.

Seeing police at the security station by the main floor exit, he crossed the wine-dark marble floor and climbed one of the marble stairways to the second floor level. There a crowd was pressed against the glass overlooking the East Lawn of the Capitol across the street.

With the polite authority of a Library docent he pushed his way through the bodies toward the window. Then he looked down and realized he had a skybox seat to the mess he had made across the street—police vans, news crews, the works.

All for naught, he thought as he stared out the glass. He had followed his precious "cosmic radiant" in the sky above Pennsylvania Avenue to the dome of the U.S. Capitol only to find an empty cornerstone.

All that remained for him now was to wait for an opportunity to escape the Library, meet Serena at their designated rendezvous, and tell her that he had failed.

Even now, the Statue of Freedom atop the Capitol dome across the street seemed to be mocking him. Made of bronze, it was six meters tall and, standing on the dome, the tallest statue in D.C. since 1863. By law no statue was permitted to be taller. Maybe that's why the statue's back was turned to the Washington Monument rising high into the sky beyond.

Or maybe not.

He caught his breath.

The U.S. Capitol was built to face west. But the Statue of Freedom faced the Library of Congress in the east. In theory this reversal was decided on so that the sun would never set on the face of Freedom, but Conrad suddenly wondered if there was another reason.

He looked again at the gleaming dome of the U.S. Capitol under cloudy skies—the cosmic center of Washington, D.C. What if the cosmic radiant in the sky that paralleled Pennsylvania Avenue didn't end over the dome? What if it kept going? In his mind's eye, he extended the radiant to the east . . . to right about where he was standing in the Library of Congress.

He turned and walked back through the crowd toward the balcony overlooking the Great Hall and looked down twenty feet below. In the center of the marble floor was a giant sunburst, around which were 12 brass inlays of the signs of the zodiac arranged in a giant square.

This must be what the Masons wanted Stargazer to find: A marker of their own design, laid directly along the path of the city's central radiant.

Conrad could feel his heart beating out of his chest.

A zodiac in the shape of a square rather than a circle symbolically linked the constellations to the flat plane of the earth, not the vast space of the heavens. And a sunburst in the center, if he recalled correctly, represented the cardinal points of the compass.

Meaning the zodiac on the floor of the Great Hall was pointing to a hidden direction on Earth—or under the earth.

The Masons moved the globe. And it was right here, under the Library of Congress.

18

OFFICE OF THE SECRETARY OF DEFENSE
THE PENTAGON

THAT AFTERNOON Max Seavers marched down corridor nine toward Secretary of Defense Packard's suite of offices on the third floor of the Pentagon. It had taken a half hour for his black Escalade to get there from the media circus at the U.S. Capitol on this overcast Monday afternoon, and he dreaded the inevitable confrontation in store.

This meeting had already been on the books. Seavers was supposed to debrief Packard after his testimony on the smart vaccine before Scarborough's committee. Only now, thanks to Conrad Yeats, Packard would be asking about what, if any, connection there was between the empty cornerstone beneath the Capitol and the bizarre codes on General Griffin Yeats's tombstone at Arlington, and how a dead American general and his elusive son could make them all look like jackasses.

Two MPs saluted as he approached the vault-like doors, and Seavers surrendered his BlackBerry to the receptionist before passing through. Packard's office was classified a SCIF, or sensitive compartmented information facility. No mobile phones, BlackBerries, or other wireless devices were permitted inside. The idea was to ensure that the most classified conversations could be held in this office in confidence, without fear of being overheard.

This afternoon the only other person in the room besides Packard and Seavers was Packard's intelligence chief, Norman Carson, Assistant Secretary of Defense C3I, who sat in one of two chairs in front of Packard's desk. A wiry egghead with thinning hair and a thinner sense of humor, Carson was in charge of all command, control, communications, and intelligence for the DOD, which these days pretty much covered all of America. He was also the executive agent responsible for ensuring the continuity of government should some unthinkable attack or natural cataclysm hit the United States.

Carson didn't bother to get up and shake hands when Seavers walked in, and Packard was already behind his stand-up desk. Seavers took his seat. The vaultlike doors closed heavily behind him in the lobby, then another set in Packard's office closed likewise, sealing them and whatever they said inside.

Packard glared down at Seavers from his desk, which looked like a giant lectern, the ultimate bully pulpit. "What the hell is going on, Seavers?"

"Security cameras in the Capitol confirm it was Conrad Yeats, Mr. Secretary. We ran the tapes through the facial recognition software. He circumvented security and bypassed the detection gates by posing as a congressman from Missouri."

"And the biotoxin scare?"

"Haz-Mat teams found an open bottle of industrial cleaning solvent in a janitor's closet. The vapors set off the false alarm. It was a diversion."

"Dammit, Seavers!" Packard said. "How the hell did you let Yeats get away?"

Seavers didn't flinch. "The Capitol Police, who are in charge of security, failed to apprehend Dr. Yeats when he escaped through the steam pipes under the complex. He popped up in the Jefferson Building at the Library of Congress. By the time the Capitol Police reviewed the security feeds, he had left the building."

Packard nodded gravely for effect, and Seavers resented this flogging for something outside his operational control, especially in front of Packard's lapdog Carson, no less. "All this after he found the cornerstone beneath the Capitol, something we haven't been able to do in two hundred years."

Seavers calmly replied, "And this is important to my initiative with the vaccine because?"

Packard ignored him and turned to Carson. "Norm, what do the symbols on the obelisk mean?"

Carson passed two copies of a leather-bound brief to Packard and Seavers that included four photos, each showing one of the obelisk's four sides.

"We worked up another interpretation of the astrological symbols," Carson said. "Based on Yeats's actions today, we now feel the symbols represent celestial counterparts to the U.S. Capitol, White House, and Washington Monument. Teams have already been dispatched to the White House and Washington Monument to search for their cornerstones."

Packard nodded. "And the number 763?"

"We confirmed it's the Major's code."

"The Major's code?"

"Major Tallmadge," Carson said. "He was George Washington's spy chief during the Revolution, although by the time he created this alpha-numeric cipher system he was a colonel."

Packard said, "So Yeats is using a code more than 200 years old?"

"He's using, in effect, the DOD's very first code, Mr. Secretary."

"And what exactly does 763 stand for?" Packard demanded. "Should I be quaking in my boots like the president?"

The Pentagon's top intelligence chief said nothing, although the look in his eyes implied that, yes, they should all be quaking in their boots. "In general terms, sir, 763 is the numeric code for headquarters. Specifically, in this context, it clearly means this."

Carson wrote a name on a sheet of paper and slipped it to the SecDef. The SecDef picked it up and stared. "Oh, gawd," he groaned, and was about to crumple it up and toss it into his wastebasket until he thought better of it. "You mean the president's paranoia might have some basis in fact?"

"General Yeats seemed to think so, sir."

Seavers, unable to read the text on the paper Packard was holding, cleared his throat. "The president is paranoid about what, Mr. Secretary? I'm afraid I'm lost here."

"We all are if this prophecy is true." Packard pulled

out a lighter and touched it to the corner of the paper.

Seavers sat forward on the edge of his seat and watched the paper burn. This stage of the briefing was news to him. "What prophecy?"

Packard said, "Let's just say we think George Washington buried something under the Mall, and every U.S. president since Jefferson has been trying to dig it up, all under the guise of building or restoring monuments over the past three centuries."

"Buried what?" Seavers pressed.

"Something very embarrassing," Packard told him. "Not just for this Administration, but for every president since Washington. Something that casts doubt on the American experiment itself, its origins and destiny. We have to stop it from coming to light."

Seavers could feel Packard studying him, clearly conflicted. Packard had brought him to DARPA to develop new vaccines and create the perfect soldier, impervious to chemical and biological weapons. That was his reputation as one of the world's greatest minds in genetic research. Coded tombstones and buried artifacts were not his forte.

Unless he knows about my great-grandfather, Seavers thought, and suddenly wondered if there had been more to his appointment at DARPA than he had given Packard credit for.

"Mr. Secretary," he said, breaking the silence, "it would help me a great deal to know what exactly you think Washington buried."

"A globe, Seavers."

"A globe?"

"A celestial globe," Packard said. "Probably about two feet in diameter. The kind of floor globe you find on a stand in the library of lavish estates."

"Like those Old World bar globes you open and inside you find liquor?"

Packard glared at him. "This has nothing to do with the Old World, Seavers."

Seavers could only shrug. "But how important can this globe truly be?"

Packard was adamant. "Nothing could be more important to the national security of the United States of America."

Seavers nodded to show he understood the gravity of the situation. "And you think Dr. Yeats has a shot at finding it?"

"He found the cornerstone of the U.S. Capitol, didn't he?" Packard began to pace back and forth behind his desk, obviously wrestling with some decision. "Seavers, I want you to find this thing before Yeats does. Or let him lead you to it, I don't care. But if he does, he'll uncover a secret he's not authorized to know. Nobody is."

Seavers glanced at Carson, who looked shocked that Packard had assigned him the task, and said, "You'll give me what I need to do this job, Mr. Secretary?"

"The president has authorized me to have the entire resources of the federal government at your disposal," Packard said. "You've got the gizmos, I'll give you some muscle, your own black ops domestic response team." Packard looked at Carson. "Norm, your ass is covered. Just give Seavers whatever intel he needs to find Yeats. It's embarrassing that he's walking around D.C., which has more security cameras than galaxies in the heavens, and we still can't find him."

"I'll track down Yeats and whatever it is he's looking for." Seavers looked at Packard and Carson. "And Dr. Yeats can take whatever he knows to the grave and join his father."

"General Yeats may have been a four-star bastard, but I always tried to treat his son like my own. So I hope it doesn't come to that, gentlemen," Packard said. "But if it does, Conrad Yeats sure as hell isn't going to be buried at Arlington with full military honors."

19

MONTROSE PARK

ROCK CREEK NATIONAL PARK

IT WAS SET for 6 p.m. However things went down at the Capitol, Serena was to rendezvous with Conrad in Montrose Park at the edge of the vast Rock Creek National Park north of Georgetown. But it was half past six already, and there was no sign of Conrad. She was worried sick.

Carrying a backpack and dressed like a college coed in a white tank top, sunglasses, shorts, and flip-flops, Serena strolled past the tennis courts, picnic tables, and playground in search of what Conrad told her would be "an unmistakable celestial marker."

And suddenly there it was: the Sarah Rittenhouse armillary, a sundial of sorts. Actually, on closer inspection, it was a classic Greek celestial sphere comprised of three interlocking rings that represented the motion of the stars encircling the Earth. The outermost band of the ecliptic featured the raised constellations of the zodiac. Piercing through the rings was an arrow that pointed to true north.

But still no Conrad.

She set her sunglasses atop her brushed back hair for

a moment and adjusted the volume of her iPod as she waited, pretending to admire the armillary. It stood on a marble pedestal and according to the plaque was dedicated in 1956 in memory of some society woman named Sarah Rittenhouse.

"Sarah Rittenhouse was some matronly preservationist who saved this park from nasty developers back in the early 1900s," said a voice from behind her. "Reminds me of somebody I know."

She turned to see Conrad in a dress shirt and suit pants, a hardcover book clutched in his hand. He looked like a university professor. "So where's the globe?"

"I'm fine, thanks." He stared at the celestial armillary. "This is where I first saw Brooke after you disappeared on me. She was walking her dog."

"We have all of three days to stop the Alignment," Serena said, frustrated. "Did you find the globe?"

"No, but I know where it is."

She started walking briskly away from the armillary, where they might be seen if they stood together too long. "You told me the globe was in the cornerstone of the Capitol."

"It was," he said, guiding them down a cobblestone walkway called "Lovers Lane" to the ravines of Rock Creek Park. "The Masons moved it for safekeeping."

"But it was already safe in the cornerstone, right?"

"Not after the British burned the Capitol down to its foundations during the War of 1812. I think the Masons felt they had to move it before the Alignment got to it. At least that's my guess."

"Your guess?" she repeated, unable to disguise her

dismay. "And where do you *guess* the Masons moved it?"

"Under the Jefferson Building at the Library of Congress."

Serena shook her head. "That site was never in L'Enfant's original plans for the city."

"No, but the cosmic radiant cuts right through the Capitol dome to the Library's Great Hall."

Serena had heard enough. Time was running out and they had nothing. "You and your blasted radiant, Conrad! We could follow it around the world a dozen times and still never find the globe."

"But the Masons knew that," he said and stopped them in their tracks near a stream that she assumed was the eponymous Rock Creek. "They knew they were 'going off the grid,' so to speak. So they left clues for Stargazer in the form of zodiacs."

"Zodiacs?"

"The Jefferson Building is a hive of them," he said. "Scholars have counted seven zodiacs, but the docents have counted eleven. I counted fifteen."

Serena stared at him. "Wait a minute. When did you count the zodiacs?"

"This afternoon."

She nearly screamed. "I'm out of my bloody mind wondering if you're alive, and you're loitering around the Jefferson Building after breaking into the U.S. Capitol across the street?"

"Calm down," he said, looking around and taking her by the arm. "I was already there, so I took advantage of the opportunity."

Serena angrily twisted her arm out of his grip. "Well,

if you found the accommodations so comfortable, why didn't you just spend the night?"

"I thought of it. But I couldn't crack the zodiacs. Then I saw the central arch to the east of the main zodiac in the Great Hall. The top of the arch is inscribed with the names of those responsible for the construction of the Library, starting with Brigadier General Thomas Lincoln Casey."

Serena huffed. "And Casey is important because?"

"He was a Mason like Washington and L'Enfant," Conrad said. "He not only supervised the completion of the Washington Monument, but he also built the Library of Congress from the ground up."

They were deep in the ravines of the park now, and Serena was wondering where Conrad was leading them.

"So you believe that Casey and the Masons built the entire Library of Congress as some kind of cosmological citadel to protect the celestial globe?"

"I do."

"It's a nice theory, Conrad, but we need hard evidence to link Casey to the last known resting place of the globe. You said it was the cornerstone of the U.S. Capitol."

"It was," he said. "And after the British destroyed the original north wing of the Capitol in 1814, it was Casey who wrote up the damage report for the Architect of the Capitol at the time, then Benjamin Henry Latrobe."

Serena knew the name of Benjamin Henry Latrobe. He had designed America's first cathedral in Baltimore for Archbishop John Carroll with input from Thomas Jefferson. Suddenly Conrad didn't seem so crazy.

"So that's when you think Casey and the Masons removed the globe from the ruins of the Capitol."

"Exactly."

"You were busy at the Library." She jabbed at the old hardcover book he held—*Elements of Astronomy* by Simon Newcomb. "Did you check out that book?"

"I'll bring it back when I break into the Library."

There wasn't much Serena could say at that point. There was no going back, and Conrad was determined to go forward. "So who is Simon Newcomb?"

"He was an admiral in the U.S. Navy and probably America's most brilliant astronomer of the 19th century," Conrad explained. "And years before Casey became Chief of the Army Corps of Engineers and built the Library of Congress, he was Newcomb's assistant. Amazing how everything connects, isn't it?"

"So you think by reading Newcomb's popular astronomy guide you'll tap the minds of the people who built the Library of Congress."

"That's the idea" he said. "Once D.C. started deviating from the original L'Enfant plan, the Masons had to find a way of communicating outside the hard landscape of astronomical alignments. So they resorted to symbols in the form of zodiacs. If I can reconcile the zodiacs with the Library's extensive renovation plans on file, I bet I can find a sealed-off access tunnel somewhere that will lead us to the globe."

Conrad paused to scope out the surrounding woodlands. Convinced they were not being watched, he stepped into some nearby brush. "Follow me."

Serena followed him through the dense foliage, her hands up to keep the branches from her face, wondering what he wanted to show her. They were off any beaten trail now. Conrad stopped a couple of minutes later in front of a small cliff in the ravines, and parted a curtain of vines to reveal the mouth of a cave.

"I used to hide out here as a kid," he told her. "There's an old Indian well in the back. The cave collapsed at least a hundred years ago, so my dad and I used to come out here and dig it out, bit by bit. Every spring we'd plant shrubs to cover any trace of the path."

Serena nodded. She wasn't even sure if she could ever find it again herself if she had to. But this cave was certainly a better safe house for Tom Sawyer here than the penthouse, which was surely under surveillance now.

She said, "Tomorrow night I'm at the Hilton for the annual media dinner and then the Presidential Prayer Breakfast the following morning. The day after that is the Fourth of July."

"I get it, game over," Conrad said. "I'm going to have to hit the Library of Congress tomorrow night at the latest if we're going to have any chance of nabbing the globe and making any kind of sense of it to stop the Alignment."

"Stop them from what, Conrad?" she pressed. "If we know what they're going to do, then maybe we don't need the globe."

"Oh, we need the globe," Conrad assured her. "And

I'm guessing the Alignment is going to do what it failed to do in 1783."

"Stage a coup?" Serena asked. "American citizens would never sit still for it."

Conrad shrugged. "What if it's a coup and nobody knows it?"

Serena grew very quiet.

"Astrological symbols are quite different than astronomical alignments," she said softly. "They're open to all sorts of interpretations, not the clean lines and calculations you're used to. Admiral Newcomb may not shed enough light for you to find the globe."

"That's OK," Conrad said. "I know an old Mason who can help us."

"A Mason?" Although Serena knew that most Masons were constructive "builders" of structures and people, their secret society had been corrupted by the Knights Templar, warriors to say the least. Worse, it now seemed clear that the Alignment itself had infiltrated and controlled the Masons at one strategic point during the American Revolution. Who knew how many of their lieutenants and informants they had left behind in the brotherhood? "Can you trust this Mason?"

"My father did."

"Like I said, can you trust him?"

"Serena, I can't even completely trust you. But our options are limited at this point. I don't even know if he's still alive."

Serena looked at Conrad, still stung by his comment about her being untrustworthy, though of course she was, wasn't she? "How are you going to find out?"

"I know someone who might know. I'll contact him at his office at 5 a.m."

"Your friend's in the office at 5 a.m.?"

"Yep."

"What are you going to do until then?"

"Camp out here," he said, looking into the cave. "You want to spend the night with me in the catacombs?"

Little did Conrad know, she thought, but she would like nothing more in this life than to hide out with him in a cave and never come out. And if God and people and the world around them didn't mean so much to her, she would.

"Tempting," she said. "But at this point it's best for both of us if I'm seen out and about and far away from you. If I can break away to join you and this Mason tomorrow, I will. But I'd rather be safe than sorry."

He gave her a funny look. "You said the same thing at Lake Titicaca."

Conrad was referring to when they first met years earlier in the Andes, and as she looked around these wild ravines she felt the same sense of mystery and foreboding.

"Well, you better have these." She removed her backpack and gave him a toothbrush, lightweight trench coat, and a change of clothing.

Conrad studied the underwear. "You know I prefer briefs."

"Please watch yourself, Conrad," she begged him. "This isn't some boy's adventure. Those are real bullets they're firing at you."

It was getting dark in the ravines now, and Serena

turned to leave while she could still find her way out. As she began to weave between the twisted branches, she thought she heard Conrad whisper something. By the time she looked over her shoulder, he had disappeared into the darkness.

20

LATER THAT NIGHT Max Seavers stood naked in the bedroom of his Georgetown house and looked at himself in the mirror. There was much to admire—his golden hair, sapphire eyes, aquiline nose, and strong chin, not to mention his rock-hard, six-pack abs. This was not the face of a monster. Moreover, it was what one couldn't see in a mirror—his towering intellect, his genius—that was intrinsically noble.

Soon, he thought, *everybody will see it.*

He heard the shower in the bathroom turn off. He walked across the plush carpet to his bed, slipped under the sheets and waited for her. As he did, he mulled over the SecDef's directive about finding this thing that Washington had buried and marveled at the absurdity of it all.

For it was in another country, in another time, that his own great-grandfather was asked to help run an organization quite similar to DARPA and to pursue similarly bizarre research for his boss, Adolf Hitler.

Before and during the Second World War, Hitler had

German scientists and archaeologists roaming the earth for evidence of the biological superiority of the Aryan race. Few were hard-core Nazis, but fewer still were about to spurn the overtures of the Fuhrer and his ax man Heinrich Himmler, who in exchange for keeping them out of concentration camps offered these academics the kind of funding and resources no university could match.

The Ahnenerbe, as the think-tank was called, was an SS agency established to prove once and for all that Aryans were not just the "master race" or pinnacle of human evolution but also the "mother race" of human civilization. At its peak it counted more than 200 scholars, scientists, and staff among its ranks. And its teams fanned out across the globe in search of evidence in places like Lake Titicaca in Bolivia, the Canary Islands, the Greek Islands, even Tibet. All these places were alleged to have been built by Aryan colonists, and research efforts soon crystallized into one final quest to find the place from which those colonists came.

That place, they concluded, was Atlantis, and its location was determined to be Antarctica. If only they could find its ruins beneath the ice, they could prove once and for all the superiority of the Aryan race and the inevitable triumph of Hitler's Thousand-Year Reich.

Toward that end, Hitler sent U-boats to Antarctica, where teams of Nazis disembarked on the ice cap in search of ruins. They also planted Nazi flags still buried to this day in order to claim the last continent for Nazi Germany.

They came back empty-handed, of course, those

who managed to come back at all. Many perished in the otherworldly cold. Those who survived had no relics to show for their pains. Some had no fingers or toes either, as they were lost to frostbite.

None of this surprised Seavers's great-grandfather, Wolfram Sievers, who considered much of archaeology the domain of crackpots. Whereas half of the Ahnenerbe was focused on the past, Wolfram was focused on the future, on genetics and human evolution. Much of his work was inspired by the American eugenics movement of the early part of the twentieth century.

Unfortunately, research required Wolfram to experiment on living subjects, which could be found in great supply among the Jews in the concentration camps. The results yielded a treasure trove of data and the creation of new biotoxins.

Hitler hoped to place the biotoxins in the tips of his V-2 rockets and launch them against the Allies. But the tide of war turned against Hitler and his Nazis, and the work of Wolfram was cut short.

In the end, Germany was split in two by invading Allied forces. "Good Germans" who had served the Ahnenerbe were free to resume their respectable chairs at elite universities. Some, like rocket scientist Wernher von Braun, were even invited to the United States to help the Americans land a man on the moon. "Bad Germans" linked to the Holocaust like Seavers's great-grandfather, however, were executed in Nuremburg for their "crimes against humanity."

Growing up in Southern California with relatives, Seavers hid his true paternity with shame. At Torrey

Pines High School he announced his resolve to dedicate his life to creating vaccines that would eradicate pandemic diseases and extend human life. By the time he was a junior at Stanford, he got the backing of venture capitalists to launch his own biotech company back in San Diego.

He made billions but ran into trouble when America's religious fanatics got in the way of his stem-cell research, which required the destruction of aborted fetuses. They called him a baby killer, these Catholic and evangelical Christian hypocrites, who themselves benefited from his drugs and who carried out "God's work" in Third World countries by administering his vaccines to the poor and sick.

It was then that he began to consider that his great-grandfather, who didn't even work on live embryos but on prisoners as good as dead, may have been misunderstood.

Politics from Nazis or the White House had no place in science, he realized, and neither did religion. But the burdens of government regulations on his company's research became too much to bear. He had nowhere to turn in the private sector—except the Homeland Security-Industrial Complex.

And it was here, outside the gaze of Wall Street and the world, that Seavers found not only billions of dollars at his disposal but the cloak of "national security" to perform the kinds of research and experiments—mostly on enlisted soldiers—that he would never have been able to pull off in the private sector. Literally decades of research had been compressed into less than 36 months.

The result was the SeaGen smart vaccine, his crowning achievement.

Now, however, like his great-grandfather, he was reduced to dealing with imbecile masters at the Pentagon, hunting for buried globes, and crossing swords with "astro-archaeologists" like Conrad Yeats.

What an insane world, he thought. *Time for a new one.*

Seavers heard the bathroom door open and saw a whiff of steam from the shower billow out. Then a long, tan leg emerged from the mist and the naked form of Brooke Scarborough stepped toward him.

Seavers admired Brooke's body as she walked over and slipped under the sheets next to him. It had been weeks since they had sex, and it infuriated him that he had to share Brooke with Conrad Yeats.

Worse, she had put him in a bind with the Alignment, which wanted her dead after she had allowed Yeats to find the code book right under her nose and slip away. He had intervened on her behalf, arguing that the death of Senator Scarborough's daughter would only bring even more unwanted scrutiny at the eleventh hour. Moreover, if there was anyone Yeats would turn to once he popped back up on the grid, it would be her. The Alignment bought his argument, and she had won a reprieve.

So far, however, Yeats seemed to be able to live without her. Brooke was certain that Yeats felt so guilty about reconnecting with Serena Serghetti that he was hiding from her as much as he was the Alignment. If so, Yeats was a weaker man than he thought.

"The president and Packard told me about the globe," he said. "Did you know this was what that tombstone and book code nonsense was all about?"

Her silence said yes. He didn't know which annoyed him more: that the Alignment had kept him out of the loop or that she had. As a biological legacy of the Alignment, he always resented it when those adopted into the organization knew more than he did. Especially the true identity of one or more of the 30 who ruled the Alignment and knew all the names and faces. In two days so would he.

"They want me to find it."

"You?" She looked at him with frightened eyes. "Have you told Osiris?"

"Of course. Nothing's changed. I simply have to keep this globe from falling into the hands of either the Church or the State. And now the federal government has given me the men and muscle to do that. Meanwhile, you're going to have to be on the lookout for Yeats. He has few places to turn now. One of them is bound to be you."

She said nothing.

It was an awkward pause, but Seavers didn't mind her discomfort. In fact, he took perverse pleasure in it and the knowledge of pleasure soon to come.

"Max, you're as cool and confident of yourself as ever," she told him. "But you only know Conrad Yeats the specimen. Not the man."

"Unlike, say, you?" he replied with ice in his voice.

She was terrified. He could see it in her eyes. "I'm

just saying that there's always a body count when people go after him."

Seavers let out a loud laugh and couldn't stop laughing. It was too funny, really.

"After tonight, Brooke, the only body you'll need to worry about is yours."

21

THE NEXT MORNING Conrad stood in his change of clothes outside the Starbucks on Wisconsin looking at his watch. It was barely 5:30 a.m., and already the line to see his old friend Danny Z was out the door.

Daniel Motamed Zadeh—"Danny Z" to friends—worked as a barista behind the counter. Danny had let his hair grow long since his days at the Pentagon and had it in a ponytail, looking like Antonio Banderas in *Zorro*. But Conrad could tell it was him even from the back of the line. Ten minutes later Conrad stepped up to the counter and looked Danny Z in the eyeballs for the first time in a decade.

"Tall nonfat latte," he told Danny as he slipped him three George Washingtons. "The name's Bubba."

Danny marked up the order specs on the outside of an empty white Starbucks cup and looked over Conrad's shoulder and said, "Next customer, please."

Just like that, they were done.

Conrad ambled over to the far counter where several patrons waited to pick up their orders—K street types, a couple of diplomats and a college intern fetching orders

for her congressman's entire staff. He couldn't help but notice the headline below the fold of the front page of the *Post* that one of the K street guys was reading:

False Bioterror Scare
Clears U.S. Capitol

Then the guy lowered his paper and looked straight at him. Conrad shifted his gaze quickly to scan the mugs on the shelves to the side. They were always coming up with new ones. He was tempted to buy a pair—one for him and one for Serena.

When a barista called the name "Bob" nobody answered. Conrad figured "Bob" was "Bubba," lost in translation.

One sip told him that was the case, and as he walked out to the street he looked at the side of his cup and noticed the peculiar markings for his latte: there were the three symbols for the constellations from his father's tombstone, along with a new, fourth symbol which Danny had inserted.

Strung together the translation on the side of his Starbucks cup read:

Boötes + Leo + Virgo = Bad Alignment.

Tell me something I don't know, Conrad wondered, but when he looked back inside the store Danny Z was no longer behind the counter. Another barista, a blonde, was taking orders.

Conrad went round back to the alley and stood by the

trash bins behind the store. It was starting to drizzle. He sipped his coffee and waited. Danny Z made slamming good coffee, although this probably wasn't what his parents in Beverly Hills had planned for their little genius when he went off to MIT.

Danny came from an Iranian family that fled Tehran when the mullahs toppled the government of the Shah of Iran decades ago. They settled in the Trousdale Estates part of Beverly Hills with other Persian Jews and pretty much kept to themselves while sending their kids to Beverly Hills High School, which eventually had so many Persians that by the time Danny was going there the school was printing its programs in English and Farsi. It was only a matter of time before the CIA recruiters called, always looking for a few good Iranians with connections to the old country. Daniel Motamed Zadeh, tired of his cars and Persian princesses and prospects for more of the same, was ripe for a higher calling and became a spy for his beloved America, the Great Satan so far as the current regime in Tehran was concerned.

Danny Z had left National Intelligence at the Pentagon a few years back under a cloud of bitter recriminations on both sides. This after he was brought on board to become, in effect, the chief astrologer for the Joint Chiefs of Staff.

Apparently Danny was under the impression that Conrad still worked for the Pentagon. The first thing he did coming out the door with a bag of trash was take a swing at Conrad with it.

Conrad ducked, spilling some coffee and scalding his hand. "Hey, Danny, I'm one of the good guys."

Danny stuffed the bag into the stinking trash bin. "Bullshit. Your name is Yeats, isn't it? Just like your old man."

"He's dead, remember?"

"Promise?"

"There was a funeral, Danny. You were the only one from the old days not there."

"Meaning what?"

"Meaning you're the only one I can trust."

Danny gave him a napkin from his pocket. "Better drink it now, it loses its oxidation and flavor in a few minutes. Don't make me waste a cup of good coffee."

Conrad wiped the cup and then his hand. He took a sip and nodded his approval.

Danny calmed down, pulled out a cigarette, and started blowing smoke, eyeing him nervously.

Conrad said, "I thought you preferred hookah pipes to sticks."

"I got religion and gave up all that shit."

"Since when are cigarettes a sacrament?"

"Since Genesis says that when Rachel saw Isaac from afar 'she lit off her Camel.'" Danny blew smoke out of both nostrils. "So you're trying to figure out your old man's tombstone like the rest of them?"

"The rest?"

"Packard's people came to me asking about the stars on the tombstone weeks ago. How else do you think I knew about the constellations? You think I'm a psychic now, too?"

Conrad looked at the once-happy Danny and wondered what must have happened to him after the DOD's intelligence branch stole him from the CIA. It was all bullshit, of course. But the Russians, al-Qaeda, the Chinese and others often timed their rocket launches, terrorist attacks, and nuclear tests to significant dates. The head of the Russian rocket program had gone so far as to state on record that he believed astrology was a "hard science." And as long as America's enemies, both real and imagined, believed in hocus-pocus, the Pentagon figured they had better, too. They plotted every day and date, both historically and astrologically, visible and invisible, in order to predict threats and prepare accordingly.

Danny was a natural, coming from a long line of mystics who allegedly traced themselves back to the Persian Empire, to the Jews exiled to Babylon and taught by King Nebuchadnezzar and his staff of astrologers six centuries before Christ. It made all the Bible-thumper evangelicals in the Pentagon wet their pants to have "the real deal" on their side. The kicker was his name was Daniel, just like the prophet who spelled out the rise and fall of the world's future empires until the end of time itself.

Conrad said, "Danny, what happened to you?"

"You don't know?"

"No."

"You don't fucking know?"

Conrad shook his head. "I heard they had you working out dates and stuff, right? I figured you got tired of the grind and living in the heads of psychos living in caves halfway around the world."

Danny took the cigarette stump out of his mouth and dropped it to the wet pavement, stamping it out.

He looked up at Conrad. "They were using my charts against special ops."

"I thought that was the idea, Danny. You think like the enemy and tell the brass, like that splinter Red Cell group of astrologers and psychics they use."

"No." Danny laughed bitterly and lit another cigarette. "They started using my charts to mount *our* special ops."

Conrad's jaw dropped. "American troops?"

"Like I'm giving 'em a regular meteorological report, only they launch an air strike when Mars is at the Dragon's Head, screw the full moon." Danny took another drag. "Admiral Temple told me they've been doing it since the Revolution. It's how we won the War of Independence. It's how we've won every stinking world war since. It's why the armed forces of the United States are invincible, Yeats."

"Invincible?"

Danny shrugged. "Stars say so."

Conrad said nothing, just watched Danny, a man clearly conflicted and depressed. In other words, after enough time at DARPA himself, Conrad was ready to believe him.

"At first, I thought they were bullshitting me, putting pressure on me. Then I decided to give them a bogus chart, just to see what happened. Next day I find out twenty Delta Force troops die, just like that. I get called in. Stars never wrong. I must have been. I promised I'd do better."

"But obviously you didn't."

Danny gave him the evil eye, offended.

Conrad glanced away at the trash bins all around them. They weren't exactly conversing in the situation room these days.

"So what was it, Danny? Another special op gone bad?"

Danny shook his head. "June 30, 2004," he said and then paused. "That's almost four years ago exactly. Holy shit! Now you turn up."

Conrad scratched his head. Four years ago Conrad was long gone from the Pentagon himself, off in the Andes doing his *Ancient Riddles* show. Then his father mysteriously resurfaced in his life, as was his pattern, and dragged him down to Antarctica.

"So what happened on June 30, 2004?"

Danny told him: "U.S. handover of Iraq."

Conrad blinked. "The Joint Chiefs had you chart the day the U.S. would return sovereignty to the Iraqis?"

"To the second: 10:26 a.m. in Baghdad, which was 2:26 a.m. here in D.C.," Danny said. "But then they fucked up. They got word of some assassination attempt in the works on the interim prime minister, Ayad Allawi. So Paul Bremer, the coalition's civil administrator, bumps up the transfer and gives Allawi the leather-bound transfer document and a handshake two days ahead of schedule."

Conrad stared at him. "And you believe that's why we screwed up the occupation in Iraq?"

"Fuck, no. But some brass in the Pentagon did. Beats looking in the mirror, I guess. It's all fucked, man. Axis of Evil. Bullshit! We found shit in Iraq. Meanwhile, the nut jobs in Iran and North Korea are building nukes and passing them around to every lowlife terrorist group. They're gonna blow up the whole fucking world. Because we got our heads up our asses."

Conrad had heard enough to know where Danny stood on the issue. Now he needed to get from Danny what he came for, without sending the poor son of a bitch over the edge.

"Danny, listen to me." Conrad took a deep breath. "I need to find SENTINEL."

Danny looked at him like he was the boogie man. "Now you wanna do business with the Masons?"

"Maybe."

"You're fucking nuts! All of you!" Danny started turning circles, waving his arms like an inmate in some asylum. "The whole world is fucking nuts!"

"Look, I told you, Danny. You're the only one from the old days I can trust. You and Sentinel."

Danny stopped turning, his eyes looking the crazier for it.

"Yeah, well he's from your old man's days, the old-old days. I heard he's dead. Him and all his Masonic bullshit."

"Is he?"

Danny finally looked like he was calming down. "Maybe. I don't know."

"If he were still alive, where would I find him?"

"Some nursing home in Richmond, I think. Near the VA hospital."

"Really?"

"We can't all go out in a blaze of glory like your old man, Chief."

They said nothing for a moment. Conrad listened to the morning rush hour picking up on Wisconsin. The sky was getting lighter, though it was still drizzling. Then Danny seemed to regain his sanity and sight. He looked at Yeats in his rumpled suit and suddenly figured it out.

"Holy shit, Yeats. That was *you* yesterday at the Capitol?"

"Maybe."

Danny shook his head. "I could have told you it wouldn't work."

"The moon in the wrong house or something?"

"Something."

"How's tonight look?"

"Seriously?" Danny worked up a quick chart on another Starbucks napkin. "Problem with you is you don't even know your own birth date. That screws things up some. But based on all your personality quirks, we always figured you for a Pisces. Definitely a water sign."

A minute later Danny showed him the chart.

It was completely unintelligible to Conrad's eyes. "And what's that supposed to mean?"

"You're fucked."

"Seriously?"

Danny nodded and stamped out his second cigarette. "So am I if I'm spotted with you."

Conrad pocketed the napkin and turned to go. "You never saw me."

"I wish," Danny said and disappeared back into the Starbucks.

22

DARPA HEADQUARTERS
ARLINGTON, VIRGINIA

THE SIX-STORY office building in Arlington that houses the headquarters of DARPA attracts scant attention from the commuters emerging from the nearby Metro station or the patrons of the neighboring fast food joints, gas stations, and multiplexes. Only the lone security guard at the entrance to the anonymous steel-and-glass office tower hints of something inside to passersby, but something no more exciting than a nondescript local bank branch.

Max Seavers was in his glass office on the sixth floor when the call came in: Conrad Yeats had turned up on the grid, and Norm Carson's team at the Pentagon wanted to move in.

Seavers called them off. "I'll handle it." He hung up and placed another call. "This is Nebulizer. I need a Medevac at the helipad. See you in ten."

Meanwhile, I'm going to need some more juice.

Seavers took the elevator down from his office to the other sixth floor—the one six stories below the building's underground parking garage. The Meat Locker on sublevel 6, as it was called, was built by his predecessor General Yeats to house an astounding discovery. The Griffter had kept it a secret even from the Pentagon. Seavers learned of its existence only upon taking over the old man's job, and its revelations affirmed in a thousand ways his choice to heed the Alignment's call and leave SeaGen for DARPA.

Seavers walked down a long tunnel to a thick metal vault. He swiped his right index finger on the scanner next to the door. He heard a lock thud and then a series of clicks as bolts moved inside. The two-foot-thick door opened to reveal a contamination room and another vault beyond.

Seavers put on a protective germ "bunny suit" and opened the second vault. Inside was a secret prison that housed one of the most unique enemy combatants America had ever captured.

His code name was HANS, and he was discovered by American troops in Antarctica in the 1940s during Operation Highjump, which was the massive U.S. invasion of Antarctica based on information gleaned from the Nazis in the waning days of World War II. Almost every major American base on the ice continent could trace its origins back to Highjump.

Hans was a corpse, the frozen corpse of a German officer who was part of a secret Nazi base in Antarctica established by the "Baron of the Black Order" himself, SS General Ludwig von Berg. It was at this base that Hitler's "Last Battalion" apparently stored biotoxins. These biotoxins had been smuggled out of the collapsing Third Reich on U-boats, along with senior Nazis, who then went on to establish new identities in Argentina.

Hans didn't talk much, but his diseased lung tissue had provided Seavers with the second most important discovery of his life: the Nazis had weaponized the 1918 Spanish flu that had killed more than fifty million humans. In the end, it also killed the Nazis safeguarding their ultimate doomsday weapon. But it breathed new life into Seavers' research and set him on his present course.

Specifically, Hans's frozen lung tissue had given Seavers the perfectly preserved live bird flu virus itself. The trouble had been converting it into an easily dispersible aerosol version. In the process Seavers also discovered a prion mutation in the corpse's brain cells. One drop of fluid drained from the tissue could create a dozen lethal injections. A simple prick by syringe or dart gun caused instant death from apparently natural disease. But it had to be used within 24 hours of extraction or it would lose its effectiveness. Hence his periodic visits to the Meat Locker.

Seavers smiled at his frozen friend. "We're going to have to make this one fast today, Hans," he said, looking forward to extracting some cells from Conrad Yeats.

23

MISSION SPRINGS NURSING HOME
RICHMOND, VIRGINIA

IT WAS A THREE-HOUR car trip for Conrad and Serena, and Conrad could tell she had grave doubts about meeting this Master Mason known as Sentinel. But dressed in her traditional nun's attire, she said nothing as they walked through the front entrance of the Mission Springs Nursing Home. The home specialized in scooping up the half-dead human leftovers from the nearby VA hospital, keeping their juices and benefits going for a few weeks, and then dumping them in the grave.

The administrator at the nursing station, seeing clergy had come to visit, directed them down the hall to 208. They came to a room with the door partially open. Conrad gave it a rap with a knuckle. It opened wide and a big nurse with the name tag Brenda came out with a bottle of urine.

"We're all done, Father," Nurse Brenda said, noticing the white collar Conrad sported under his trench coat, courtesy of Serghetti Couture.

They entered the room and there was Reggie "Hercules" Jefferson, who had gone by the name Sentinel for as long as Conrad could remember. Herc, short for Hercules, was one of his father's few true friends from the Air Force, maybe his only one. Born in New Orleans, Herc's father was a bricklayer who became a Tuskegee Airman, one of the first African-Americans to fly for Uncle Sam.

Herc wanted to do even better and aspired to be an astronaut. But NASA wasn't ready for an African-American Apollo pilot, so he ended up flying Hercules C-131 transports on black ops missions for General Yeats. In time he, like most anybody associated with Conrad's old man, literally crashed and burned in an impossible landing that snapped his spinal cord and left him crippled for life at the age of 40.

That was thirty years ago.

Before Conrad could say a word, Herc said with a low, gravelly voice, "Took you long enough, son."

"I finally figured out that it was you who carved my father's tombstone."

"Just like your daddy wanted."

Herc was an unlikely Mason, not of the dead white male variety. His family claimed to have descended from a line of slave Masons since the Revolution. General Yeats believed it, having witnessed both Herc's encyclopedic knowledge of Masonic esoterica and his advanced skills as a stonecutter and site planner for forward-based military ops. As for Herc's claim that his family had blood ties to Founders like Washington and Jefferson, who allegedly had had affairs with female slaves, that seemed like wishful thinking to Conrad when he heard it from Uncle Herc as a boy. Looking at him in bed it seemed even more fanciful now.

Conrad said, "The globe's not in the cornerstone of the Capitol building."

"Of course not. Casey moved it after the War of 1812. I could have told you that, boy."

Conrad sighed. "You could have come to the funeral."

"On these legs? Besides, your old man and I never thought I'd make it this far. We thought you'd be on your own. Had to build a message into the tombstone and hope you'd be smart enough to figure it out. Guess you ain't."

"So how long have you been waiting for me?"

"How long since the Griffter died?"

Four years, thought Conrad, ashamed for having not even thought of Uncle Herc until now. Conrad could see that Herc had expected him to pay a visit as soon as his dad died. But Conrad had been wrapped up in his own worries following the death and destruction in Antarctica. Little did he know that poor Herc had been waiting here all this time, scratching sores in the bed his father had put him in.

There wasn't much Conrad could say, so naturally Serena said it for him, getting directly to the business at hand. "Hello, Uncle Herc. I'm—"

"I know who you are, Sister Serghetti," old Herc said. "Pleased to meet you."

"We figure the globe is buried beneath the Library of Congress," she said. "Casey and his son Edward, who was responsible for the interiors, appear to have left clues in the form of zodiacs as a map. But Doctor Yeats can't crack the secret, and we hoped you could."

Her bold Australian accent immediately perked up old Herc, and he smiled at Conrad approvingly. "She's a handful, ain't she?"

Conrad glanced at Serena. "That she is. Now, about the globe—"

But Herc asked Serena, "So you think we Masons are all devil worshippers?"

"I think you worship knowledge," she said without batting an eyelash. "The danger comes in ever learning but never coming to the knowledge of truth."

"We ain't a religion, Sister Serghetti. We promote enlightenment, not salvation."

"Thereby making an idol of enlightenment," she countered. "The very temptation that Lucifer offered Eve in the Garden of Eden."

"So you *do* think we worship the devil."

She smiled. "In a roundabout way, yes."

Conrad said nothing as a heavy silence filled the room.

"You know, Yeats, your girl reminds me of another lady named Anne Royall," Hercules finally said. "She was America's first prominent female journalist, a real rabble-rouser screaming about government corruption and all in the 1800s."

"Anne Royall?" Conrad repeated.

"Yeah, she used to live on B Street near 2nd Street and the Capitol back in her day," Herc said. "Her husband, Captain William Royall, was a Freemason. For years their basement was used as a secret meeting place for Masons dedicated to preserving the federal city's alignment with the heavens. But in time they couldn't even preserve the house. Got torn down by the Army Corps of Engineers."

Conrad could feel a tingle racing up his spine. Something was coming. He could see it in old Herc's eyes. "Why did the Army Corps of Engineers tear down Anne Royall's old house?"

Herc smiled. "Casey had to raze it to make room for the Library of Congress and the laying of its northeast foundation stone in 1890."

There it was. He looked at Serena, who got it, too: *The Masons moved the globe to the basement of Anne Royall's house. Then they built the Library on top of it. The house was gone, but not the basement. It was buried under the Library of Congress.*

Then Conrad thought of something and frowned. "The radiant I've been tracking cuts across the Library's Great Hall in a southeasterly direction. Shouldn't the basement be somewhere under the northeastern corner of the building?"

Hercules nodded. "It is, but the access tunnel is in the southeast corner."

"What access tunnel?" Serena pressed.

"Go get me my file, and I'll show you."

Conrad and Serena looked around the small room and saw only a wooden dresser with an old picture of Herc and Conrad's father from their glory days.

"It's inside the back."

Conrad walked over, removed the backing from the picture and peeled out a very old and thin schematic that had been folded several times over. He brought it over to Herc, who motioned for him to unfold it.

"Ain't hardly readable, but I can interpret."

It took a minute, but when Conrad was done he and Serena found themselves looking at plans, elevations, and details from the Jefferson Building. They were stamped "Edward Pearce Casey, Architect, 171 Broadway, New York" and signed by Bernard Green "Superintendent & Engineer" for the Library of Congress.

"See, the radiant crosses the sign Virgo across the zodiac on the floor of the Great Hall," Hercules pointed out with a gnarled finger. "At the end of the day, when it comes to the federal district, it's all about Virgo. The whole city is aligned to the Blessed Virgin in the sky."

"I beg to differ," Serena said. "The astral virgin is Isis, not Mary, despite attempts by Vatican astronomers to Christianize her in the Middle Ages. As such, the zodiacs are part of a deterministic philosophy of astrology that worships fate, not free will. And there can be no human rights without the recognition of free will."

"Maybe it means all that to some people," Herc said. "But to Masons the Virgin represents the hearth and home, the milk of the breast and the promise of the harvest. Like the New World to the Founders."

"Well, then your stars are sexist."

Herc seemed delighted with Serena. "You got a point, Sister. Anytime you deal with God or the stars, it seems you gotta have a Virgin. Very important." He looked at Conrad. "You ain't gonna pull this thing off without a virgin, son, and now you've got two of them—one in the heavens and one real live wire here on earth."

24

HERC AWOKE with a start in his bed later that afternoon at the nursing home. He had dozed off after the Griffter's son and the nun had left. He lay still pondering everything they had discovered, wondering if he should have said more.

Because there was certainly a lot more he *could* have said.

Slowly he reached his shaking hand under his bed and pulled out an old dagger with Masonic letters. It had been passed down through the generations, and he was told it once belonged to George Washington. He wondered if that was true. The only reason he kept it under his bed these days was to make sure some orderly didn't steal it.

He had intended to give the dagger to the Griffter's kid but forgot. His memory was slipping, along with just about everything else.

He heard footsteps and slipped the dagger under his gown as two young orderlies appeared at his door with a wheelchair and Nurse Brenda chirped that it was time for his physical therapy.

As they wheeled him down the hall, he noticed that he was feeling a bit queasy. Damn nursing home food.

"I know you want to keep the feeding tube in, sweetie, but your mother is trying to tell you she wants to leave this earth," Nurse Brenda was telling the daughter of the woman down the hall as they passed by.

Forget the feeding tube, Herc thought, they just needed to give that woman some water. She was going to die of dehydration, not dementia.

Suddenly Hercules realized they had passed the physical therapy room, and when he looked ahead they pushed him through two double doors to the parking lot outside where an ambulance was waiting.

"Hey, where you taking me?" Herc said as the orderlies lifted him up and dropped him on a gurney inside the ambulance.

A blond doctor with a syringe inside welcomed Hercules as the doors closed and the ambulance moved off. "I'm disappointed we missed Dr. Yeats," the man said. "But maybe you could tell us where he's going?"

Herc said nothing, although his gown was wet. He must have pissed in his pants. That's because he saw the other guy strapped down in the ambulance—young Danny Z, his mouth gagged and eyes wide.

"Don't know who you talking about, Doctor. Now please tell me where we're going."

"For a ride, Mr. Hercules," the man said with some amusement. "If you help me, you might get off. If you don't, then I'm afraid you'll suffer the same fate as your friend here."

Danny Z started to scream as the doctor slipped a long needle into Danny's neck.

"A body is a terrible thing to waste," the doctor told Danny as he slowly pushed the syringe. "So I'm only going to melt your brain."

25

GEORGETOWN BALLROOM
WASHINGTON HILTON

"A FUNNY THING happened to me yesterday on my way to Capitol Hill."

There was laughter in the Georgetown Ballroom at the Hilton Hotel as Serena Serghetti addressed the Washington Press Corps at the annual Media Dinner on the eve of the annual Presidential Prayer Breakfast.

"I was testifying about human rights in China, or lack thereof when it comes to your personal body parts and organ transplants, when I realized that the Chinese are right."

The room grew quiet, just a few forks clinking on plates as the journalists enjoyed their choice of beef or salmon. Meanwhile, here she stood as an ambassador for Christ covering up a federal crime in progress. The guilt was almost too much to bear.

"If a human lives for four score years and the state is forever, then the state should be able to do whatever is necessary for the so-called greater good," she explained. "But if it's the soul that is immortal, as that old Oxford don C. S. Lewis used to say, then it's the state that is passing away. Which means individual rights are para-mount."

She was getting nervous as she saw the clock in the back of the room. Secret Service teams with dogs would be sweeping the hotel in a matter of hours and then the security would clamp down like a fortress, and nobody would be able to come in or go out until the president left the breakfast in the grand ballroom at 10 a.m. If Conrad didn't get back soon . . .

"The whole point of 'one nation under God' in the American pledge of allegiance is recognition that the government isn't God. Individual rights are the basis for the foundation of the United States, and much of this philosophy came from American preachers like Thomas Hooker, who argued for the 'priesthood of believers,' insisting that since the Holy Spirit resided in the heart of every person, each person should be able to vote and live their conscience. In short, we're the government. You and me and all the people."

She looked at the sea of faces in the room, many of them familiar talking heads on TV who would have plenty to talk about if they only knew the truth.

"Sometimes I wonder if my evangelical friends in America have forgotten this. Are we people *of* faith in the halls of power? Or are we people who have faith *in* the halls of power? It's an important distinction. One leads to an open, diverse society. The other leads to something like we have in Russia today, where the for-mer KGB spy agency has effectively taken over the gov-ernment. One begins to wonder if something like that could even happen here."

She was thinking of the Alignment and the average American citizen. The Romans had bread and circuses. The Americans had TV and the Super Bowl. The members of the "chattering class" represented in this room were part of this Great American Conspiracy. But they also reported on it and thus shaped it. Which is why she had accepted this invitation in the first place.

"All of this underscores the primary role the Fourth Estate or free press performs in a democratic society, for it is you who inform the electorate and help us make sense of our world so that we, the people, can decide the fate of nations, not the other way around."

It was over soon enough and she was standing before a line of appreciative journalists. And then Brooke Scarborough walked up.

Serena hadn't seen her until now in the room, and never in person. She was much . . . taller than she expected, with very big hands that now clasped her own.

"Sister Serghetti," Brooke said. "I think we have a mutual friend who is in trouble."

Serena feigned ignorance, but knew from Brooke's eyes that each woman completely understood the other.

"You'd tell me if you've seen Conrad, wouldn't you?" Brooke pressed.

"Ms. Scarborough, I had assumed that you would be the first person Dr. Yeats would go to if he were in trouble. Are you no longer together?"

It was Brooke who feigned ignorance now, as she was forced to move off and let the person behind her say hello to "Mother Earth," but even out of sight Serena could feel Brooke's eyes watching her every move.

26

JEFFERSON BUILDING
LIBRARY OF CONGRESS

CONRAD LISTENED to the soft strains of Mozart on his iPhone's earbuds as he walked along Constitution Avenue in the rain. The dome of the Jefferson Building at the Library of Congress gleamed proudly under dark skies tonight, its grandeur almost eclipsing that of the U.S. Capitol across the street. It was already a few minutes past midnight, which meant it was already July 3, and meant he was running out of time. He turned up the collar of his trench coat and walked into the researchers entrance.

The guard on duty looked up from his station and immediately recognized Conrad from all his previous, legitimate visits to the Library over the years. Conrad's heart sank. Good ol' Larry was shaking his shaved head, whistling the spooky theme song to Conrad's old reality series *Ancient Riddles of the Universe*, which could be seen only in syndicated reruns on late-night TV and which said everything Conrad needed to know about Larry's social life.

"The Library closed to the public at 5:30 p.m. and to

researchers at 9:30 p.m., Dr. Yeats. Only congressmen or their staff allowed now. You know the rules."

"Still a little wet behind the ears, Larry, as you can see." He wiped his wet hair back and put on a smile, his gut churning at the thought that Larry might get hurt.

"If you'd just stick to the tunnels connecting all the buildings here, Dr. Yeats, you'd stay nice and dry on a night like this." Larry, unable to resist, had to repeat the show's tag line. "After all, 'the truth is DOWN there.' "

"You know I'm claustrophobic, Larry. Besides, I needed some fresh air."

"What you need is to get yourself a date," Larry said. "Say, whatever happened to that blonde Nazi babe from Fox News Channel? She didn't like your salute?"

"My salute's just fine, Larry. It seems I have trouble following orders."

Larry chuckled, but Conrad could tell he was disappointed. The guard's head was filled with images of Conrad in Egyptian pyramids and Mayan temples, with beautiful graduate "researchers" assisting him on his digs—when they weren't working auto shows. What on earth was an astro-archaeologist like Dr. Conrad Yeats, "the world's foremost authority on megalithic architecture and the astronomical alignments of Earth's oldest monuments," doing roaming the musty hallways of Washington, D.C.?

Conrad emptied his pockets of his wallet and keychain and made a face.

"Let me guess," Larry said. "You forget your user card again?"

Conrad nodded. In truth he had a bogus ID card with another name, which he obviously couldn't use now. And even if he had his own ID, Larry wouldn't be able to swipe it without all sorts of "apprehend and detain" directives popping up on his screen.

"I won't be long in the stacks," Conrad promised, looking at his watch. "Just give me twelve minutes."

Larry looked doubtful as he handed him a clipboard. "Just give me your John Hancock and ID number."

Conrad scribbled a signature, put down a bogus six-digit number and hoped that Larry would manually key it in later.

Larry took the clipboard without a glance. "Come on through."

Conrad turned up the volume of his iPhone and approached the multisensor detection gate. Serena had told him this particular piece of music would throw off the new brainwave scanners the feds had installed around the Mall. As he passed through the gate, he watched Larry study the thermal-like images on the bank of monitors. It was the curious monitor at the end Conrad kept an eye on, which could detect what the feds called "hostile brainwave patterns." The colors changed, and Conrad could see that Larry saw it too. But Larry's voice betrayed nothing, and his hand hadn't reached for the silent alarm yet.

"Your iPhone, Dr. Yeats."

"Oh, I'm sorry." Conrad removed his earbuds and

handed the iPhone to Larry. "You want the fedora and bullwhip, too?"

"Hee, hee."

Larry passed the phone through the detector, but Conrad only motioned to pick it up along with his wallet and keychain.

"You have yourself a good evening, Dr. Yeats. Don't go reading so many old books you scare yourself shit-less."

"Too late," Conrad said as he walked away.

"Hey, Dr. Yeats," Larry called after him. "You forgot your—"

Conrad turned, pressed the remote on his keychain and heard the crack of the iPhone explode behind him. Larry started coughing, and Conrad waited for the invisible knockout gas to work. But it wasn't. Larry staggered a bit, down but not out. He was reaching for his radio to call for help.

Damn sufentanyl, Conrad thought. So much of its effect depended on the biology of the individual.

Holding his breath, Conrad marched over to Larry and gave him a good, sharp chop to the back of the neck, knocking him out the old-fashioned way.

"Sorry, Larry."

Conrad removed Larry's radio transceiver along with his iPhone and earbuds and walked away. He looked at his watch as he entered a low hallway with yellow walls and white trim. Larry would be up in a few minutes if he wasn't discovered sooner.

Conrad's twelve minutes had just been cut in half.

27

JONES POINT PARK
VIRGINIA

ACROSS THE POTOMAC at Jones Point near Alexandria, Max Seavers looked over schematics at his makeshift command post inside the old lighthouse while the special warfare dive team searched the sea wall below for the original foundation stone.

According to the crippled vet they broke under torture, the Masons had moved Washington's globe from the cornerstone of the U.S. Capitol to an even more auspicious location "back in time": the very first boundary stone that Washington laid for the Federal District itself.

Seavers's own research confirmed that it was Daniel Carroll, the man who sold Washington Capitol Hill, who laid the stone here with Washington and an old black astronomer named Benjamin Banneker.

Today Jones Point is a big municipal park under the shadow of a giant bridge. For several years the bridge had proved to be a security headache for the feds, but it also proved to be a perfect cover for Seavers and his special ops team of Marines.

They were part of an elite 86-man unit known as

Detachment One, oriented toward amphibious raids, at night, under limited visibility. "Extreme circumstances" were their theater of war, and they were trained and equipped to carry out special missions including embassy evacuations, airfield seizures, underwater demolitions, and down-pilot rescues within six hours of notice.

Normally, they fell under Naval Special Warfare Squadron One, which operated out of the U.S. Special Operations Command.

Now they were under his command.

The lighthouse door opened and a Marine stepped inside from the rain, which was picking up now.

"The dive team found the foundation stone, sir. It's embedded in the seawall."

"Bring it up," Seavers ordered.

28

CONRAD PASSED UNDER a thick arch and entered the Great Hall. He felt a tight knot in his stomach as he stepped onto the huge zodiac embedded in the marble floor and faced east toward the Commemorative Arch leading back to the former entrance to the Main Reading Room. He was acutely aware of the six security cameras, two visible and four hidden, all watching him. But what he was looking for was invisible and in a moment he would be, too.

Conrad looked back over his shoulder, due west, toward the library's main entrance. Were it open, he would see the gleaming dome of the U.S. Capitol. And were it visible to the naked eye, he would see a radiant from the center of that dome pass through the zodiac on which he was standing, cutting through the signs of Pisces and Virgo and projecting to a point beyond the arcade at the east side of the Great Hall.

Conrad followed the radiant under the archway to the other side. The air smelled like bubble gum—the peculiar odor of the antiseptics they used to scrub the floor. To his right and left were two working antique elevators used by the Library staff. Above each elevator was a mural by the American Symbolist painter Elihu Vedder, one depicting the effects of good government and the other the effects of bad government.

The message was clear: America faced two possible and diametrically opposite fates.

The fresco above the staff elevator to the right showed America in all her glory, with full leaves in bloom and fruit in season—a land flowing with milk and honey. The fresco over the service elevator to his left depicted a barren America, bare trees, and a bomb with a lit fuse under the rubble of overturned marble and monuments.

Conrad considered the two opposing fates.

He walked to the staff elevator beneath America the beautiful and pressed a black button. The doors opened to reveal an ornate cage with a marble tile floor, brass bars, and glass. Conrad stepped inside and looked at the column of five buttons: 2nd Floor, 1st Floor, Ground, Basement, Cellar. He glimpsed the horror of America the damned before the doors closed and the elevator began its descent.

When the elevator doors opened again in the musty cellar of the Library, Conrad could see the staff elevator on the opposite side of the gray linoleum floor, just a few yards away. He was about to step out when he heard something down the corridor, out of his field of vision. He stayed in the car and pulled out a telescoping rod with a mirror, carefully sticking it out of the elevator at floor level. The mirror showed another security guard coming his way, probably to use the elevator.

Conrad retreated to the back of the elevator and took

out the radio he lifted from Larry at the researcher's entrance. He pressed the Channel 6 button and waited.

There was a crackle down the hall. The sound of approaching footsteps stopped. A voice said, "Kramer here."

Conrad kept the talk button pressed, to avoid the guard hearing his own voice coming out of the speaker. Conrad said in a soft voice, "Central Security. A sensor in the Asian Reading Room is acting up again. Need a visual check."

"Copy," Kramer said, backtracking in the opposite direction.

Conrad waited for the steps to die away before he crossed the cellar floor to the staff elevator on the opposite side and pried its doors open. He stuck his head into the shaft and looked up to see the bottom of the staff elevator stopped at the basement level overhead. Then he looked down and could see the bottom of the shaft six feet below. Feeling the doors pressing him on both sides, he jumped.

He landed on an iron grate embedded in the floor, heard a painful pop and immediately dropped to his knees. For a second he could have sworn he blew his Achilles tendon. But it was only an ankle sprain. It would hurt like hell, but it wouldn't slow him down.

He heaved on the grate with his fingers. The heavy iron bulkhead lifted an inch or two, revealing a narrow crawl space and steep well that dropped into nothingness. He slid the grate with a heavy scrape across the floor. He wanted to avoid severing a finger as he lowered it. But in doing so, he dropped it the last quarter inch and it fell with a deafening thud. He froze. Had any of the audio sensors in the floor above picked up the sound? He closed his eyes and waited for a few seconds. His pulse thundered in his ears. Nothing.

He opened his eyes and looked down into the well. He then heard a hum and looked up to see the elevator coming down on top of him. He quickly jumped into the crawl space.

He waited in the darkness until the elevator started back up. Then he reached up and with a strong tug pulled the grating shut. At one time the staff elevator could descend to this subcellar level. But years later the Architect of the Capitol decided it was an error, that the shaft was in fact unfinished and abandoned by Casey, so the Army Corps of Engineers ordered modifications that raised the floor. When the Library was closed for a 12-year renovation in the 1980s and 1990s for its centennial, the hollow was used only to house a modernized electrical power plant.

Conrad looked around, the light from the shaft overhead dimly illuminating his makeshift command center. His pocket sonar had confirmed a tunnel on the opposite side of the north wall of the well.

He could barely contain his excitement as he unrolled the Primasheet explosive from the lining of his jacket and stuck it on the wall. He then attached the wafer-thin cardboard backing and popped in the remote fuse.

He had honed his skills in demolition over the years through numerous illegal explorations of Egyptian and Mayan pyramids. But this was no Third World dust bin. This was the Library of Congress of the United States of America. And he was about to detonate an explosive device on American soil, in a sacred national institution no less.

If he properly attached the Primasheet, the explosion would blow in one direction—into the tunnel on the other side of the wall. That was the beauty of it—you could shape, direct, even stand next to it with only a piece of cardboard in between. If you did it right.

If he was wrong, Conrad could burn the place down and himself with it. Actually, even if he was right, he could still die in a matter of minutes. But at least he would know why.

He stepped behind another wall, which his radar had proved rock solid, and looked at the remote detonator in his hand—his cell phone. He then made the sign of the cross, did a Hail Mary, and pressed speed dial button No. 2.

29

THE RAIN WAS DRIVING down hard at Jones Point as Seavers watched the crane plop the dripping foundation stone onto the ground. He marched over while the Detachment One divers shone lights on the sides and he examined the markings.

"This is it. Drill it."

The demolitions diver came over with a drill and started boring a core sample. But a minute later he shook his head.

"It's solid, sir. There's nothing inside."

Seavers felt the frustration rising inside him. "Then split it open."

The divers looked at each other, as if some higher permission was necessary to open the original foundation stone for the Capitol of the United States of America.

"Split the goddamn rock!" Seavers shouted.

The diver hit the drill and made four holes before he took a special pick and gave one big whack. Seavers heard the clink of the metal to stone, heard the crack spiderweb across the surface and watched as the stone crumpled open into solid chunks.

He could only stare as the wind and rain whipped off the Potomac.

The Mason lied! That goddamn cripple!

Just then his cell phone rang. It was his office. This was an official alert. The voice on the other end said, "Something's going down at the Library of Congress, sir."

Conrad Yeats!

Seavers shouted into the phone: "Seal the whole frickin' Library, I don't care if you have to kill all the Capitol Police to do it. Nobody gets out. Nobody. I'm on my way."

30

THE BLAST HAD BLOWN Conrad back against the wall and the grating up the elevator shaft. The grating struck the bottom of the elevator car on the floor above, creating a series of sparks that set off a dozen different fire alarms and the sprinkler system. Then it came back down toward the well. Conrad crouched for cover as the grating landed with a deafening crash. He put his hands to his ringing ears and choked on particle-filled air.

When the dust settled, he could hear alarms blare overhead and his radio squawking like a duck. Every sector was rushing to the shaft. He stood up and, stepping through the debris, peered anxiously into the swirling dust through his goggles to see stone steps declining steeply into the earth.

He left behind another gas explosive with a sensor to slow his pursuers and started down the steps. The air coming up from the bottom of the passageway was cool and dank. Conrad felt a chill. The end of the stairs loomed abruptly from out of the shadows.

A wrought iron gate blocked the bottom of the stairs.

Conrad kicked the gate open. It was the only damn thing that had opened as planned so far.

There before him was a long sloping tunnel with a dirt floor. He broke out his flashlight and started sprinting, catching his sprained foot on a tree root and falling face down into the dirt. He picked himself up and started running. Suddenly it dawned on him that the topography beneath his feet was that of George Washington's time.

Despite the nonsense of this hill's alleged supernatural origin, Conrad sensed the logic of everything as he neared the end of the tunnel. As the city grew bigger, monument by monument, the entire American republic had been built upon Washington's dream.

As he reached the bottom of the hill and the end of the tunnel, he was drenched in sweat, barely able to breathe. The path he had followed, illuminated a dozen feet at a time with the beam of his flashlight, came to an abrupt halt at a wall. There was a small marker with a symbol—the constellation of Virgo—and an iron gate, beyond which lay the vault.

Conrad stared at the star pattern for Virgo on the wall. He had seen one like this only once before in his life, at the bottom of the earth in Antarctica.

"The Beautiful Virgin," he said aloud, and then heard himself laugh as he remembered old Herc. For all their genius, America's founding fathers had peculiar fantasies. He slapped another Primasheet patch with a five-second timer on the gate and blew the vault open.

Dust filled the tunnel, forcing Conrad back. Suddenly he heard another explosion from behind and realized that security forces had set off his flash explosive. They were entering the tunnel. Conrad took a deep breath, choking on the dust, and ran headlong through the cloud and into the vault.

The vault was a large bunker similar to those beneath the Pentagon, dominated by a big stone table with an old model of the city on it. He recognized the White House and U.S. Capitol and the Washington Monument. But to the south was an enormous, never-built pyramid.

It's a monument to America itself, Conrad realized. Roman numeral markings at the foundation of the pyramid struck him as odd at first glance.

But he had little time for closer inspection. At any moment security forces would be entering the tunnel outside.

A few feet beyond the table was what he was looking for: a golden celestial globe, like something out of Dutch master cartographer Wilhem Bleau's studio in the sixteenth century.

This was the original globe that Washington kept in his study at Mount Vernon for years before it disappeared, Conrad knew instantly. Not the inferior papier-maché replacement from London that Washington later commissioned as America's first president and which now stood on display in the estate's museum.

Or at least Conrad prayed to God it was the real deal.

Conrad dropped to his knees and felt the smooth contours and constellations of the globe, marveling at its three-dimensional, holographic look. The artifact itself would fetch a small fortune at auction.

The corner of his eye caught a glint of metal on the table beside the globe. He looked over and saw a silver plate—*the* silver plate made and engraved by Caleb Bently, a Quaker silversmith, upon which the U.S. Capitol's cornerstone was set.

That's why the U.S. Geological Survey could never find the cornerstone with metal detectors. The Masons had taken the plate when they moved the globe.

He read the engraving on the silver plate:

> This South East corner Stone of the Capitol of the United States of America in the City of Washington, was laid on the 18th day of September 1793, in the thirteenth year of American Independence, in the first year of the second term of the Presidency of George Washington, whose virtues in the civil administration of his country have been as conspicuous and beneficial, as his Military valor and prudence have been useful in establishing her liberties, and in the year of Masonry 5793, by the Grand Lodge of Maryland, several lodges under its jurisdiction, and Lodge No. 22, from Alexandria, Virginia.

THOMAS JOHNSON,
DAVID STUART,   Commissioners
DANIEL CARROLL,
JOSEPH CLARK, R.W.G.M.—P.T.
JAMES HOBAN,

STEPHEN HALLET   Architects
COLLEN WILLIAMSON,   M. Mason

Conrad's hands began to shake as he slipped the silver plate into his coat pocket and looked at the globe.

The fate of the world is in your hands, he marveled, recalling Washington's words. *Let's see what the world has to offer me.*

He ran his finger along the 40th longitude of the globe, feeling for a seam. When he found it, he traced it to a spring-loaded latch. He pulled the latch and stared in amazement as the globe split open.

PART THREE

JULY 3

31

CONRAD RAN OUT of the vault at the same time two red laser beams shot through the dust at the end of the tunnel and federal agents in night goggles poured in. The agents started firing as soon as they spotted Conrad. The sound of the shots in the ancient tunnel was muffled, but Conrad felt the force of bullets whiz past his ear and plow into the wall behind him. He hurled a flash puck down the tunnel. It exploded with a bright light, blinding the agents temporarily and buying him a moment to escape.

Conrad ducked back inside the vault and searched for a second, secret exit. The Masons usually had one somewhere. He found it behind a wall-sized tracing board depicting the entrance to King Solomon's Temple with two giant pillars on either side. The rich gold hue gave it the look of a Byzantine icon, and it was very heavy. Conrad needed to give it a good hard shove with his whole body to slide it even two feet across the floor. But when he did, an opening in the wall behind the board revealed a small spiral staircase.

This picture of the Temple portal was itself a portal.

The smell was rank as Conrad ran up the spiral staircase and into a sewer tunnel. He was a hundred yards down, sloshing through God knows what, when he found a stairwell to street level. A moment later he burst out a metal door and found himself not in some alley between a couple of federal buildings like he had hoped, but inside a small book bay in the Main Reading Room of the Jefferson Building.

Damn.

He could feel his heart pounding in the silence of the cathedral-like room. Father Time and his clock said it was a quarter past midnight. The life-size statues of history's greatest thinkers looked down on him from near the top of the dome. The room was empty. Not even a lone Library or Congressional staffer was around here this time of night. Security cameras would catch him the second he stepped out from the alcove and into the open.

His only choice was to turn left and run along the stacks of books through the exit to the yellow corridor which led back to the researcher's entrance. Overhead he noticed what looked like a large metal duct running along the ceiling of the corridor. It was the conveyor belt that distributed books throughout the Library and U.S. Capitol complex.

He followed the beltway to two metal doors, which automatically slid open to reveal a large processing room. Large bins of books surrounded a conveyor belt on which blue bins carried books to an elevator-like chute. They were too small to carry a person. There was no escape.

He pulled out the parchment he had taken from inside the celestial globe and gazed at it. On one side was a strange sort of celestial chart or star map. The other side was blank save for a signature at the bottom—President George Washington.

He stared at it intently to burn it into his memory. Then he folded it several times over and removed a book from a bin—*Obelisks*, of all things. He carefully inserted the star map into the spine of the book and placed it back in a blue bin. Glancing at the code key sticker on the wall, he tapped a four-digit code into the chute's keypad and sent the book on its way to join the millions of others in the Library of Congress, the world's largest.

As he watched it disappear he heard the doors slide open from behind and turned to see Larry the security guard stagger in, gun waving at him.

"Hands up where I can see them, Professor Yeats." His voice broke above the low hum of the processing equipment.

"Larry," Conrad said, slowly raising his arms. "This isn't how it looks."

"I'm sorry, sir. But it looks pretty bad. You can't just go around stealing books."

"Larry, it's not a book. It's something very different."

The doors opened again and Max Seavers stormed in with a gun pointed at him.

"Excellent job, officer."

Larry nodded, his eyes on Conrad. Then Conrad watched in horror as Seavers turned his gun to the security guard and shot him in the head.

"Larry!" Conrad shouted, but the bullet had already

blown splinters of skull fragments and brain against the machinery. Stunned, Conrad watched the security guard crumple to the floor.

Seavers bent down and picked up Larry's gun. "So you found the globe, Yeats."

Conrad put this reference to the globe together with the brazen slaying he just witnessed and instantly knew that Max Seavers was not acting on behalf of the United States but the Alignment. And Seavers knew he knew.

"Yeah, it's in front of the Cartography Room," he said, referring to a public display globe in the basement of the Library's Madison Building. "I can show you if you want."

"Your file said you were a cool one in a tight spot," Seavers said with a hint of admiration. "There might even be a place for you in our organization if you hand over whatever you found inside."

"Oh, so they didn't tell you? I bet the Alignment's having second thoughts about you already. What happens to you when you can't deliver what I stole?"

That seemed to touch a nerve. Seavers pointed Larry's gun at him. "I'm thinking this poor son of a bitch you killed got a lucky shot off as he went down and hit you in the heart."

"Really? Because I'm thinking I have a better chance of walking out of here alive with what I know than you do with what you don't. And all your billions won't save you."

"No, but maybe this will," said Seavers as he extended his gun to Conrad's chest and fired.

The bullet pushed Conrad back against the conveyor

belt, knocking two blue bins to the floor. He slid down, breathing hard as Seavers marched over.

Conrad lay there, the world spinning around. Then he felt Seavers's hands patting him down. He opened his eyes a crack to see Seavers remove the silver cornerstone plate from Conrad's inside coat pocket.

As Seavers stared at it in wonder, a small piece of metal fell from it into his hand. Seavers studied it before realizing it was the slug from his gun, and that the silver plate had stopped it cold.

Conrad grabbed Seavers's balls and squeezed hard. Seavers winced and fell back, then swung Larry's gun at him.

Conrad slammed Seavers's hand against the conveyor belt and the gun went off. They wrestled as Conrad tried to pry it loose from Seavers's grip. Again he slammed the back of Seavers's hand against the belt. This time the fingers loosened and the gun dropped onto the belt.

Seavers tried to grab it, but Conrad tackled him from behind, driving him into the machinery. Seavers tried to strike back, but seemed to have caught his finger in some gears. With a shout Seavers pulled out his bloody hand, sending a severed finger flying through the air.

The finger landed on the conveyor belt, Seavers helplessly watching it make its way to the inner recesses of the Library.

Conrad grabbed his hair and slammed his head against the conveyor belt. Seavers crashed to the floor, out cold.

Conrad quickly fetched the severed finger from the belt before it disappeared and put it in his pocket. At some point, if he ever survived the night, it might prove useful when the police ran the ballistics on who shot Larry.

He then pried loose the silver cornerstone plate from Seavers's other hand and stood up and stared at the two bodies on the floor, aware of shouts outside growing louder.

32

WHEN THE U.S. CAPITOL POLICE burst into the processing room on the main level of the Jefferson Building, Sergeant Wanda Randolph found three bodies on the floor: Max Seavers, a security guard with bloody hair matted across his face, and a third man with a bullet hole in his shaved head—obviously the perpetrator who detonated the explosives.

A few minutes later, outside the researchers entrance on 2nd Street, she watched the coroner zip up the corpse of the stranger when Officer Carter, one of her R.A.T.'S., walked up.

"So who is he?" she asked.

"They're telling me his name is Dr. Conrad Yeats," Carter reported. "But I couldn't run the security feeds through the facial recognition software to confirm, because somebody up there pulled them."

Wanda could feel her blood begin to boil. "Did they make that secret tunnel in the subbasement disappear, too?"

"No, but there's a detachment of Marines down there now."

"Marines?"

"Sealed the tunnel off and won't let us in."

She looked on as two emergency technicians used backboards to immobilize an unconscious Max Seavers before placing him on a stretcher and securing him in the ambulance for transport to George Washington University Hospital.

"This is our turf, Carter, not theirs."

"Sure, and you can bring that up with the president next time you lunch with him," Carter said. "Meanwhile, what do we do?"

The EMTs moved the big stretcher with Seavers to the side and put the folding one with the security guard on the bench seat next to him in the back of the ambulance. An attending paramedic was on hand to check his wound.

"That guard is our only chance of finding out what really happened in the processing room," she said. "I'll see what I can get out of him before he goes into surgery. You keep working the DOD detail. They can sweep the tunnel clean but they can't seal it off forever."

The ambulance was getting ready to go. The first EMT had gone behind the wheel and the second one was about to close the doors in the back.

Wanda sprinted up before the doors shut and flashed her card from the ERMET. "I'm a certified EMT-2 and need to talk to the security guard if he comes to," she said to the attending EMT. "What's his status?"

"Looks like he's lost a lot of blood, but I couldn't find the entry wound. I was going to clean him up some more on the way over and start a transfusion."

"And Dr. Seavers?"

"Lost a finger and consciousness. Possible concussion from a nasty blow to the back of the head."

"I'll handle it. You stay in touch with the ER up front with the driver," she said as the EMT closed the doors on her.

The ambulance shot out down 2nd to Pennsylvania with its lights full on and siren blaring. Wanda, seated on an uncomfortable, foam-padded vinyl seat with one hand on a stainless steel grab handle, looked down at the guard.

He lay on a fold-out stretcher, held with three straps and a white blanket. She adjusted the light blue pillow behind his head.

The guard stirred and she held his hand. His hair was matted with blood.

"He shot me," he groaned, eyes still closed.

"I know," she told him. "His name was Conrad Yeats. But you killed him. They just zipped up his body and sent him to the morgue."

"No, him."

He lifted his finger and pointed to Max Seavers in the other gurney, who was just beginning to stir with consciousness.

"Max Seavers?"

The guard nodded and seemed to pass out again by the time the ambulance pulled up to the emergency entrance on 23rd Street. The ER at George Washington University Hospital, just blocks from downtown D.C.'s monuments and government complexes, was a Level 1 Trauma Center. It was where President Ronald Reagan was rushed after being shot in 1981, the year Wanda was born, and it was where she herself had been sent on more than one occasion for smoke inhalation and suspected carbon monoxide poisoning from the subterranean tunnels she frequently explored beneath the city.

A reception team was waiting to transfer the guard and Seavers to the ER. The security guard was carried in first while Wanda helped the hospital paramedics roll a moaning Max Seavers into the ER.

Seavers seemed to be regaining strength quickly, and Wanda bent her ear to listen to what he was trying to say. Then she noticed his bloody finger stump pointing to the empty gurney inside the ER.

"Don't worry," she told him. "The guard made it out alive, too. Probably in surgery already."

Seavers's eyes widened and he bolted upright, startling her and the attending ER technician. He angrily pulled the IV drip out of his forearm and looked around.

"You stupid bitch," he said to her, his eyes on fire. "That was Yeats in the ambulance. He pulled a switch!"

She ran out of the ER and saw a discarded, bloody uniform stuffed into a trash bin. The security guard from the Library of Congress was gone.

33
HILTON HOTEL
WASHINGTON, D.C.

CONRAD, now wearing a white dress shirt and raincoat stolen from a doctor's locker back at GWU Hospital, got out of the cab at Dupont Circle. He walked several blocks in the drizzling rain up Connecticut toward the Hilton, which even at 1 a.m. was swarming with cabs, limos, and security as visitors from around the world were checking in for the next morning's Presidential Prayer Breakfast.

The way it was supposed to work, Conrad would walk into the lobby, ride the elevator to the tenth floor and go to room 1013, where Serena had already seen to it that he was checked in under an alias, Mr. Carlton Anderson. Then he was to call room service using the room phone and order a pastrami sandwich. Some mole on the staff under her control would then let her know that he had arrived safely and she would come to his room and see what he found in the globe and plot the best way to get it to the president at the prayer breakfast.

The problem, he immediately discovered upon

entering the Hilton, was that his picture was on every
TV screen in the hotel bar. News reports called him a
"person of interest" in connection with a terrorist attack
on the Library of Congress, in which a Capitol Police-
man was slain. The FBI was pinning the blame on former Pentagon analyst-turned-Starbucks barista Danny
Z, now an "Islamic extremist" and the "mastermind"
behind the attack.

Those bastards, Conrad thought.

He slipped into the mainstream of boisterous late-
night patrons and followed them past the gift shop to
the elevator banks, which were packed with still more
people. It was a mob, many of them smiling and making
conversation.

Who are these people? he wondered. *And why were
they alarmingly cheerful at this hour?*

Conrad stood in the middle of the mob, aware of a
few glances from a couple of bodyguards around the
president of some African country. He just had to grin
and bear it.

It took three elevators before one opened with
enough room for him. He stepped in, saw that every
single button was lit up, and sighed. It would be a long
ride up. At every floor it stopped, a couple of people
would step off, and four more would be outside waiting
to catch the elevator on the way down.

"Suck it up!" ordered a loud one from Texas, whose
wife, a petite blonde, kept eyeing Conrad. "Always room
for one more for Jesus!"

Finally, it was just him and the couple from Texas.

"Thought you could escape, huh?" the husband said,

smiling. His nametag read Harold from Highland Park, Texas. "My wife says she knows you."

Conrad stood there, flat-footed.

"She says you're Pastor Jim. You wrote that book *A Church of One*."

Conrad paused for a moment and smiled. "So you liked it?"

"No, but Meredith did," Harold said, and turned toward his wife, whose lipoed waist and silicon breasts defied the laws of natural aging. She could have been anywhere from 30 to 50 years old, depending on where she was between her Botox injections. "See, honey, I told you we'd meet all the big shots here."

"You look much younger than your picture," she said and squeezed his arm enthusiastically. But her husband Harold didn't seem to notice.

Conrad remembered something Serena always used to tell him and said, "Now don't go looking at the outside, Meredith. The good Lord looks at the heart."

She sighed. "So true, Pastor Jim."

The elevator door opened on the tenth floor, and Conrad exhaled as he stepped off along with Harold and Meredith. He turned down a hallway and walked briskly to Room 1013, hearing Meredith's heels clack behind him. He looked over his shoulder to see the couple wave good night and enter their room across the hall. He looked both ways and then inserted the coded plastic key card Serena had given him to unlock the door.

Once inside he immediately picked up the phone on the nightstand and called room service. "I'd like a pastrami from your all-night menu. Thanks. Oh, and a Sam

Adams." Then he went to the bathroom and turned on the shower.

As the water heated up, Conrad removed the silver cornerstone plate from inside his raincoat. He rubbed his thumb over the dent from the bullet Seavers intended for his heart.

He placed the silver plate on the dresser next to a golden ticket that Serena had left for him. The embossed letters read:

57th Annual
Presidential Prayer Breakfast
Thursday, July 3, 2008

Next to the ticket was a 10 x 14 souvenir reproduction of *The Washington Family* portrait by Edward Savage. Apparently Mr. Anderson had taken a day trip to Mount Vernon and the new museum. There was even a sales slip from the gift shop.

Nice, Serena.

Then he took a shower and found a complete wardrobe hanging for him in the closet. Instead he put on a bathrobe and waited for Serena, hoping she'd really bring him that pastrami because he was famished.

As the minutes passed with no Serena and no pastrami, he found his eyes drifting back to the souvenir copy of Edward Savage's portrait *The Washington Family*. He had used it to find the globe. Perhaps it held some secret to the meaning of the contents of the globe, namely, the star map.

But the only thing new he noticed in the portrait was

the column—or rather, two columns on either side of the panoramic view of the Potomac. Mount Vernon, of course, had no columns like that.

He remembered the giant Masonic board depicting King Solomon's Temple in the secret chamber beneath the Jefferson Building. It, too, had similar columns. But something about those pillars was different from Savage's. He couldn't put his finger on it, but he was sure of it.

Then it hit him: The columns at the entrance of King Solomon's Temple had two orbs on top of them.

Two globes.

The Savage portrait hinted at it all along. That's why there were two suns on the celestial map.

There's a second globe!

But, of course, he realized. They always came in pairs.

Old Herc must have known there were two. Why didn't he tell me?

He looked again at the Savage portrait, realizing that if there were two suns representing two globes, there were probably two landmarks designating their location. If Martha Washington's fan pinpointed the cornerstone of the U.S. Capitol in the east then perhaps . . . yes, young Eustice—a virgin, no less, at least in symbol—was holding the L'Enfant map at the western horizon. Her fingers pinched the horizon just behind the starburst in the guard of Washington's sword—surely a symbol of the sun.

That would place the location of the landmark somewhere in . . . Georgetown.

Only there was no celestial landmark in Georgetown, at least none that Conrad knew of, and he knew them all, or so he thought.

Conrad sat quietly, running through any correlation he could think of when he heard a knock at the door.

He rose to his feet and walked over to the door. He looked out the peephole to see Brooke standing in the hallway.

His heart stopped.

"I know you're in there, Conrad," she said. "I saw you in the lobby. Please let me in. Everybody's been looking for you, and I've been worried sick."

Conrad, his mind racing ahead to Serena's impending arrival and the resulting fireworks, realized it was better to have Brooke inside the room than outside, so he opened the door.

Brooke came in wearing an expensive but modest dress that still managed to show off her amazing figure. Her eyes swept the room, resting on the silver cornerstone plate on the dresser. She wrapped her arms around him and kissed him.

"Thank God you're OK, Conrad. Where the hell have you been? What's going on? The police have been asking questions, the FBI, and now your face is plastered all over the news. My news director called me and asked me if I had seen you and said you were about to join America's Most Wanted."

"You'd never believe me."

"Try me."

"The feds think I attacked the U.S. Capitol and Library of Congress and killed some people."

Her eyes widened. "And did you?"

"Well, yes. But I didn't kill the people they say I did."

"You just killed different people?"

"Yes."

"Oh, my God, Conrad. You better tell me everything."

34

GODDAMN YOU, Yeats.

Minutes after refusing treatment at the hospital, Max Seavers was back at the Library of Congress. He ordered it sealed in the name of national security. Kicking over what was left in the secret chamber Yeats had discovered, he nursed his bandaged stump of a finger and examined the split-open celestial globe in the corner.

The globe was an incredible work in its own right, Seavers thought, and looked like it had been fashioned from a single block of fiery bronze or copper.

But the globe was empty.

Yeats had gotten away with whatever was inside.

Until now Seavers had convinced himself that the Alignment's quest for the celestial globe was a distraction from its mission. But now that Conrad Yeats had cut off his finger and gashed his head, he was furious. The smooth, unruffled veneer he had cultivated since his days at Stanford had been punctured forever. Never again could he do a handshake deal with somebody without the knowledge that he was missing something, even if it was only the tip of a finger. For that he would always hate Yeats.

Worse, Seavers knew he would have to report his failure to Osiris, something he had never had to do before.

Seavers stared at the globe in morbid fascination for a full minute before he heard footsteps and turned. It was the wide-eyed black cop, Sergeant Wanda Randolph, nipping at him like some federal terrier with two of her R.A.T.S. The Marines shouldn't have let her in.

"Sir, we've got a problem."

Once again, he'd have to set her back on her heels. "You lost the suspect again, Sergeant?"

"The security tapes from the processing room where you were shot, sir. They're gone. Without them we can't verify your story."

"Why don't you stop trying to cover your ass and start looking for Yeats, Sergeant. While you're at it, maybe you could find my finger, too."

He saw the fury in her eyes, which he actually thought made her more attractive.

"Yes, sir," she said.

The sergeant turned and vanished into the tunnel.

Seavers waited until she was gone before he turned his gaze to the Masonic mural depicting King Solomon's Temple on the opposite side of the chamber. The two pillars in front with the orbs atop caught his eye. Like a gateway.

He walked over and ordered two of his Marines from Detachment One over. They lifted the mural away to reveal a small alcove with a Mason's compass symbol to the side. He pushed it and the wall slid open.

So this was how that son of a bitch Yeats got away.

Whatever cool he still possessed disappeared as he ran through the damp tunnel like a madman, even though he knew the chance of catching up to Yeats was nil. A minute later Seavers emerged through a metal door into an alcove in the corner of the ghostly, empty Main Reading Room.

He stopped and looked around. And it suddenly hit him that the silver plate and whatever else Yeats may have taken could still be in the Library, buried somewhere among the thousands of stacks with millions of books. Even if he found Yeats, it could take days or weeks to find whatever the Alignment wanted, if ever.

He looked up at the statues of the world's great teachers ringing the dome looking down at him. He could almost hear their jeers at his failure.

Suddenly all the anger, the frustration and fury building inside him burst forth. In that moment he knew he would do whatever it took to get back whatever Yeats stole from him—starting with his own dignity.

You goddamn bastard, Yeats. I'm going to slice you alive and make you eat your own brain.

He listened to the deafening silence around him, feeling only his raging pulse. And vibrating cell phone.

He had a text message from Brooke:

YEATS AT THE HILTON.
ROOM 1013.

Seavers smiled. He wouldn't be making that call to Osiris after all.

35

"**My father** always said your father was one sick bastard," said Brooke, who sat on the bed after Conrad finished the pastrami sandwich that room service finally delivered and recounted the events since his father's funeral. Everything except Serena, which admittedly was leaving out a lot. "You can't actually believe you're a sleeper agent sent by George Washington into the future to save America? This isn't about the future of the republic, Conrad. This is about your father continuing to mess with your mind from the grave."

Conrad paced back and forth, aware of Brooke looking at him like a crazy person and all the while expecting a knock on the door from Serena.

"Brooke, this is what I know: Washington entrusted a secret to Robert Yates, a secret passed down through the generations to my foster father, who then spent the better part of my childhood training me to unlock it. And I also know that the L'Enfant map, the celestial globe, and the people trying to kill me are for real."

"Who is trying to kill you, Conrad?"

"I told you, the Alignment."

She sighed. "A mystical group of warriors who use the stars to chart the rise of their master civilization?"

"Yeah, and Max Seavers is one of them."

She blinked. "The head of DARPA?"

"Yep. This belongs to him." Conrad showed her the finger of Max Seavers.

"Oh, my God!" She stared at it in horror and looked like she was about to vomit. "What have you done?"

"Relax, he's alive." Conrad pocketed the finger in his bathrobe. "Which is more than I can say about the guard he shot in the head."

Brooke sat still on the bed, her eyes darting back and forth as if she was processing everything he was telling her. He realized just how crazy it sounded. But at some point he was going to have to deal with the feds, and Brooke through her father Senator Scarborough was his best shot for exoneration. Unless, of course, he wanted to spend the rest of his days hiding out in a monastery and refurbishing toner cartridges.

"Show me this document you found inside this globe."

"I hid it somewhere."

She narrowed her eyes. "You don't have it with you?"

"No, but it had a kind of star map on one side and George Washington's signature at the bottom of the other side."

"And this is the reason you walked out on me and got mixed up in this crazy conspiracy? Some map and a signature?"

"Maybe," he said. "I think the star map was originally

drawn in invisible ink. But it's what's on the other side that got me into trouble."

"But you said there's nothing on the other side, just a signature."

"I think the rest of that side was written in dissolvable ink. Washington sometimes signed iffy contracts in an ink that would dissolve after a while, effectively making them disappear."

"And you found this invisible-visible parchment in a golden celestial globe?"

"It looked more like copper, really, but yes. And I think the star map leads to the other globe."

Her eyes widened. "There's another globe?"

"Yeah, but I don't know where just yet. I can't believe I was so stupid. There are always two—a celestial globe and a terrestrial globe. Even the old Mason knew it, I could see it in his eyes, but he said nothing."

He was aware of her looking at him in shock and awe. Shock at his lunacy and awe that he apparently thought it was true.

"Do you hear yourself, Conrad? How am I or my father or anybody else supposed to believe you? Show me something other than chopped-off fingers to back up your story, Conrad!"

"How about this?"

He showed her the silver cornerstone plate. The markings captured her attention immediately. He recalled her family had some Masonic background.

"This is the cornerstone plate, Conrad. You actually found the cornerstone of the U.S. Capitol."

"I told you I did."

She looked up at him, hope in her eyes. "No, you don't understand. *This* is a legitimate story. This is something you unveil on July 4, a piece of Americana. I'll get you to tell your story on Fox. Whatever crazy-ass stuff you add, well, nobody can deny you found this."

"Or that I was the one responsible for the incidents at the Capitol and Library of Congress."

"Let me work on this, work with my dad, bring you in somehow."

"Bring me in? You make me sound like a dog you're afraid is going to come in out of the rain and crap on your carpet."

"If the paw fits, Conrad. Now get dressed."

Conrad walked into the closet and removed his bathrobe. He slipped the finger from Max Seavers into his expensive suit pants and put one leg in after the other.

"Say, Brooke," he called out. "What was his name?"

"Whose name?" she answered from the bedroom, sounding preoccupied, like she was on the phone.

"Your dog's name."

"His name was Rusty," she called back absently as she spoke quietly in the bedroom.

That's right, he thought, remembering that day in the park. Her dog was named after some early American scientist her father admired—David Rusthouse or something like that.

Conrad slid his belt through the last loop of his pants, eager to bolt. Any minute Serena would walk in and find him with Brooke, and then he would have still more explaining to do. But the reality was that after what happened at the Library of Congress tonight, nobody was going to believe anything he had to say. Not Serena nor the feds.

His only hope was to find that second globe. To do that he had to find some kind of landmark in Washington, D.C., that aligned with the setting sun, just like in the starburst on George Washington's sword at the western edge of the L'Enfant map in the Savage portrait.

The problem was that the land at the western edge of the district was developed as residential housing or preserved like Rock Creek Park. In other words, there were no obvious monuments or landmarks he could think of.

And then it hit him.

Ritty. The name of Brooke's dog wasn't Rusty. *It was Ritty.*

As in David Rittenhouse, a famous astronomer during the founding of America who worked closely with Ben Franklin and Benjamin Banneker.

As in Sarah Rittenhouse, the grand dame who two centuries later "saved" Montrose Park in Georgetown from development.

But what was Sarah Rittenhouse *really* trying to preserve the parkland for?

Conrad felt his pulse explode:

The terrestrial globe!

The armillary dedicated to Sarah Rittenhouse was in fact the landmark he was looking for—a monument to the terrestrial globe that Washington buried somewhere below!

How could I have missed it?

Then he knew the answer: In his mind he had always associated the armillary sphere with Brooke's dog, who was urinating on the memorial's base that day he followed the canine back to Brooke's shapely legs and they reconnected.

He quickly tucked in his shirt, and then froze.

How could Brooke forget her own dog's name?

Suddenly their meeting in the park—their entire "reconnection"—smelled like a setup from the start. She must have known that he liked to jog in the park and simply put herself in his path. The irony was that he must have jogged past that armillary a thousand times and never imagined its secret. And neither, he guessed, did Brooke.

Brooke had stopped talking in the bedroom.

From behind Conrad could hear the *click* of a slider. Slowly he turned and saw her pointing an automatic pistol at him.

"I'm sorry, Conrad." She shook her head. "That fucking dog."

36

CONRAD STARED IN SHOCK at the 9mm Glock in Brooke's manicured hands, his mind trying to make sense of how he could have so thoroughly misinterpreted the nature of their relationship, and how long he had before whomever she called arrived.

"You've got to understand, Conrad, I had no choice," she said. "But you, you still have a choice: Give up the globe or die."

She's either with the feds or the Alignment, he thought. If it's the feds, he could live with it. *But, God, not the Alignment*.

"Some choice," he said, and coolly walked into the bedroom. Brooke followed him, and he could sense her gun pointed at his back until he sat down in a chair and looked up at her. "So everything we had was a lie?"

"No, Conrad," she said, her voice shaking with emotion. "Everything *but* us is a lie."

"Like you and Max Seavers?" he said, putting it out there.

"Tell me where you put the star map from the first globe, Conrad, and I'll let you go before he gets here."

Damn. She's Alignment.

He said, "What about the second globe?"

"Max doesn't have to know. But I need something to give him."

Conrad nodded, trying to figure his way out of this. "Does your father know about any of this?"

"No. He's a Mason. That's why it was a coup for the Alignment to nab me as a teenager and then use me to get to you, the son of General Yeats."

"But I'm not his son. Not his real son."

"No, you're much more special," she said. "I know about Antarctica, Conrad. I know about your blood."

Conrad looked at her. "What about my blood?"

"It's the basis for Max's flu vaccine."

Conrad started. "And how's that?"

"Max came to DARPA to genetically engineer the perfect American soldier," she said. "Along the way he discovered certain immunities to disease in the bloodlines of native Americans, specifically the Algonquin Indians. Immunities that had been diluted over the generations. So Max launched a global DNA testing program to connect the lost cousins of the Algonquins in the Americas, Europe, Africa, the Middle East, and Asia. It was called Operation Adam and Eve. By studying the mutations in Y chromosomes and mitochondrial DNA, Max was able to reconstruct their tribal migrations throughout the globe and trace their roots to Antarctica and one common ancestor: You."

"Me?"

"You're more American than any of us, Conrad. The last of the Atlanteans."

"Atlantis?" Conrad had thought he was ready for anything, but not this. This was over the top even for Brooke. "What on earth are you talking about?"

"You may be of this earth, Conrad, but whatever is in some of your dormant DNA strands isn't. You're one in six billion. Why else do you think your father was so hell-bent on going to Antarctica in the first place? Or didn't Her Holiness, Sister Serghetti, and her friends in Rome tell you?"

No, she hadn't, Conrad thought, and he hoped to God she was going to beat Seavers to the room so he could personally hash this out with her.

"So I take it you're not going to help me with the feds?"

"The Alignment IS the federal government, Conrad. That's what I'm trying to tell you."

"You cannot seriously expect me to believe that every low-level grunt in the federal government is Alignment."

"No, but they all work for the Alignment, whether they know it or not."

"Not me," he said and with a quick move of his right arm grabbed her arm holding the gun, slammed her body against the wall with his own, and then with a hard twist snapped her wrist.

"Ahh!" she cried, but wouldn't drop the gun. She was almost as tough, physically, as Seavers.

He gave her a sharp elbow in the stomach, spun out as she doubled over and then hit her on the neck, sending her to the floor.

He picked up her gun and pointed it at her head as she slowly rose on all fours.

"You broke my fucking wrist, Conrad," she said.

He dug the barrel of the gun into her temple. "Why do the monuments line up with the stars tomorrow, Brooke? Why now? Why 2008?"

"Something about the transit of Venus or something."

Conrad knew the transit of Venus—when Venus crossed the path of the sun to the naked eye on Earth—came once every couple of hundred years. But when the transit came, it came in pairs—eight years apart. As it happened, the world was in the middle of such a transit. The first crossed the sun in 2004, the year he and Serena had their adventure in Antarctica. The next transit was due in 2012. There wasn't anything scientifically significant about such a conjunction, but it held great meaning to the ancients.

"We're between the two transits, Brooke. Why 2008?"

"Something about solar years and the number 225. It's all Alignment esoterica. I'm not at that level."

But Conrad was. The planet Venus takes about 225 Earth days, or about 7½ months, to go around the sun. At the same time, Venus took more than 243 Earth days to turn on its own axis, making its days longer than its years. Conrad subtracted 225 from the current year, 2008, and came up with 1783.

"Newburgh," he said, recalling the coup attempt Washington allegedly quelled in 1783 at his final winter encampment. "It has something to do with Newburgh."

"I don't know!" Brooke screamed.

He kept pressing her. "What's the connection to my

family, Brooke? What did Robert Yates have to do with it? Was he responsible for this?"

Brooke bared her teeth. "He was nobody, Conrad, a side note to history like you want to be. He was the god-damn lawyer."

Conrad paused. "For what?"

Brooke rammed her head into his, and with a scream lunged for the gun in his hand. Caught off-balance, Conrad fell back and brought the butt of the gun down on the back of Brooke's head, knocking her out.

With a heave he pushed her body off him and dragged it to the bed. He then tied her hands to the posts, spread-eagled, as she came to.

"What's going to happen tomorrow, Brooke?"

"I don't know," she moaned. "Only that the Alignment is going to make it happen."

"Not good enough." He tightened the knot around her broken wrist until she winced in agony.

"I'm just trying to save your life!" she cried.

"Funny way of showing it," he said, waving her gun in her face. "Now, for the last time, what's going down tomorrow?"

Her voice, when she finally spoke, had a dead tone. "Max is going to release a weaponized bird flu conta-gion."

Conrad stared at her. "Where?"

"Somewhere on the Mall, I don't know. But it's got a 28-day incubation inhibitor so that it won't jump human-to-human until August 1. Everyone will assume it origi-nated at the Olympic Games in Beijing."

"So Seavers kills a billion Chinese," Conrad said.

"What happens to all the Americans who get saved with his vaccine?"

"You know that, thanks to Congressional gerrymandering, there are only seventeen competitive districts left in America that can swing a national election. Undesirables, including representatives, get their vaccines turned off and die. By the time the voters elect replacement officials—Alignment types—it's too late. A democratically elected coup."

"And this thing from Newburgh is their moral, if not legal justification."

"Oh, God, I loved you, Conrad."

He gagged Brooke and left her writhing on the bed as he placed the gun on the dresser and walked to the door. He slowly opened it and looked down the hallway just as the ding of the elevator sounded.

He quickly walked across the hall and knocked on the second door to the right. It was Meredith from Texas who answered. "Harold, it's Pastor Jim!"

Harold was in the bathroom, vomiting up his dinner.

"May I come in?" Conrad said, stepping inside and closing the door behind him. As he did, he looked out the peephole and saw Max Seavers walking toward his room.

37

THE ELITE CLUB ROOM on the tenth floor of the Hilton was on the same level as Conrad's room, but Serena felt a world away. What she had hoped to be a brief meet-and-greet after the media dinner had stretched into the early hours of the next morning. It was against her nature to not sympathize with and pray for those in need, whatever their station in life. And it was also the perfect alibi for her whereabouts during those hours between the media dinner and the prayer breakfast.

A Hollywood producer was confessing to her that his reason for attending the Presidential Prayer Breakfast was to meet well-heeled "Christian coin" to fund "family movies" to cover his alimony payments and cocaine habits. As he spoke in hushed tones, she couldn't help but steal glances at the large flat-panel TV screen on the wall flashing pictures of Conrad and the swarm of police outside the Library of Congress. The dateline flashed July 3, 2008, across the screen, and it was clear the story was going to dominate the morning news shows in an hour or so. This was what America was going to wake up to.

Dear Lord, she prayed, *I hope he's OK.*

Her iPhone vibrated and she looked down to see a text message from Benito that Conrad had made it to his room and had called the hotel's room service. Serena let out a low sigh of relief. She wanted to bolt right then, and struggled to maintain a calm expression before this reprobate of a producer who saw American Christians not as a flock to be fed but a market demographic to be fleeced. His "career," it seemed, consisted almost entirely of living off other people while he indulged his talent for making box office flops.

That moment a concierge walked over to tell her that there was a gentleman outside the club lounge who would like to see her. *Could Conrad really be that stupid and have left his room?* She casually stood up and politely excused herself, pausing only to shake a few hands on her way out.

Max Seavers was waiting for her in the foyer, along with two Secret Service agents.

"What did you do to your finger, Max?" she said, trying to hide her alarm. "And is that a gash on your forehead?"

"Follow me," he said sternly.

He led her down the hallway to the third door on the left—the room she had reserved for Conrad. She tensed up.

The game's up, girl.

The door was open and two more Secret Service agents were inside. But she couldn't see Conrad.

Only Brooke Scarborough, tied to the bed, spread-eagled, a bullet hole in her head.

Oh, my God, she thought with a shudder. *Conrad, what have you done?*

"I'm sorry you had to see this, Sister Serghetti, but I need to ask you if you've seen Conrad Yeats at the hotel."

"No," she said, still staring at Brooke. "What does he have to do with this?"

"He's a wanted man," Seavers said. "This was his room. He checked in under the alias Carl Anderson. I thought you might know something."

"I don't."

Seavers turned to the Secret Service agents. "Not a word to Senator Scarborough or anybody until after the prayer breakfast," he ordered. "We have a killer on the loose. We don't want to give him a heads-up that we're onto him by creating any unusual disruptions. Seal off the room and post two security guards outside the door. I want room-to-room sweeps during the breakfast while everybody is downstairs in the ballroom. This killer isn't getting out of this building."

The lead special agent nodded. "Yes, sir."

Seavers took her by the arm and escorted her out the door.

"Where are you taking me, Max?"

"Somewhere safe," he told her. "There's no telling what this maniac might do."

He led her down the hallway to a service closet that turned out to be an express service elevator. It linked the small kitchen of the 10th-floor club room to the hotel's main kitchen on the ballroom level. They took it all the way down and emerged in the service corridor between the back of the ballroom stage and the main kitchen.

Waiting for them were six Secret Service agents, who instantly formed a protective ring around them.

They turned down another hallway behind the back of the ballroom, a curving corridor with wood-paneled walls and portraits of every president and first lady since George Washington. Step by step they passed through succeeding epochs of administrations until they came to the portraits of the sitting American president and his wife and then a small, unmarked door.

Inside was a special VIP room with red carpets and gold walls that reminded Serena of a funeral parlor. The president's advance Secret Service detail was there. So, too, were Secretary Packard, Senator Scarborough, and several Chinese officials, all awaiting the president.

"Sister Serghetti," said Packard. "You know Senator Scarborough."

She was caught off guard but smiled and shook the hand of the father of the dead woman she had just seen. "How are you, Senator?"

"On behalf of the Presidential Prayer Breakfast, I'd like to personally thank you for offering up the opening prayer."

"The honor is mine, Mr. Senator."

"And this is Mr. Ling, China's top Olympics ambassador. Max Seavers is going to show him and all the Olympics delegates some real fireworks tomorrow on the Fourth."

Mr. Ling was all smiles. "I told my wife I was going to see the Fourth of July from the ultimate skybox—the observation deck of the Washington Monument. She didn't believe me."

Senator Scarborough looked at his watch. "Well, Mr. Ling and I have to get backstage. Sister Serghetti, you simply walk out when Bono is finished performing and open the breakfast in prayer. The rest of the program will take care of itself."

Serena nodded. "Yes, Mr. Senator, thank you."

She watched Scarborough leave with Ling and two Secret Service agents. It was just her, Seavers, and a glaring Packard in the room now, along with the president's personal advance team.

"What the hell is going on, Seavers?" Packard burst out.

"We found the body of Senator Scarborough's daughter in a room checked out to Yeats. Yeats murdered her."

"God Almighty!" Packard said. "This is a nightmare!"

"I don't believe Dr. Yeats murdered Ms. Scarborough," Serena said quickly. "Not for one second. Dr. Yeats is an American patriot of the first order and comes from a family of patriots. I also know he had feelings for her and would never kill without just cause."

Packard looked at Max Seavers. "What's Yeats doing here at the Washington Hilton of all places, anyway?"

Seavers said, "We believe his primary target is the president, sir."

"What!" Serena cried. "You can't be serious."

She was astounded, considering his relationship with Conrad, that Packard seemed to think it plausible.

"I suggest you mass e-mail a photo of Yeats to all agents on the premises immediately, Mr. Secretary," Seavers pressed. "He's wanted not only for the death of a security guard and an attack on the Library of Congress, but now the slaying of a U.S. senator's daughter. And the senator will have all our heads if we fail to apprehend Yeats."

That was enough for Packard, whose purse strings were controlled by Scarborough as chairman of the Senate Armed Services Committee.

"OK, do it."

Max Seavers nodded, clearly proud of himself.

Serena realized that Seavers had cleverly managed to turn the one person she and Conrad needed to reach— the president of the United States—into the one person he would never be able to get close to.

"What about Sister Serghetti, sir?" Seavers asked. "She has a history with Yeats and might pass along intel to him. Or some key or means to escape."

"That's absurd, Mr. Secretary." She then looked at Seavers. "You want to frisk me, Max?"

Seavers motioned to a couple of the stone-faced Secret Service agents but was cut off by Packard.

"This is the Presidential Prayer Breakfast, goddammit," Packard said. "Sister Serghetti is in the program for the opening prayer. We can't hold her, Seavers. We'll just watch her."

A Secret Service agent walked up and said, "Mr. Secretary, the presidential motorcade is two minutes away."

"I'll be back in a minute to walk with the President to

the ballroom." Then Packard offered her his arm. "Ladies first."

"Thank you, Mr. Secretary."

Packard looked back at Max Seavers and the security detail. "After the breakfast we'll meet here with the president and break the news of his daughter's slaying to Senator Scarborough," Packard barked. "By then you better pray that you've got Yeats in custody. Now go find that goddamn bastard."

38

IF CONRAD had his way, right now he'd be digging for the second globe beneath the Sarah Rittenhouse armillary in Montrose Park. He had already figured out that the secret access tunnel had to be the cave that his father had shown him as a child, and that the globe was probably at the bottom of that old Algonquin well in the back. It all made sense now, every wacky thing his crazy ass father had put him through.

But by 5 a.m. all entrances and exits to the Hilton had been sealed off in anticipation of the president's arrival. He was trapped in a hotel room with Harold and Meredith from Highland Park, Texas.

The most he could hope for now was to warn Serena and the president about the second globe and Seavers's plan to release a bird flu contagion. His best shot at reaching them was the prayer breakfast. And thanks to some bad blowfish the night before, Harold was going to be saying his prayers in the toilet while Conrad—or rather "Pastor Jim"—escorted Meredith to the breakfast.

Together they stood in the long line of thousands of prayer breakfast attendees who had emerged from packed elevators and stairwells to follow the directions of young ushers in blue blazers down two escalators to the ballroom level for the 57th Annual Presidential Prayer Breakfast. And dead ahead, just before the ballroom's open doors, the Secret Service had set up an elaborate and impenetrable security checkpoint.

"This is just like the end of time when God's angels will separate the sheep from the goats," Meredith joked.

Conrad chuckled nervously. He had pulled a switch with the tickets back in Harold and Meredith's room, taking Harold's ticket and leaving him his own. But he also had the silver cornerstone plate. Whatever hope he had of slipping through the checkpoint would vanish as soon as he tripped the metal detectors and drew unwanted attention.

Meredith slipped her arm under Conrad's and looked up at him starry-eyed. "Ooh, I feel so dangerous, Pastor Jim!"

As the metal detection gates at the checkpoint began to loom larger, Conrad felt his chest tighten. There was no way the trained agents were going to miss the fact he looked nothing like Harold's picture unless Meredith distracted them first.

"Hey, Meredith," he said, and removed the silver cornerstone plate from his inside breast pocket. "This souvenir I bought from Mount Vernon. I want you to have it."

"Why, thank you, Pastor Jim!" she said and took it from his hand and ran a perfectly manicured fingernail across the surface. "How pretty! I'll treasure it," she cooed and slipped it into her little pink purse.

When they reached the security gates a few moments later, Conrad could see there were checkpoints about ten feet apart. Armed agents in windbreakers stood at one table next to the first gate.

"Please empty your pockets and place any metal objects on the table," said a young female officer. "Thank you."

Beyond the gate an impossibly large black agent stood with a wand in his hand for full body scans.

"Oooh, this is so exciting," she said to the officer as she emptied her purse. "Oh, wait, hon, you go through first, I better turn this over," she said and pulled out the cornerstone plate from her purse. "Don't want to set off any alarms with my souvenir."

Conrad presented his ticket, walked through the metal detector, and looked back to see the officer return the cornerstone plate to Meredith.

"Please move on, ma'am."

Conrad let out a low breath as Meredith bounced over to him with a smile. He calmly led them away from the security checkpoint and toward the open doors of the giant ballroom. Soon as they crossed the threshold, he tried to ditch her.

"I'm at table 232," he told her. "Where are you?"

She had trouble letting go of his arm. "I'm over in the 700s."

"I just realized something," he said. "That souvenir

I gave you—I had promised it to someone else. I feel horrible."

"Oh, now don't you worry about a thing, Pastor Jim." She looked disappointed, but gave it back without a second thought. "You gotta be a man of your word."

Conrad smiled at her as they parted ways. "You're a saint."

Seavers left the gold room with a couple of Secret Service agents and marched toward the security checkpoint outside the ballroom. He showed the agents on duty Yeats's picture. None of them had seen him.

"Are you sure?" Seavers pressed one young man, who had hesitated.

"I'm almost positive," he swore, though Seavers could see the doubt in his eyes.

"Almost?" Seavers seethed.

Just before he killed her, Brooke had told him that Yeats had discovered the existence of a second globe. Seavers knew he had to find out what Yeats knew and stop him before he told the good sister or the feds.

Seavers then heard some kind of row and turned to a man being frisked at the metal detection gate by two agents.

Seavers hurried over. "What's going on?"

"We flagged his ticket—Carl Anderson."

Seavers looked at the man. He obviously wasn't Conrad Yeats, but the man must have had contact with him. "I take it your name's not Carl?"

"My name's Harold," the red-faced man said. "I don't

know how I got that ticket. Look, my wife is already inside with Pastor Jim Lee. You know, the bestselling author?"

"Does Pastor Jim look like this?" Seavers held up the photo of Yeats, which looked familiar enough to startle Harold.

"That's him!"

"Not quite," Seavers said. "You just handed off your wife to a terrorist wanted for the slaying of law enforcement agents and attacks on America's most sacred landmarks."

"Dear God!" Harold cried. "I didn't know! You have to believe me!"

"Can you recognize your wife, at least?"

Harold shot him an angry look. "I'm pretty sure I can."

"Then take me to her in the ballroom," Seavers said.

The gigantic ballroom was as big as a football field. The domed ceiling a couple of stories high only added to the aura of an indoor sports stadium.

Conrad, now free of Meredith, slipped between hundreds of round tables with white cloths and gold chairs toward a table to the right of the stage. It was near the staff door to the hotel's main kitchen, where hundreds of waiters shuffled in and out.

He picked an empty seat at the table, the least desirable chair because its back was to the stage, but perfect for him. He sat down and faced the wall by the kitchen entrance and six smiling table companions: a young couple from California, an older self-proclaimed "Lake Wobegon" couple from Minnesota, a middle-aged rabbi from New York, and a tall black woman from D.C. It was a United Nations of faith.

"You're never going to see anything good looking this way," joked the rabbi. "Would you mind passing the cantaloupe? They pray later."

Conrad looked down at the table full of fruit, pastries, juices, and coffee. Because of security issues and the crowd, everything had been prepped beforehand, and he had to remove a clear plastic wrap from the chilled plate of cantaloupe.

"Here you go," he said and passed it over. As he did, his eyes swept the ballroom for Serena. She was already on stage with various generals and senators, including the presumptive Democratic and Republican party nominees for the presidency in November. They were waiting for the president.

Most everybody else in the ballroom was seated, except hundreds of waiters attending to the tables. Conrad helped himself to some coffee and looked over the navy blue program with gold leaf trim in front of him. The opening prayer was to be offered by Sister Serena Serghetti following a contemporary rendition of "Amazing Grace" by the rock group U2's lead singer, Bono.

Conrad was about to pour himself a second cup of coffee when the young California man, who was Asian-American, said, "You might want to think twice about that. Security won't let you go to the bathroom while the president and first lady are in the ballroom."

"Thanks, I'll hold off . . ."

"It's Jim," the man said, offering his hand and Conrad shook it. "Jim Lee."

Conrad cocked his head. "Like Pastor Jim, the best-selling author?"

The black woman and the rabbi snorted a giggle. Conrad didn't get the joke.

"Pretty much," said Pastor Jim. "That's me."

"Oh!"

Conrad suddenly realized that Meredith from Texas had known from the start he wasn't Pastor Jim.

The old-timer from Minnesota said, "Is it true that there are more Christians in China than America, Pastor Jim?"

"Yes," said Pastor Jim. "But my family is Korean."

"From Seoul?"

"Burbank."

The old-timer, realizing he perhaps made some sort of faux pas, nodded enthusiastically. "You people make good citizens."

"Thank you." Pastor Jim smiled.

The black woman next to Conrad said, "He sells almost as many books as Bishop Jakes, you know."

Conrad nodded absently and, scoping the room for any sign of Seavers, said, "You sure don't see this kind of event in any other country on Earth."

"You mean elected officials acknowledging they're not God?"

"You got it," Conrad said, surprised by her dig. "You must work for one of them?"

"All of them. I'm a sergeant with the Capitol Police."

"I'd have never guessed," Conrad said slowly. There

was something very familiar about her. But if she was feeling likewise she wasn't showing it. "Tell me, is it true what they say about politicians here in Washington?"

"What's that?"

"That the only ones with convictions are in jail?"

"You're funny! I'm Wanda, by the way. Wanda Randolph."

"J-Jack," he said, glancing over at Pastor Jim, who was now talking to the rabbi.

She put out her hand. "Pleased to meet you, Jack."

"The pleasure's mine."

The instant Conrad grasped her hand he knew it belonged to the woman who held his in the ambulance the night before, the same one who pumped several bullets his way in the tunnels beneath the U.S. Capitol a couple of days ago.

She knew it, too. Her smile froze and she looked down at his hand, not letting go. Her eyes widened like she had just been shocked with an electric buzzer.

"This your first time here, Jack?" she asked him, even as she glanced over her shoulder at the small army of plainclothes security surrounding the ballroom.

"First and probably last," he told her, not taking his eyes off her.

"Why is that, Jack?"

"I just feel like I don't belong, you know? Like I'm a criminal here with all the saints."

There were glances around the table. Then a few vigorous nods.

"We all are, brother," said the man from Minnesota. "But too few of us are honest enough to admit it and seek forgiveness at the foot of the cross. Isn't that right, Pastor Jim?"

Pastor Jim, his mouth full with an almond croissant, could only nod.

Conrad looked at Wanda as her hand reached into her purse. He slipped both of his own under the table and for a wild second was ready to upend it if necessary.

But her hands emerged with a card and a pen. "I know from the ballistics report that you didn't kill my man Larry last night," she whispered to him as she wrote a phone number on the back of her card. "But I can't yet prove that Max Seavers did." She slid the card across the tablecloth to him.

"What's this?" he asked.

"That's the number to Prison Fellowship. It's a charity that ministers to men and women behind bars. You're going to need it if you don't scram this second."

Conrad looked at her. "And why is that?"

"Because I see Max Seavers and two Secret Service agents walking straight toward our table."

From the stage Serena saw Max Seavers, too, and decided to jump the gun on the prayer breakfast by standing up, walking to the microphone stand, and offering up her opening prayer a good seven minutes ahead of schedule.

"Let us rise for the opening prayer," she said, and bowed her head, aware that the president hadn't arrived yet and that she had caught the senators on stage off guard. But there was nothing they could say at this point as everybody in the ballroom rose to their feet and effectively blocked Seavers from reaching Conrad.

"Almighty God," she prayed. "We make our earnest prayer that Thou wilt keep the United States in Thy Holy protection, and Thou wilt incline the hearts of the citizens to cultivate a spirit of subordination and obedience to government, and entertain a brotherly affection and love for one another and for their fellow citizens of the United States at large. . . ."

She kept her eyes open, along with every member of the security detail stationed throughout the ballroom, and she could see Seavers seething in the back, craning his neck as he searched for Conrad.

". . . And finally that Thou wilt most graciously be pleased to dispose us all to do justice, to love mercy, and to demean ourselves with that charity, humility, and pacific temper of mind which were the characteristics of the Divine Author of our blessed religion, and without a humble imitation whose example in these things we can never hope to be a happy nation. Grant our supplication, we beseech Thee, through Jesus Christ our Lord, Amen."

As soon as everybody sat down again, Seavers, a furious frown on his face, marched toward the corner of the room where Yeats sat. Bono, who was supposed to open the breakfast with a song before the opening prayer, now began to sing "Amazing Grace."

This prayer breakfast was like an absurd nightmare,

Seavers thought, walking among the well-dressed deluded whose minuscule brainwaves were directed to a deity that did not exist, and who actually believed that the Founding Fathers sought to establish a Christian nation. That Conrad Yeats believed he could find refuge here was even more absurd.

Yeats had his back to him as Seavers approached and recognized the policewoman from the Capitol. Was there any place he could avoid that woman?

Seavers glared at Sergeant R.A.T.S. as the two Secret Service agents took positions behind her opposite Yeats. Seavers then placed his left hand with the stump of a finger on Yeats's left shoulder.

"Time's up, Yeats."

But instead of Yeats, Seavers found himself staring at the face of a Latino server, who was holding a pot of coffee.

"This is Pablo, our server," Sergeant Randolph explained. "We had an extra seat and in the spirit of this event invited him to join us in prayer."

"Goddamn you, where is he?" he said, drawing sharp glances from nearby tables.

"Relax, Dr. Seavers," she said, eyes like daggers. "Where's he going to go? He's not armed and you've got an army of security people down here."

Seavers snapped his head and scanned the ballroom for Yeats as the Irish lilt of Bono's voice swelled to an unearthly decibel level. No sign of him, only servers with coffee and breakfast items heading into and out of the kitchen entrance.

"The kitchen," he barked.

39

BY THE TIME Serena followed the president out of the ballroom after his remarks to the attendees, it appeared from the anxious faces of the Secret Service agents in the hallway that her prayer had been answered and that Conrad had escaped.

"I heard you did a good job with the opening prayer, Sister Serghetti," the president said as she followed him and his Secret Service detail past the portraits of previous leaders. "Wish I had heard it myself."

"I simply recited the official prayer that George Washington offered for the United States of America in the year 1783," she said. "It was printed in the program."

The president frowned and said nothing more until they entered the gold room, where Packard was waiting beside an American flag and a small spiral stairwell that led to a secret outside door and the president's waiting limousine.

"You've got sixty seconds before I step outside," the president said.

Packard broke the news. "That item we've been searching for is waiting for you in the Oval Office, but it's empty," he said, providing no particulars with Serena present. "Brooke Scarborough is dead. Conrad Yeats killed her and is at large on the premises. Seavers is sweeping everything room-by-room."

The president looked at her. "And I'm to understand that the Vatican has been helping Dr. Yeats?"

"No, Mr. President, but I have," she said boldly, seeing the shock in Packard's face. "You should, too. And he did not kill Brooke Scarborough."

She slipped her hand inside her blouse and removed Washington's letter to Stargazer. Packard looked like he was going to pass out at the very sight of it.

"I had hoped to press my case with you once I had everything, Mr. President, but I'm afraid I don't." She handed him the letter. "But you have everything I do, sir."

The president looked it over and handed it to Packard. "DARPA will analyze this?"

"Right away, Mr. President."

Serena watched Packard slip it inside his dress uniform pocket. She doubted it would ever see the fluorescent light of a lab at DARPA or anywhere else if Packard were foolish enough to pass it along to Max Seavers.

She said, "What you'll find out, Mr. President, is that Dr. Yeats is simply following the orders of George Washington, commander-in-chief."

"I'm the commander-in-chief, Sister Serghetti," the president said emphatically.

"What I'm trying to say is that he believes he is serving the highest interests of the republic. If you could offer him immunity from prosecution, he might come in and give you whatever he took from the globe."

"I appreciate that, Sister Serghetti, and maybe yesterday we could have cut him some kind of deal," the president said. "But now that he's been caught detonating explosives on U.S. landmarks, slaying federal agents, and has murdered the daughter of one of America's most prominent senators, well, I don't think even I can help him. I swore an oath to protect America."

"No, Mr. President, you swore an oath to protect the Constitution."

The president was not pleased with her impudence. "I'll say a prayer for Conrad Yeats, Sister Serghetti. God bless you."

"And you, Mr. President."

With that the president marched up the spiral staircase behind two Secret Service agents. He was followed by Packard, who looked back at her with undisguised animosity. She saw a square of light thrown on the curving wall and heard the roar of running engines outside before the thud from an unseen door left her alone in the room.

She pulled out her cell phone and pressed a button. Benito answered. "Bring the car around. We're leaving."

40

INSIDE THE HILTON'S underground parking garage, two policemen stood on either side of the service door as dozens of waiters carried crates of fruit, muffins, and croissants from the prayer breakfast to awaiting vans, which in turn would deliver the food to local homeless shelters.

One of those waiters was Conrad Yeats. He carried not one but two boxes of ice-packed fruit on his shoulders to the nearest van, but he never went back inside. Using the vehicle line to shield himself from the policemen, he walked out into the garage in search of Benito so he could hitch a ride in Serena's limo with the Vatican emblem and secret cargo compartment.

The garage was alive with activity now that the president had left and the senators, congress members, and foreign dignitaries were free to leave as well. The limousines and SUVs were already lining up to pick up their VIPs in front of the hotel entrance.

"Conrad Yeats?" a voice called from the shadows.

Conrad cursed himself for having ended up in a well-lit place in the garage. He turned to see a young brunette whose face he recognized but whose name he had forgotten. She was in her mid-20s, an aide to a female senator from California.

"Hi, there!" he said, faking excitement as he walked over to her.

She frowned at his generic response. "It's Lisa from San Francisco," she said. "And what are *you* of all people doing at a prayer breakfast?"

"Mending my ways, Lisa."

He pulled out a knife he had taken from the kitchen and put it to her side as she gasped. He hated himself for doing this to her, but he had no choice.

"OK, I confess," he whispered in her ear. "I haven't really changed. If you scream or make a sound, I'll kill you. You've seen the TV reports. You know I will."

"Please," she begged him. "I'll be better for you next time. You can wear the fedora and I'll learn to like the whip."

"Quiet," he said, jabbing the knife in the fold of her skin. "You're going to help me get out of here, Lisa. Nod if you understand."

Lisa nodded.

Seavers stationed himself outside the main entrance of the Hilton and watched the VIPs get into their taxis, limousines, and SUVs. The prayer breakfast was over, incident-free as far as its guests were concerned. The announcement about Brooke Scarborough's death would not reach them until they were on their way back to Kansas or Iowa or wherever the hell they came from. By then, of course, the Alignment's agenda would be unstoppable.

The only X factor, he thought with rage, was the elusive Yeats.

Seavers watched the junior senator from California and her aide get into her limousine and drive off as a sleeker limousine with a Vatican flag pulled up. He turned his head to see Serena Serghetti emerge from the front entrance and make her way to the open rear door and climb in.

Seavers motioned two Secret Service agents to the limousine. They halted the driver and swept the underside of the car with long, extended mirrors.

The rear door opened and Serena stepped back out and watched the scene. And because she did, a small crowd behind her did also.

"Lose something, Max?" she asked, putting on a great show of being held up. "I confess I brought out a couple of chocolate croissants for Benito. He loves them so."

"Tell your driver to open the trunk," Seavers demanded and walked to the back as two agents drew their guns.

He was aware of the scene he was causing with the curious dignitaries, but he didn't care, even when a press photographer started taking pictures. He knew he couldn't force her to open up—the car had diplomatic plates, after all—but if she didn't the world would know she was hiding something, and so would he.

Her swarthy driver came out and, getting the nod

from Serena, opened the trunk. Besides a garment bag and small suitcase, it was empty.

Serena put her hands on her hips and an amused expression on her face for the cameras. "You want to search those, too, Max?"

Seavers turned red with rage when one of his agents came up. "Sir, we found something," he said and led Seavers to the rear seat of the cabin.

Seavers then waved the good Sister over from her photo op and pointed into the limousine. "Open that seat compartment or I'll tear it open with a knife. Your choice."

"Max." She turned serious. "You do understand that in some countries I've been forced to smuggle out missionaries and political prisoners. If you let the press and public know about this, then some of those prisoners will lose their last option."

"Your choice, Serena."

She leaned into the back of the limousine and felt for a hidden latch that released the flap beneath the rear seat. As it opened, she was pushed back by one of the Secret Service agents.

"Step back, please, ma'am," he said and pointed his gun into the secret compartment.

But it was empty.

Seavers burned inside as Serena turned to face him with her beatific smile. "Told you, Max."

Aware of the television cameras, he leaned over and whispered. "Your friend the fugitive is a murderer and an American traitor. You don't want anything to do with him."

"No, Max. I don't want anything to do with *you* anymore. You can keep your vaccines." She got inside and nodded to Benito to go.

Seavers watched the limousine drive off and turned to the Secret Service agent who had examined the secret compartment. "Did you place the GPS nano tracker on her person?"

"Yes, sir. Stuck it under her shoulder when we hustled her down to the holding room. She'll never know."

"Have a team follow her signal," Seavers ordered. "At some point she's bound to lead us to Yeats."

Serena leaned back in her seat and breathed a sigh of relief as Benito turned the limousine onto Connecticut.

"You OK, *signorina*?"

"Now that I'm breathing, yes. But I don't know where Conrad is."

Benito looked up in the mirror. "He was in that limo ahead of us back at the Hilton."

"No, there was a senator in that limo. I saw her get in."

"But Dr. Yeats was driving," Benito said. "He found me in the underground garage and told me to give you a message."

Serena sat on the edge of her seat. "Give it to me."

"He said he will meet you at Sarah's house."

As Conrad drove the senator's limousine, he listened carefully to the senator gossip with Lisa about some of the individual speakers at the breakfast even as she expressed being moved by the event itself. Lisa said very little. He had warned her that he was strapped with explosives and that any attempt to alert the senator or send a text message from her cell phone would blow them all up.

It worked until they crossed Washington Circle.

"What's that knocking?" the senator asked Lisa.

Conrad could see Lisa squirm in his rearview mirror.

"Could be the 87 octane level of the gas, ma'am," he told the senator, pulling into a Union gas station across the street from the Ritz-Carlton. "Let me check, maybe top off the tank with some premium."

"You should have done this earlier," the senator barked as he stepped out in his chauffeur's uniform and walked to the pump.

A minute later, the knocking got even louder inside the limousine.

The senator looked out the window and couldn't see the driver. "Find out where he is, Lisa."

But her aide started breaking down in tears for no reason.

"I don't have time for this today, Lisa."

The senator opened her own door and saw the gasoline hose in the limousine's gas tank, but no driver. The knocking, she realized, seemed to be coming from the trunk. She stepped out and walked to the trunk and opened it.

There was her driver, tied up and gagged.

❖ ❖ ❖

By the time Seavers and his men arrived at the gas station, two D.C. cops were questioning the senator's aide, who apparently knew Yeats from their previous, albeit brief, relationship and provided a detailed description. An ATM camera across the street at the SportsClub fitness center, meanwhile, had captured Yeats on video.

Where are you going, Yeats? Seavers wondered as he climbed into his SUV and they drove off. *To the second globe perhaps? To meet your lovely Serena?*

"You set it up so I can track the nun on my own phone?" he asked the driver, a Marine named Landford from Detachment One.

"Yes, sir," Landford replied. "Check your Google Maps."

Seavers looked at his cell phone and followed the red blip that represented Sister Serghetti. It was moving up R Street past Montrose Park. Then it stopped.

He looked closely at the screen and clicked the zoom button. Slowly the fuzzy pixels sharpened and he realized he was staring down at a statue of some kind. He clicked on the image and a Web page automatically popped up with a picture of the Sarah Rittenhouse Armillary.

The armillary, he realized, staring at the image of the sun dial-like sphere on its marble pedestal. *The second globe that Brooke had told him about, the one Yeats was after now, could be buried beneath the armillary!*

"We're here, sir," said the driver in the mirror.

Seavers looked out his window to see the armillary a mere 20 or so feet away from the street, potentially holding a treasure but in plain daylight for all to see.

But there was no sign of Serena or Yeats.

He looked back down at his phone. The red dot—the GPS tracker—was still stationary, still blinking next to the armillary.

"She must be under the armillary," he said. "There must be another entrance, a sewer line or something beneath the monument. Get the drill team from Jones Point over here and send a plainclothes unit to sweep the park."

"Excuse me, sir," Landford said, hanging up his phone. "We picked up a call from the National Park Service station inside the park. An officer nabbed a man in a chauffeur's uniform fitting our APB."

A few minutes later Seavers entered a small, damp NPS station, which stunk from the dung of the horses in the stables. The watch officer escorted Seavers to a small holding cell, where the man in the chauffeur's uniform sat in the corner.

"Yeats!" Seavers shouted.

The head looked up and Seavers found himself looking into the wrinkled, warted face of a homeless man who had traded his rags for a suit.

"You imbeciles!" Seavers shouted to the watch officer.

But the watch officer was talking on his radio. "Copy that," he said and switched it off before addressing Seavers. "Looks like your man stole one of our horses, too."

41

CONRAD LEFT his police horse at the old Peirce Mill. He then walked along the creek at the bottom of the ravine in the direction of the cave. That cave, he was now convinced, would lead him directly to the final resting place of the terrestrial globe beneath the Sarah Rittenhouse Armillary.

As he crossed the creek, exhausted but determined, he thought of Washington's crossing at Valley Forge and the courage that saw America through the Revolution. It was that same courage and resolve which must have driven Washington on the fateful night in these woods when he stood up to the Alignment to save the republic.

George Washington galloped through the woods on his horse in the rain. It was almost three o'clock in the morning when he cleared the trees and came to an abrupt halt by the wharf in Georgetown.

Slowly Washington led Nelson to the old stone house, listening to the old war horse's hoofs clapping lightly in the night. He tied him to a hitching post and walked to the front door, anonymous in his civilian raincoat and hat. Even so, he could not hide his regal bearing as an officer and gentleman.

He knocked on the door three times. He paused a moment and again knocked. He tried the latch and the door opened on its own. Washington stooped to enter, his towering 6-foot-3-inch frame filling the doorway, and stepped inside.

The man he was to meet, his top forger, sat limply in a chair by the flickering fireplace, blood on his face and a bullet hole in his forehead. On the rough-hewn table before him were charts, maps, and documents.

"A treacherous affair, this new republic." A voice spoke from the shadows. "Who knows where it will end?"

Washington grew very still, then slowly turned his head.

Several feet away, beneath a doorway, stood a mountainous silhouette. He was a bull of a man, with a ruddy face and white, curly hair. His eyes were black and soulless. The man drew a pistol from his coat and aimed the barrel directly at Washington. "You should not have tried to fool the Alignment." His voice, though familiar, was not easy to place. "Now tell me where your copy of the treaty is."

"There on the table," Washington said warily. "I came to pick it up."

"Liar." The man emerged from the shadows.

"You!" Washington said, staring at one of his most loyal officers through the years. The man was a former

Son of Liberty. A Patriot. One of the original members of the Culper Spy Ring who helped Washington beat the British in New York. His top assassin.

"This is a forgery," the assassin said as he picked up a document from the table and waved it in Washington's face.

Washington felt a surge of dread. He knows. How does he know?

"The ranks of the Alignment are everywhere. Its destiny and America's are one." The assassin leveled his gun at Washington's chest. "Now sit down next to your friend."

Washington did as he was told. Dawn was still hours away, and the room was very dark. He removed his hat and coat and set them on the table, revealing the ceremonial Masonic apron he was wearing, and sat down opposite the assassin.

"A lot of good your brotherhood of builders did you," the assassin sneered. "What match are they against the warriors of the Alignment?"

Washington watched as the assassin unfolded the forged document on the table and examined it by the light of the fire.

"Brilliant," said the assassin approvingly. "This looks exactly like the amended and updated treaty you are to sign and exchange with the Alignment for the original treaty. Except that you used that special ink that becomes invisible after a few days, rendering your signature meaningless because the articles of this treaty will, in effect, disappear. By the time the Alignment would have discovered your treachery, you would have no

doubt destroyed the original treaty. Was old Livingston here your man in the Alignment?"

Washington said nothing.

"You always did like to play the double spy game." The assassin turned, holding the official treaty that Washington was supposed to sign. *"And what did you intend to do with this?"*

The assassin held up the amended treaty that Livingston had copied, the one that would have bound Washington and America to an unthinkable fate.

Washington stared at the fire wordlessly. *That infernal treaty!* he thought. *I never should have signed the first one ten years ago.*

"No matter," said the assassin. *"Your game is nearly up. Our friends will be here soon. They will decide if you attend your ceremony tomorrow."*

He was pointing to a flyer posted on the wall inviting all to join the president and members of Congress on a procession from Alexandria to the top of Jenkins Heights for the laying of the cornerstone of the new United States Capitol building.

Washington could feel a cold chill coming on, the life of the republic passing away.

"How about some ale?" Washington asked.

"Always the cipher, General," the assassin said. He reached for some glasses on a shelf and for a moment turned his back. *"So what drink shall it be? Fate or free will? Destiny or liberty?"*

"I choose freedom," Washington said, leaning back in his chair until his feet came up toward the table. *"I can't help it."*

Washington rammed the table with his feet into the assassin's back, driving him into the wall. Several glasses crashed to the floor. The assassin turned, his face a bloody mess as his arm swung up with his pistol. Washington rose from his chair, his left hand deflecting the pistol as his right knee came up into the assassin's groin. The assassin's head jerked forward, his leg hooking behind Washington's, sending them both crashing to the ground. As Washington went down with him, he reached for the wrist of the hand that held the pistol, smashing his fist into the side of the assassin's neck, aware of the pistol exploding between them.

There was the distinct smell of burning flesh and the assassin lay still, dead.

Washington got to his feet, picked up the official treaty and tossed it into the fire. He signed the forgery and slipped it into his overcoat. Then he paused.

The rain had stopped outside.

"Blast it," he cursed, realizing that he had to hurry for his rendezvous with the Alignment to exchange his forgery for their copy of the countersigned and amended treaty he first signed ten years ago. It was the only binding document left, and, God willing, would shortly be in his possession.

In the center of the Federal District was a hill known as Jenkins Heights. Washington had always known it as Rome, because a century earlier a Maryland landowner named Francis Pope had a dream that a mighty empire to eclipse ancient Rome would one day rise on the banks of the Potomac, which he called the Tiber.

Washington, steeped in the history of the land he surveyed as a youth, knew the hill's history stretched well before that, and he felt as if he were riding back in time as old Nelson climbed the hill for the exchange of treaties.

Long before Europeans colonized the New World, the Algonquin Indians held tribal grand councils at the foot of this hill. The Algonquin were linked by archaeology to the ancient Mayans and by legend to the descendents of Atlantis. The chiefs of their primary tribe, the Montauk Indians, were known as Pharaoh, like their ancient Egyptians cousins. And the word was spelled like it was in the old Arabic languages 10,000 years ago, meaning "Star Child" or "Children of the Stars."

Which was why Washington had chosen this hill as the heart of the new federal city, and why his handpicked surveyors Ellicott and L'Enfant had oriented the proposed Congressional House to the star Regulus in the constellation of Leo—key to both Atlantis and Egypt—and the entire federal city to the constellation Virgo, like Rome.

Washington himself was ambivalent about astrology.

As a Mason, he felt it made sense that new cities and churches and public buildings be aligned to the stars, if only to acknowledge the necessity of heaven's blessings on so vast and corruptible an earthly enterprise as the founding of a new republic. And it made sense to him to cast astrological charts for the laying of cornerstones *at the most opportunistic, astronomically favorable moments, such as the time set for the laying of the cornerstone of the U.S. Capitol on this very hill at 1 p.m. later that day. The stars, after all, were more permanent fixtures in the heavens than the passing politics of men.*

The officers of the Alignment, however, were no builders like the Masons, but rather warriors who traced their origins to Atlantis and who had infiltrated and manipulated the armies of various empires throughout the ages. They used the stars to wage war and destroy those they considered their enemies. Moreover, their astrology was not elective, like his, employed only to make the most of a favorable astrological climate. No. Their astrology was fixed, fatalistic, and filled with doom—a self-fulfilling prophecy. They never considered the irony that they were merely using the stars to justify their actions.

At strategic points in history, the Illuminati, the Masons, and even the Church had served as ignorant hosts to the infernal ranks of the Alignment, who had now set their sights on the federal government of the new United States. During the Revolution, even Washington himself had gone so far as to rely on certain officers trained in their arts to turn the tide of battle.

It was a mistake he had lived to regret.

They were waiting at the top—12 representatives of the Alignment on horseback with torches. They included officers, senators, and bankers Washington knew well, but clearly not as well as he had thought.

Washington rode up to the group, stationed around a trench dug for the laying of the cornerstone.

A few feet beyond the trench was the golden celestial globe.

The official Alignment negotiator, known by the pseudonym Osiris, ran his hands around the smooth contours and constellations of the globe until it cracked open to reveal the wooden axis that kept the two halves together. He pulled the globe apart and removed the axis. It was hollow.

"The treaty, General," he said.

Washington handed over the forgery he had brought with him from the old stone house, complete with his signature as president of the United States.

Osiris rolled it up into a scroll, placed it inside the axis and closed the globe. Then Osiris handed over the original treaty signed in Newburgh in 1783, back when Washington was commander-in-chief of the Continental Army and the United States of America and its Constitution did not yet exist.

Washington slipped the Newburgh Treaty into his pocket, then watched as the sealed globe with the forgery penned with dissolvable ink was lowered to the bottom of the trench into a hollow stone block. On the reverse side of the forgery was something the assassin back at the stone house missed: a star map in invisible ink that would reveal itself later should the globe ever see the light of day.

But that would be centuries from now, Washington thought.

Mortar was poured on top of the trench to seal it. Then a few spades of dirt to cover it. Come morning a silver plate marker would be placed at the bottom of the trench and on top of it the cornerstone to the U.S. Capitol.

"You have what you want," Washington told them. "Why not be rid of me?"

"You have been indispensable, sir. And we salute you. If only you were of more sturdy character, you would have let us crown you, and then you could have led us and America into her destiny this generation instead of forcing her to wait for another."

"America will prove you wrong," Washington said.

Four soldiers were posted to guard the celestial globe until the cornerstone-laying ceremony, and the 13 officers dispersed in every direction. Four each to the north, south, and east, and one lonely horseman, Washington, to the west.

It took Washington a half hour to reach the wild outskirts of the Federal District and make it to Peirce Mill along Rock Creek. He followed the winding waters through rocky ravines and dense, primeval woods. At the end of his journey was a cave, hidden among the dense ferns, shrubs, and other foliage. A shroud of gray moss and tangled vines over the entrance made it all but invisible.

Washington tied Nelson to a hickory tree, parted the curtain of tangled vines and stepped inside, where a flicker of light was visible in the distance. He followed the cave to the end, where a larger cavern or hollow appeared and a shaking Hercules, his most trusted slave, *held a torch over an ancient Algonquin well surrounded by several barrels of gunpowder.*

Washington gazed at Hercules and the round sack-cloth by Hercules' buckled shoes. He bent down and removed the sackcloth to reveal another copper globe.

The globe was almost identical to the one he had just seen buried atop Jenkins Heights. But this one was ter-restrial, originally paired with its sister but now sepa-rated for a special purpose. He stared at the unique to-pography the cartographer who crafted the globe had carved so long ago, marveling at it.

Washington moved his finger along the 40th par-allel on the globe, feeling for the seam. He found the spring and the globe cracked open. He removed the signed document from his overcoat, placed it inside the globe and closed it up. Then he nodded to Hercules, who knotted some rope around it and lowered it down the well.

Washington watched as the coil of rope by Hercules' feet unwound. Deeper and deeper the globe descended until it rested at the bottom of the well. Putting on his Masonic apron, Washington took out a trowel and threw a simple spade of dirt into the well. Then he sat down on a barrel of gunpowder and held the torch as Hercules rolled up his sleeves, picked up a shovel and began filling the bottom of the well with dirt.

Every now and then Hercules would pause to dust himself off, and Washington could only marvel at his slave's fine clothing, gold pocket watch, and ornate buck-les. Hercules was probably the best dressed slave in the

United States. It was a shame to involve him in all this nasty business.

"Do you realize you are a finer specimen of fashion than I am, Hercules?"

"You allow me to sell leftover foodstuffs, sir."

"And your profit?"

"About $200 last year, sir."

Washington shook his head. This was a new world.

Finally, they lowered two kegs of gunpowder down the well, and left a long trail of powder behind them as they exited the cave.

Outside in the dark, Washington took in the fresh air and looked at his nervous slave.

"You'll be going back to Philadelphia by way of New York," Washington told Hercules and handed him an envelope intended for Robert Yates, chief justice of the New York Supreme Court. "You know where the designated drop box is buried?"

Hercules nodded. "Just outside that farm."

"That's right," said Washington. "You best be going now. We'll talk again when I'm back in Philadelphia."

"Yessa," Hercules said, and ran off through some branches to his horse and untied him.

Washington watched Hercules gallop off and then turned to the cave and removed his pistol.

Washington raised his arm and leveled his pistol at the cave. "God save America," he said and fired a single shot.

There was a flash from somewhere deep inside the cave, and then a deep, thunderous explosion, setting off several more as the entire back of the cave collapsed. A blast of dust and the smell of sulfur billowed out from the mouth of the cave, burying the globe until Kingdom Come or until Stargazer could come for it, however fate would have it.

When the smoke cleared, Washington was gone.

Conrad found the cave on the other side of the creek behind its cloak of vegetation. He parted the curtain of roots and entered the damp passage. It felt like he was going back in time, searching for his lost childhood, his origins, his father. In a way, he was. Because here in this cave everything came together: *Tom Sawyer*, those many days with his dad digging out the cave, even the Sarah Rittenhouse Armillary in the park a hundred feet up where he used to jog.

It was always here, he marveled. *All this time.*

There was a movement in the dark, then the blinding glare of a headtorch. Conrad blinked for a moment until he saw Serena's angelic but dirty face, a halo of light behind her, and a shovel on her shoulder, ready to bring it down on his head.

"Thank God, Conrad," she said. "You made it. I wasn't sure if I got your directions right."

He wanted to wrap his arms around her, tell her how much he loved her and drag her away from all the nonsense that kept them apart. Instead, he grabbed her by the throat.

"You dirty, pretty liar," he told her. "You knew there were two globes all along, and you didn't tell me."

"They always come in pairs, Conrad," she said, choking. "Terrestrial and celestial. I assumed you knew that."

He tightened his grasp. "Or maybe you and your friends at the Vatican wanted to keep them for yourselves."

"Please, Conrad, I know you didn't kill Brooke."

He looked into her dark, smoky eyes and let go.

She gasped for air.

"Brooke," he muttered, remembering his last glimpse of her tied to the bed in the hotel room, feeling the hurt of what must have happened to her after he left pressing down on him. "Seavers did it, I swear."

"I know," Serena said, swallowing hard, trying to catch her breath. "Here, take this. We don't have much time."

She handed him a shovel.

42

SARAH RITTENHOUSE ARMILLARY
MONTROSE PARK

IT WAS JUST AFTER 7 P.M., the sun setting over the horizon, when the corporal from the Army Corps of Engineers crawled out of the sewer on R Street near the armillary to break the news to Max Seavers, who had the area roped off by his disguised Detachment One Marines.

Seavers, who was hunched over a geological survey of Rock Creek Park in the relative quiet of the playground by the armillary, had noticed the drilling had stopped. "What's wrong, Corporal?"

"We tagged something, but we're not sure what," the corporal said. "So we're tripping right now."

"English, Corporal."

"The casing—er, the tube we dropped down to set off the charges, developed a spur of some kind. So we're bringing the drill bit back up. Once we've tripped the bit back up, we'll send down a mill to bore out the casing. After we retract the mill, the bit will have to be tripped down again."

The only thing Seavers understood was that this was going to cost him even more time. And he had already allowed Yeats too much. "How long is this going to take, Corporal?"

"It's going to cost DARPA about a hundred grand for the new drill bit and about a million for the day as far as the GSA is concerned," the corporal said. "We've got seventy-five men and a lot of equipment down there, sir. This is a massive operation to throw together so fast."

"I didn't ask about the cost, you penny-pinching bureaucrat," Seavers seethed. "I asked how long."

"The trip is going to take about twelve hours each way."

That was 24 hours from now, Seavers realized, just when he was going to be accompanying the Chinese Olympic officials to the Washington Monument.

"That's unacceptable, Corporal. How much further do you have to go?"

"About two hundred feet before we hit what looks to be a cavern, although it's partially collapsed," the corporal said. "But we've hit the harder, more resilient metamorphic rock that's in the way, sir. It's got schists, phyllites, slates, gneisses, and gabbros."

At this point, Seavers knew more about the geology of America's fourth oldest national park than he ever wanted to. Designed for the preservation "of all timber, animals, or curiosities . . . and their retention, as nearly as possible," the park was 15 kilometers long and almost two kilometers wide, a sanctuary for "many and rare and unique species," according to the act of Congress that created it.

Those species right now included Conrad Yeats and Serena Serghetti.

"Hold on, Corporal," Seavers said, and radioed Landford at the mobile command post. "Where is the NPS in the hunt for our terrorists?"

"Nothing yet, sir," Landford reported. "But they've got all available rangers and police on horseback and foot sweeping the creek area."

Unfortunately, as Seavers now knew, Rock Creek itself ran almost 53 kilometers, and the entire Rock Creek "watershed" covered almost 50,000 acres. Worse, it cut through deformed metamorphic crystalline rocks that were dotted with innumerable sinkholes, caves, and caverns. A quarter of the area was within the boundaries of the federal district, making it a virtual urban Tora Bora in which Yeats could hide for some time.

Seavers looked down at his geological map showing the vast cave systems throughout the area. He was positive Yeats and the nun had followed one of them to wind their way back beneath the armillary. At some point, if he didn't beat them to the globe, they would have to come out, and when they did, he wanted them captured immediately.

But he was taking no chances.

"Corporal, you're done drilling," Seavers said. "We're going to drop a suitcase bunker buster bomb down the casing. It should easily penetrate the remaining two hundred feet of rock to hit the cavern."

The corporal looked shocked. "You drop a mini bunker buster, sir, and you'll probably collapse the cavern, burying whatever it is you're looking for."

"We can always dig it up," Seavers said. "I just don't want it going anywhere."

43

THE WALLS of the ancient well were lined with stone, which made Serena wonder if it had been used for something sacred or ritualistic. It appeared to have been originally constructed with pure Algonquin muscle, probably two or more Indians working side by side. As such it was wide enough to accommodate both her and Conrad. He did the digging while she hauled up the dirt.

"Mother Superior always told me that if you ask God to move your mountain, don't be surprised if he gives you a shovel."

"Did she also teach you to lie and cheat, too?" Conrad asked with a grunt, digging his shovel deep into the dirt. "You knew Brooke was Alignment from the start, Serena, didn't you? But you didn't warn me. You didn't lift a goddamn finger until after I found my orders as Stargazer from Washington."

"What did Brooke tell you, Conrad?"

"That Seavers is going to release a bird flu virus at the Olympic Games in Beijing next month." He tossed a shovelful of dirt into a bucket. "Actually, he's going to release it tomorrow at the National Mall. But the contagion won't start until the Olympics so that everybody will assume it started in China. America gets to give the smart vaccine to its friends and deny it to its enemies at home and abroad. Seavers is just the Alignment's trigger man for the Apocalypse. The globe we're after is what they're going to use to somehow justify the 'cleansing' and their New World Order."

Like a dark shadow the revelation came upon her and she shivered.

"The bird flu," she repeated. "Oh, my God, Conrad. I should have known. As a linguist I should have known."

"Known what?"

"The word *influenza* comes from the Old Italian," she said. "It means a 'bad alignment of stars.' The ancients associated the outbreak of plagues with astronomical conjunctions."

"Yeah, well, this time the Alignment is going to make it happen."

"We have to stop him, Conrad. But how in the world are we going to get to him?"

"We're never going to find that needle in that haystack," he said, breathing hard. "There are going to be a half million people picnicking on the Mall for the concert and fireworks. And security has never been tighter."

As she watched him redouble his digging, Serena tried to make sense of this new revelation. Suddenly, she said, "I know where he's going to do it."

Conrad stopped digging for a moment, to catch his breath and listen.

"I heard Seavers talking to a Chinese official at the

prayer breakfast. He's going to the top of the Washington Monument when all the visiting Olympic officials go up to see the fireworks. We have to call it in to the president and Secretary Packard."

Serena tried her cell phone, but of course there was no signal, not this deep under the earth.

"Like they're going to believe us, anyway," he said, and she heard a definitive clank of the shovel.

She got down on her knees and helped him clear the remaining dirt away to reveal the bottom of the well. She felt her stomach turn over.

"It's not here," she said, desperation in her voice. "The globe is gone. We have to leave and warn the White House about Seavers. We have no choice now."

"No, it's here." Conrad wiped his brow and looked up the walls of the well. "I know it. We haven't gotten below the water table yet. Step back."

Serena moved aside as he lifted his heavy shovel into the air like a man with a sledgehammer at a county fair about to ring the bell and impress his girlfriend. "What are you doing?"

"This is a false bottom." He brought the shovel down on the stone bottom of the well. Sparks flew from the thunder of the blow. Conrad lifted the shovel up again and brought it down even harder, and she heard a loud crack. "Help me lift these out."

It took a half hour to haul up the stones, and another hour of digging before Conrad's shovel produced a distinctive clink. He had struck something metal.

It was the globe.

Conrad set the shovel against the wall of the well, pulled out a cigarette from the pocket of the shirt he had lifted from a homeless man and lit it.

Serena stared at him. "What the bloody hell are you waiting for!" she said, worried that Max Seavers and his armed dupes could be on top of them any moment.

Conrad took a slow drag from his cigarette and blew out a perfect ring of smoke. She watched the "O" hang in the air, expand and break up as it floated away into nothingness. Finally, he spoke:

"Brooke said something else back at the Hilton."

She could feel her stomach tighten. He always did this—chose the worst moments to bring up something he had been turning over for hours, days, weeks, or even years. "Not now, Conrad. Please."

"She said you knew something about my blood. Something you've always known. Something I had to see to believe."

Serena took a deep breath, walked over, and removed the cigarette from Conrad's mouth. She took a slow, deep drag, returned the cigarette and blew smoke back in his face. "You really want to play this game now, of all times?"

"Yep."

She got down on her knees in the bottom of the well and started digging desperately with her hands while Conrad watched her. "It's not your blood so much as your DNA."

"You had my DNA analyzed?"

"After Antarctica," she said, her voice tightening.

"What did you take from me?"

"A lock of hair," she said. "We can do this later, Conrad. Please help me. Help yourself."

"Why did you have my DNA analyzed, Serena? You didn't really believe what my father said there, did you? There's nothing special about my DNA. You don't think I had myself tested? I've seen the numbers, read all the tables. No unusual strands or combinations, Serena."

"Conrad, you're impossible!" She could see the top of something metallic just beneath the dirt.

"You know something I don't, Serena? You usually do."

"It isn't explained in analysis, Conrad. You have to see it."

"What the hell are you talking about, Serena?"

She rose to her feet and looked at him. "You want to know, Conrad? Fine. Your DNA strand spirals to the left."

"Of course it spirals. That's what the double-helix is all about."

"Except that the DNA of every indigenous organism on planet Earth spirals to the right."

She watched his hard face, watched his penetrating eyes study her, until his mouth softened and he dropped his cigarette and stamped it out. "So what do you believe, Serena?"

"I don't know what to believe now, Conrad. Only that I love you and want to be with you if we get out of this mess. I realized that the moment I thought it was you who was dead in the room and not Brooke. But we have to pull out whatever is under our feet and get it before Seavers does, or we're history."

She wrapped her arms around Conrad's neck and leaned up and kissed him full on the mouth. She could feel her heart pounding out of her chest and his arms wrapped around her waist, pulling her tight. Then he slowly let go and she looked up at his face, grim with determination.

"Let's dig this thing up."

44

CONRAD DUG a channel around the globe with his hands while Serena brushed the surface protruding from the dirt with a rag. Soon the outline of North America, etched across the northern hemisphere, came into view.

"Look!" Serena said excitedly. "This is clearly the terrestrial globe—it shows the land, not the stars. How do you open it?"

"Like this." Conrad pushed the blade of his knife under the edge by the equator and pressed hard. There was a crack and the hemisphere began to move beneath his hand, opening like a lid to reveal a sealed wooden cylinder. "Here it is."

They climbed out of the well and knelt on the dirt floor of the cave. Conrad removed a scroll from the wooden cylinder and began to unfold it.

"You're smudging it with your dirty hands," Serena scolded. "Let's get out of here and look at it someplace safe."

"Your hands are just as dirty as mine, Serena." He refused to budge. "And no place is safe until we know what this thing says. Right here, Serena, right now. Information, not preservation."

She flashed a light on the document. "I hate you."

"Get in line, it's a long one." He angled the document to the light.

The paper was like the star map, almost a parchment. But this was no map. Rather, it was a formal document, written in English, with a bold sort of preamble. Certain dates and titles from 1783 had been amended and initialed in 1793.

"A Treaty of Peace," he began to read, "concluded this Present Day ye eighteenth day of September One Thousand Seven Hundred & Ninety Three between the Regency of New Atlantis and its Subjects and George Washington President of the United States of North America and the Citizens of ye Said United States." He looked at Serena. "The Regency of New Atlantis?"

"The Alignment," Serena said. "A regency is simply a person or group selected to govern in place of a monarch or other ruler who is absent, disabled, or still in minority."

"So they're saying there's some new Caesar waiting in the wings to take over the world?"

"We in the Church prefer to call him the Antichrist."

The preamble was followed by a series of articles Conrad had a hard time following. He handed her the treaty and took the flashlight.

"You're the linguist and expert on international treaties, Serena. What's this New Atlantis?"

"The federal government," Serena said, scanning the articles. "This treaty says that the federal government has the right to secede from the United States on July 4, 2008, and form its own entity, New Atlantis, the very superpower that Sir Francis Bacon predicted would arise in the New World through its technology and power. The United States of America would be dissolved and power would be returned to the states."

"Holy shit. If it's legal, this thing's nuclear."

"You mean neutron: the regimes would change, but D.C. and all public lands acquired by the federal government since its inception—about one-third of the country, mostly in the West—would remain as territories of New Atlantis, including all U.S. military bases both here and around the world. Meaning the New Atlantis would have the means to enforce its will on the former United States and the rest of the world."

He shook his head. "The U.S. Supreme Court would never back it."

"How could it?" she said. "If anything, this Charter is not only unconstitutional, it's *anti*-constitutional. It clearly holds itself as both the precursor and successor to the U.S. Constitution. But it definitely looks genuine. As such, it's an embarrassment to America and casts doubts on its very founding at a time when its critics are wondering whether the world is better off without it. No wonder every president since Jefferson has been after this. What I can't understand is why Washington would ever sign such a thing."

She handed it back to Conrad, who looked at the bottom. There was an endorsement of the articles dated April 23, 1783, by George Washington, commander-in-chief of the Continental Army. Lastly, there was a second endorsement dated almost a decade later, September 13, 1793. This was followed by the signature of President George Washington and the official seal of the United States of America—or rather the front of the seal. Opposite thereto, were twelve signatures and the reverse or "New World Order" side of the seal.

One seal, Conrad thought, *and two Americas.*

"I can see why he'd sign it," Conrad said, the years of American history drilled into him by his father kicking in. "Put yourself in Washington's boots in 1783."

"But to endorse it as president after the U.S. Constitution was ratified? What was he thinking?"

"He was thinking like most Americans that the federal government and its lands were all of a few square miles of marshland on the Potomac, dwarfed by the giant states like Virginia, Pennsylvania, and New York. He had no idea it would consume the continent as an empire with warships controlling the seven seas and military garrisons around the world and in space."

Conrad looked at the two seals, the eagle and talons for the United States and the pyramid and Lucerific eye for the New Atlantis, and recalled what Brooke had said: The Alignment wasn't merely a shadow government, it was the government. Or, rather, *the other side* of the federal government. It always had been; it just hadn't come to light—yet.

"What's wrong, Conrad?"

"I know why the Alignment signed this and why Washington had to go along at the time. And it's obvious why every president aware of its existence has tried to keep it from coming to light, if only to preserve the

Union. But to a large extent the Alignment has already succeeded beyond its wildest dreams and the federal government is so strong—taxes to boot—that in a *de facto* way America IS the New Atlantis. So, aside from some historical or perverse moral justification, what possible reason could the Alignment have for risking its agenda to grab the treaty?"

"I can think of twelve, Conrad."

She showed him the signatures of those representing the Regency of the New Atlantis.

Conrad looked through the signatures. Members of Congress, American patriots, Founding Fathers who supported a strong federal government. "Holy shit. These names."

"Some of the most famous in America, along with some I've never heard of," she said. "These are the ancestors of those who are going to make the Atlantis prophecy happen one way or another. This is what Washington was trying to warn us about, and to do it he used L'Enfant's layout of the city and Savage's portrait in the National Gallery and the letter to Robert Yates for you to open more than two centuries later. To lead us to this Newburgh Treaty and its signatories. So we could know the families, trace them to the present day and have a fair idea of who its leaders are."

Conrad said, "Which means if we can find their descendants today . . ."

"We can find out who is behind what's going to happen—who Seavers is really working for—and stop them." Serena paused as she scanned the treaty, her face pale.

Something had struck her, and Conrad realized it wasn't in the body of the charter. Rather, it was one of the signatures.

Conrad brushed off bits of loose dirt that had fallen onto the treaty from the ceiling. He looked at the names again, starting with Alexander Hamilton, and one in particular, the designated Consul General of the Regency, jumped out at him: John Marshall.

Conrad's mind whirred. Marshall, a lawyer at the time of the Revolution, became chief justice of the Supreme Court within a year of Washington's death and over the next 30 years did more than anybody else to expand the powers of the federal government. Then he made the connection:

Marshall was also a cousin of Thomas Jefferson and, as such, the sitting president's great-great-grandfather on his mother's side.

"Holy shit!" he said as the walls began to shake violently. "We've got to get out of here."

Serena grabbed her backpack as the roof of the cave started to collapse. Suddenly smoke filled the cave. Then everything went black.

PART FOUR

JULY 4

45

AN UNDISCLOSED LOCATION

CONRAD WOKE UP in complete darkness, a black hood over his head, chilled to the bone. He sensed he was deep underground and could feel the low rumble of large, powerful machinery nearby. Something very sharp was pressing on his chest.

"Serena?" he called out.

He heard a laugh. It belonged to Max Seavers. "You're an inspiration, Yeats, I'll give you that."

Then the black hood came off and Conrad looked up to see Seavers standing over him, pointing an ornate dagger at his chest. Conrad tried to move, but his arms and legs were strapped to a restraint chair, bolted to the floor of a windowless room with stone walls and a metal door.

"Do you like my dagger, Yeats?" Seavers said, pushing the point into Conrad's sternum. "Your old friend Herc gave it to me before he died and joined Danny Z in the Great Beyond. He said it once belonged to a legendary 33rd Degree Mason of the Scottish Rite or some such, and that the Masons used the dagger in rituals to initiate candidates into a perverse system of levels or degrees by which they replicate themselves. Apparently the candidate for the First Degree is hooded and brought into the Lodge. There, at the point of a dagger, he undergoes ritual questioning. Welcome to my Lodge, Yeats. Maybe you can work all the way up the ranks like Herc."

As he struggled to get his bearings, Conrad remembered what Brooke had told him about the weaponized bird flu virus Seavers was going to release, and what Serena said about Seavers hosting the Chinese at the Washington Monument for the fireworks.

"The Fourth of July concert on the Mall," Conrad said. "You're going to release your contagion on Chinese officials during the fireworks. At the only moment in history that the monuments will be directly below their designated stars."

"Impressive, isn't it?" Seavers said as he walked out of sight behind him. "I was surprised to discover there's actually some science behind what you allegedly do for a living as an astro-archaeologist. The stars in the sky rotate like some giant odometer every 26,000 years or so. Washington one-upped the Egyptians by ordering his chief architect L'Enfant to align the sites of as-yet-constructed monuments not to the position of the key stars of their day, but to their positions on this day, July 4, 2008, when the Regency of New Atlantis could make its claim and dissolve the United States."

"Tell me something I don't know, Seavers."

Seavers obliged. "When my masters in the Alignment thrust this great responsibility upon me, I knew that I had to make it special for them, seeing as they actually believe in mystical astrological signs and all. So I took a page from your book and decided to coordinate our strike with the heavens."

"Is that what you call killing, what, a billion Chinese and a third of the world's population?"

"It's written in the stars, sport. Today the sun begins a 28-day path across the skies from Washington, D.C., to Beijing, where it will experience a total eclipse at dusk on August 1, exactly seven days before the opening ceremonies of the Olympic Games. My time-delayed virus on Earth mirrors the sun's path in the heavens like some cosmic fireball. As above, so below. By the time they light the Olympic torch, the first symptoms of the global human-to-human bird flu pandemic will appear, igniting international chaos and cries to build a new Great Wall to quarantine China. Poetic, isn't it?"

"You're deranged."

Conrad craned his neck to see a dozen syringes, needles, and tubes laid out on a table along with rolls of adhesive tape, bags of saline solution, handcuffs, and leg irons. He shivered. "Are you really going to use all that on me, or is it just for effect?"

Seavers put on a pair of surgical gloves, selected a vial and held it up to the fluorescent light. "This is for somebody else."

As he spoke the door opened and two lab technicians rolled Serena in on a gurney. She was strapped down flat and showed little movement.

"You bastard!" Conrad snarled.

Seavers slid the vial into a syringe gun and put it to Serena's neck.

"This is a special formula of the bird flu virus minus

the incubation inhibitor," Seavers said. "Tell me where you put that star map you stole from the celestial globe or I pull the trigger and Sister Serghetti is the first to die."

"Don't you dare, Conrad," Serena warned from the gurney. "You know all those stories through the ages about Christian martyrs? This is one of them. But if you cave to this bastard, he'll just off us and it's plain murder. We'll be as much his victims as the ones who get the bird flu."

Not if we survive, Conrad thought, and he wondered why Seavers wanted the star map. It only led to the terrestrial globe and the Newburgh Treaty, which Seavers already possessed. "It's inside a book at the Library of Congress."

"Shut up!" Serena screamed.

Seavers dug the syringe gun into Serena's carotid. "Tell me the title of the book, sport."

Conrad shifted in his restraining chair. In pressing the point of the dagger to his chest, Seavers had nicked one of the straps. Conrad felt it would tear and snap with enough force, but that he still wouldn't be able to free his hands or feet.

"It's in a book called *Obelisks*," Conrad said, hearing the desperation in his voice and seeing the disappointment in Serena's eyes.

"You bloody fool," Serena said in defeat. "I hope you've made your peace with God."

"You know I did," Conrad said. "In Antarctica. But not with you."

"And you won't in this lifetime, you wanker," she

said. "But when I wake up in the next and see the face of Jesus, I want to see yours, too." She began to utter something in Latin.

Seavers began to laugh. "Are you performing last rites for your beloved Yeats?"

"For you, Seavers," she said. "Because there's no air conditioning where you're going."

"Now, now, Sister Serghetti," Seavers said, in a soothing tone Conrad found very creepy. "Even Jesus forgave his enemies when he was dying on the cross."

"Well, you can go to hell, Seavers!" she screamed. "You have no excuses. You know exactly what you're doing."

Max Seavers's face screwed up into a twisted mask of pure hatred, and Conrad anxiously watched him walk to the instrument table and return with a roll of duct tape.

"That mouth." He tore off some tape and slapped it across Serena's lips. "Somebody in Rome should have shut you up a long time ago."

Then he plunged the syringe gun into her neck again, this time deep enough that Conrad could see a trickle of blood.

"Give me the call number for the book, sport, or I shoot."

"I don't know the call number," Conrad said, panicking as he saw Serena struggle, her eyes wide and her cries muffled. "But it's an old book and there can't be more than a couple of copies in special collections. I'm telling you the truth."

"We'll see when I come back from my previously

scheduled engagement," Seavers said and pulled the trigger.

Serena's neck twitched like she'd taken a bullet.

"No!" Conrad shouted.

Seavers laid the syringe gun down, studying Serena as he spoke to Conrad. "She'll be fully infected within a few hours unless I administer the vaccine. But once she starts showing symptoms nothing can save her, not even my own vaccine, and she'll be dead by dusk. So you better pray to her God that I find that map. Or you'll watch her die before your eyes, and then I'll kill you."

With that Seavers walked out past two Marines posted outside the door, which rumbled shut and locked with a thud.

46

THE NATIONAL MALL

MORE THAN 20 security checkpoints had been set up around the National Mall in preparation for the day's Fourth of July parade and festivities, which slowed an impatient Seavers on his way to retrieve the star map from the Library of Congress. That map, together with the Newburgh Treaty, was his insurance policy just in case he pulled the trigger on the bird flu contagion and Osiris suddenly decided he was of no further use to the Alignment.

Sitting in the rear of the black SUV with a Marine driving, Seavers pulled out a laptop computer from his briefcase and called up the Library of Congress website. He typed in the name of the book on obelisks that Yeats had given him. It was in special collections on the second floor of the Jefferson Building. He jotted down the call number.

He then removed the folded Newburgh Treaty from the left breast pocket of his suit jacket and reviewed the signatures, some famous and others obscure. He typed the names into his laptop to cross them against current U.S. political leaders. He wanted to see where the genealogies matched ancestor with descendant. A far more detailed analysis would be required later on, he knew, but almost immediately several names popped up and surprised even him.

"Well, would you look at that?" he said to himself with a soft whistle.

First, there was the sitting U.S. president himself, a "man of faith" that Seavers would not have guessed in a million years. Could he be Osiris? The president's lineage didn't necessarily mean he was Alignment, only that it was likely.

Then there were the leading Democratic and Republican presidential candidates. Both had blue-blood family ties to the Alignment, ensuring that whoever was elected in November would stick to the Alignment plan. These names he more readily accepted as leaders of the Alignment.

Finally, there was Senator Scarborough—a real shocker since Brooke had been led to believe otherwise. So had Seavers.

He could only imagine what Scarborough was feeling now that the senator most surely had been given news of his daughter's death. And Seavers could definitely thank his lucky stars that Conrad Yeats was taking the rap. As soon as he grabbed the star map he would call in the orders to kill Yeats, before anybody in the Alignment could interrogate him.

Seavers shut the laptop and looked out his window. It was going to be a hot and sticky day.

By the time he walked into the special collections room at the Jefferson Building, his shirt was soaked with sweat. The Library was closed to the public today but not to members of Congress and the executive branch. He flashed his ID to the lone female staffer at the desk, wrote out a request for the *Obelisks* book and waited. She returned with a copy.

He took the book to a cubicle and opened it. Nothing!

He returned to the desk and asked the woman for the second copy. She checked her computer and said, "It's still in the carts, we haven't shelved it yet."

As calmly as he could, Seavers said, "Well, do you think you could check the carts? Please."

She flinched at his intensity. "It may take me a few minutes. We only have a skeleton staff today."

Seavers said nothing, and quietly fumed for almost fifteen minutes before she returned with the book.

"Here you go," she chirped. "It was between—"

"Thank you," he said, cutting her off and taking the book to the opposite corner of the room, out of her line of sight.

He cracked the book open and found the paper folded lengthwise and tucked inside the spine, in the space between the cover and the binding. He unfolded it and saw Washington's signature on one side and the star map on the other.

Seavers reluctantly had to give Yeats credit for not only finding both globes but thinking clearly enough to hide the star map among the millions of books at the Library of Congress as a bargaining chip.

But now that chip was cashed.

Seavers pulled out his BlackBerry and made the call. "This is Seavers. Terminate prisoner 33."

47

SERENA HEARD THE DOOR to the cell open and looked up from her gurney as two Marines, their faces all business, walked in. One of them went to the table with the syringes. The other marched straight for Conrad in the restraining chair and started thumping Conrad's left forearm with his finger, looking for a vein.

She tried to shout, but her cries were muffled by the duct tape across her mouth.

"You strapped him so tight, you cut off his circulation," the Marine complained to his comrade. "I can't find a vein."

The other Marine, who was preparing an IV apparatus, said, "Keep poking him with a needle until you find a gusher."

Serena watched as the Marine attending to Conrad loosened the strap on his left hand to allow for more blood flow. Still without luck, he then tried the right arm and struck blood with a needle. He slipped a catheter into Conrad's vein. The catheter tube was connected to two bags of a clear solution.

Conrad glanced at her and then spoke to the Marines.

"Max Seavers was responsible for the deaths of Brooke Scarborough and a Capitol Police officer," Conrad said. "And he's going to be responsible for a billion more if you don't help me."

Either the mention of Brooke or the CP seemed to get their attention. But it didn't slow their work. The Marine with the syringes placed them in order. "He gets sodium pentothal sedative first, then the potassium chloride to paralyze him, and then the lethal injection."

Serena suspected the Marines wouldn't even need the lethal injection, because the only thing potassium chloride paralyzed was the heart: it stopped it cold. She started squirming in her straps, moaning as loud as she could. But the Marines ignored her.

Conrad said, "Seavers is working with terrorists against the U.S., and now you're working for them, too."

The Marine securing his catheter said, "Then why are you the one on death row in a black ops prison?"

"Because I know what Seavers is going to do," Conrad said. "He's going to release a weaponized flu virus on the Mall today during the fireworks."

The Marine looked at him in disbelief. "On Americans?"

"On a Chinese delegation watching the fireworks from the Washington Monument. They won't become infectious until the Olympics when it spreads worldwide."

Something in the Marine's eyes told Serena that he knew at least enough about Seavers to consider Conrad's story in the realm of the possible. "And what are we supposed to do? Let you go?"

"No, call the Pentagon. Tell them you have a message

from me for Secretary of Defense Packard. My name is Conrad Yeats. And that's Serena Serghetti."

Serena nodded up and down as the Marine walked over to her. He turned her gurney around so that her feet touched the wall and he looked down on her face with amazement. "Holy hell, I think it's Mother Earth!"

The other Marine scowled. "You can't possibly believe him, Hicks."

"No, I really think it's her," Hicks said, and suddenly turned red-faced as he stared at her. "Remember those . . . pictures . . . I downloaded from the Internet."

"That was her face on some stick model's body," the other Marine said. "This one's got curves."

Serena felt the bewildered gaze of Hicks. "Look," Hicks said. "It can't hurt to at least call in a potential security threat."

With great relief Serena watched Hicks turn for the door when suddenly the other Marine shot him in the back of the head. Hicks's arms went up in shock, and then he went down with a crash.

Serena stared at the dead Marine sprawled on the floor face down. The other Marine, obviously Alignment, holstered his sidearm and picked up a syringe with a nasty yellow-greenish color to it. Serena started to panic as the Marine took the syringe over to Conrad, who looked at her with determined eyes.

"Good thing the Pentagon ordered up that stockpile of bird flu vaccines," the Marine said and pushed the syringe into the catheter.

Serena watched the yellow-green line of fluid wind

its way down the long tube toward Conrad's arm. The Marine watched it, too.

"Say night-night, Yeats," the Marine said when Serena used her feet to push off the wall and launch the gurney into the Marine's back.

The Marine shouted in surprise and turned to strike her.

As he did, Conrad snapped his left hand free from the loosened strap, yanked the catheter out of his right arm and plunged it into the Marine's groin.

"You son of a bitch!" the Marine grunted, eyes wide in shock as he pulled the catheter out. But it was too late. Whatever he had intended for Conrad was in his system now. His eyes glazed over and he collapsed next to his fallen fellow Marine.

"And then some," Conrad said, and began to unfasten the rest of his straps.

Serena's heart leapt as Conrad stood up and wobbled, weak at the knees from the hours in the restraining chair. He staggered to the Marines and lifted their swipe cards and guns. Then he walked over to her and with a quick yank pulled off the duct tape.

"Let's go," he said.

Her lips stung, but finally she could move them as Conrad freed her.

"I can't go, Conrad. If I've got the bird flu, I'm going to infect everybody. I may have already infected you."

"Impossible," he said, and she watched him take a Masonic dagger from the table and put the blade to his forearm. "I'm immune."

"What are you doing?" she cried as he slit his arm. A scarlet line of blood oozed out.

"Brooke said Seavers used my blood for his vaccine."

She stared at him. "And you believe her?"

"You said my double-helix spirals to the left instead of the right." He took an empty syringe and unwrapped a sterile needle and drew his blood out. "Should I believe you?"

He offered her the syringe filled with his blood.

"But it's just your blood, Conrad. It's not the vaccine. We don't know if it will work."

"It can't work if we don't try."

She took the syringe from him and ran the needle along her arm until she found the right spot. She hated getting shots, but her travels throughout the Third World long ago made them a regular part of her life. She had rolling veins but not deep, which meant she wouldn't have to penetrate far beneath the skin.

"Do you want me to do it?" Conrad asked impatiently.

"No, I've got it," she said and stuck herself with the needle.

Slowly she pushed Conrad's blood out of the syringe and into her vein. It felt warm and strange. Then she pulled the needle out, put her thumb on the puncture and held her arm up.

"So how in bloody hell do we get out of here?" she said, standing up. "Those swipe cards can't open every door in this facility."

"No, but I bet this will," Conrad said and held up a finger—Max Seavers's missing finger.

48

CONRAD LED SERENA through the dark corridor to another metal door, the sixth they had encountered. They hadn't seen any more Marines, and security cameras were nowhere to be found. But Conrad was beginning to wonder if they were ever going to get out of there, much less in time to stop Seavers.

He used Seavers's severed finger to open the door and walked into a round conference room dominated by a circular stone table and thirteen white marble busts in alcoves evenly spaced along the wall. In the center of the table was the terrestrial globe.

"The lair of the Alignment," Serena said. "These busts look to be the work of Houdon."

"Who?" Conrad asked, his eyes searching for another way out, but he couldn't find one.

"Houdon," Serena repeated. "A French sculptor during the Enlightenment who made famous busts of Washington and the Founding Fathers. I've seen his work on exhibit at both the Louvre in Paris and at the Getty in Los Angeles. Only these aren't America's Founding

Fathers. These faces belong to the other Founders, to the Alignment."

Something about the dimensions of the room struck Conrad as familiar and he felt drawn to an empty section of wall between two of the busts. As he stood there, his eyes adjusted enough to make out the faintest outline of a doorway. He pushed it with his hand and the previously invisible door slid open.

"I'll be damned," he said. "This is just like the shafts in the sublevels of P4 and the Great Pyramid."

"The Great Pyramid?" she repeated.

"When I was under the Library of Congress, I saw a monument the Masons proposed in the same chamber that held the celestial globe," he said. "Some kind of American Memorial, like they feared the worst and wanted to preserve their memory—and America's—through a monument that would stand as long as the pyramids. This is where I think both they and the Alignment knew it would be, wherever we are. So the Alignment basically graded the site. All it's waiting for is the pyramid on the surface."

"And it's going to go up as soon as America falls," Serena said.

"We've got to hurry," he said. "If this is like P4, then I know the way out."

He started for the door but Serena didn't budge.

"I told you, Conrad. I can't go with you. I can't risk spreading bird flu contagion on the surface and doing the Alignment's dirty work."

He stared at her. "But I gave you my homegrown

vaccine, Serena. If it didn't work, you'd be showing symptoms by now."

"We don't know that for sure, Conrad. And I can't take that risk. You're going to have to stop Seavers yourself."

"And what are you going to do in the meantime?" he demanded.

"I'm going to stay here and wait for you and the cavalry to come back." She walked up to him, tears streaming down her face, and kissed him. "But if we get out of this alive, I'm going to walk out of here with you and walk away from my life as a nun. If you still want it, we're going to start a new life together."

He looked into her wet eyes. "What about the Church?"

She wiped her eyes. "I was supposed to betray you, Conrad, to use you to find the globes and take them from you. Please forgive me," she begged. "You have to believe I'm sorry."

Conrad could see she was. "But you always told me you believed that the Church is the hope of the world."

She shook her head. "Jesus is the hope of the world, Conrad. And the hope of the Church. We are called to be the Church and serve people in His name. I don't have to be a nun to do that. And I don't want to go on without you. I told you. I knew it the moment Max took me to your room and I expected to see your body instead of Brooke's."

"You swear to God?" he said.

"You know I don't like those kinds of oaths, Conrad. But, yes, I swear before God." She then threw her arms around him and hugged him tight. "Conrad, go."

He hesitated, then gave her a pistol and swipe card. "In case you change your mind," he said and shut the door, leaving her alone with the globe and the faces of thirteen dead white men.

Serena stared at the faces of the thirteen marble Houdon busts. The founding fathers of the Alignment in America. They were so lifelike that she half-expected them to speak to her in the shadowy chamber.

And then one of them did.

It was the second to her right, a face oddly strange and familiar.

When she leaned forward to study the face, she suddenly recognized it.

She gasped. "Oh, my God."

Remembering the names from the Newburgh Charter that she had memorized, she now knew why Cardinal Tucci wanted the globe at the Vatican.

Dear Lord, my promise to Conrad.

She paced before the globe and her jury of the deceased, praying to God for some answer. The shot that Conrad had given her was clearly kicking in, and she was feeling stronger, more alert. So alert that it frightened her.

The Americans already had the celestial globe that the Masons had buried beneath the Library of Congress. If Conrad succeeded in stopping Seavers, as she prayed he would, then the Americans would have both globes. But if he failed, she now realized that the Alignment would control not only America but also the Church.

With a heavy heart she knew what she had to do.

Conrad, forgive me.

Conrad ran through a maze of corridors until he reached a door without a biometric keypad that would require the finger from Max Seavers. That suggested he was reaching the outer, less secure perimeter. He only needed to use one of the Marine's swipe cards to unlock it. He cracked the door open and sighed at what he saw: another dark corridor. When he was sure it was clear, he made his way out.

This corridor was different, and he immediately sensed it was some kind of neutral bridge between the Alignment's secret bunker and the larger world. At the end of it was a pinprick of light and a dull roar. He edged cautiously toward the door that emerged in the light when suddenly it was flung open. A Metro engineer stepped in and froze when he saw Conrad.

"Shit, you military people always scare me," the engineer said, "skulking around down here like shadows."

"And because of us you get to celebrate Independence Day," Conrad said and kept walking, without looking back.

Conrad emerged from a utility door onto a lower platform of the L'Enfant Plaza Metro Station. With no less than three Metro lines intersecting here, it now made complete sense why the Alignment chose the bunker below as their place to meet. But he was spotted across the platform by a D.C. police officer instantly, whose hand went to his mouth as he radioed in.

Conrad ran up the escalators to a food court tunnel, where four more policemen were coming toward him.

The underground food court connected him to the Loew's L'Enfant Plaza Hotel, and when he cut across the lobby he emerged into the bright light of day and blinked.

There must have been several thousand motorcycles and leather-clad bikers revving their engines in front of him. Their black leather jackets said Rolling Thunder, and the backs of their bikes boasted American flags.

Conrad caught up to the rear of the group and scanned the nearest tattooed and bearded bikers prepping their machines. He found an old-timer in his sixties with a handlebar mustache and beer gut wearing a black "Ancient Riddles" T-shirt. He was wiping the chrome fork of his BMW chopper.

Conrad stole a helmet on the ground and brazenly walked up to the man. "Hey, partner, my bike's busted and I could use a lift," he said as he offered his hand. "I'm Conrad Yeats."

The rider rose to his surprisingly tall six-foot-four-inch height and looked down at him. "Anything for the Griffter's kid. My name's Marty. Hop on."

Conrad jumped on the chopper as Marty hit the accelerator and they rode off to join the others in the parade.

49

THROUGH THE SIGHT of her sniper rifle atop the National Archives, Sergeant Wanda Randolph watched the tail end of the Independence Day parade march down Constitution Avenue. She scanned the crowds for any sign of Conrad Yeats. America's most wanted criminal was presumably still on the loose after yesterday's Presidential Prayer Breakfast.

More than 22 government agencies, including the U.S. Capitol Police, U.S. Park Police, and Washington Metropolitan Police Department, were coordinating security: There were jets overhead, chemical sensors in the subways, Coast Guard boats on the Potomac, and more than 6,000 cops and troops on the streets.

Members of the 49th Virginia Infantry Regiment Civil War reenactment group now marched below to the cheers of onlookers, from babies to grandparents. It had been a morning of high school and military bands, and the Civil War types prompted as many smiles as the group that usually followed them.

Wanda could hear them now—the roar of thousands of Harley Davidsons revving down Constitution, their riders in jeans and leather jackets. Rolling Thunder was a motorcycling group that supported veterans. Today they had come out in full force, headlights blazing and American flags extending from the back of their bikes.

Her eyes followed them down Pennsylvania as they turned onto Constitution, one oddball biker in sunglasses after another. Several times she had to look away from the glare of the sun bouncing off the medals on their vests and the chrome on their bikes.

One neon yellow-and-chrome chopper with two riders caught her eye, and she followed it to the turn when another glare off the chrome blinded her for a split second. When she caught up with the chopper again on Constitution, it had only one rider.

What happened? Where'd he go?

She jerked her rifle back to the parade turn at Pennsylvania and Constitution and scoped the crowds. Nothing. And then she saw the small pump station building behind the crowd.

Dang, it was him, she thought. *It had to be. Conrad Yeats.*

She wanted to believe that Yeats was one of the good guys, but regardless of which hat he wore—white or black—he was about to get himself picked off by her or another sniper unless she could bring him in safely.

"Code red," she yelled into her radio. "Pump station."

She scrambled off the roof and out the National Archives, ran a block to the station and burst inside. Two Metro cops were down, knocked out, and a hatch to the sewer was open. Six FBI agents, plainclothes types from the crowd, swarmed in as she pulled out a map.

"The SEAL will pick him up in the sewer," one of the agents said.

But the SEAL swimming up and down beneath Constitution reported nothing. "He may have gone deeper," crackled the radio, the voice of a SEAL breaking up. "Shit, he's in the Tiber."

Long after the hill beneath the U.S. Capitol had ceased to be called Rome, the river upon which ships ferried marble from the White House to the Capitol retained the name Tiber Creek. And to this day the Tiber still runs beneath Constitution Avenue along the northern edge of the National Mall.

Conrad sloshed through knee-high water in the ancient sewer built of brick masonry. About 30 feet wide and ten feet high, the old sewer ran along the upper portion of the bed of the old Tiber Creek. Conrad could feel its rotting floor planks give way under his shoes and prayed he wouldn't step into a hole and get sucked into the bog, never to return to the surface.

He remembered the Tiber from a consulting gig when the feds asked him how to preserve downtown D.C. as the ancient Egyptians had preserved the pyramids. The Tiber, like the Nile, ran in front of the Capitol and through the Smithsonian.

The whole Mall, in fact, was one giant flood plain. The east wing of the Natural History museum, Conrad had discovered, was already sinking and pulling away from the main building because the Tiber still coursed beneath the Mall. Only a carefully built and even more carefully camouflaged levee kept the Mall from being under water. The feds did a great job planting trees on it to hide it. Only by lying down on the steps of the Lincoln Memorial and looking out toward Constitution Avenue could you see the levee with the naked eye.

Inside the old Tiber Creek sewer, however, there was very little to see. Conrad looked around the battered side walls and the stone arch ceiling over the river channel, which had seen better days. The brick was crumbling and refuse from the more modern sewer line—cut in the 1930s—was raining down on him.

The sewer emptied out near the Washington Monument, where the east branch of the Potomac used to be before the feds filled it in. It was here Conrad started his search for a planned tunnel that may or may not have ever been built to the monument.

The "Capitol Fourth" concert was just getting underway on the National Mall when Max Seavers arrived at the Washington Monument, which was closed to the public today due to security concerns as well as a very special "private function"—a White House reception for Chinese Olympic officials.

Seavers checked his cell phone GPS, which confirmed that the aerosol canister containing his bird flu was in place and activated. Once everybody was inside the elevator, he'd speed dial the silent detonator and the revolution would be over before anybody even suspected it had started. The very thought that he could kill billions with the push of a button gave him a special kind of thrill, but not nearly as much as the knowledge that his vaccine would make him a savior to the rest of the surviving world.

He slipped the phone back in his pocket, next to the folded Newburgh Treaty.

"Dr. Seavers!"

Seavers turned to see the enthusiastic head of the Olympic delegation, Dr. Ling, walk up with a smile. "I saw you yesterday at the president's prayer breakfast. Very moving."

Seavers smiled, assuming Dr. Ling was being polite and that the Chinese had learned from the mistakes of the former Soviet Union when its leaders allowed a Polish pope and a cowboy American president to undermine their entire empire and bring it to collapse. The only reason he didn't release the virus at the prayer breakfast—his first choice—was that it was too easy to trace back to him as "ground zero." This plan was much simpler: The Chinese Olympic delegation would go up to the observation deck to enjoy the fireworks and by the time they came back down they'd be infected with the weaponized bird flu virus. The virus would incubate for 28 days until it made its day-and-date world premiere at the opening ceremonies of the Olympic Games in Beijing. From there it would fan across the world. And everybody would blame the Chinese.

Genius, he thought.

"Well, if you liked the breakfast, Dr. Ling, just wait until you see the fireworks! The National Symphony Orchestra plays Tchaikovsky's '1812 Overture' for the finale. The piece is accompanied by live cannons—four

105mm Howitzers set off by the U.S. Army Presidential Salute Battery."

Seavers led a delighted Ling and the small line of Olympic officials to the monument's new elevator. The glass cab held 25 passengers, and would take 70 seconds to go up to the observation deck at the 500-foot level. Special panels in the doors were timed to turn from opaque to clear at the 180-, 170-, 140-, and 130-foot levels, allowing passengers to view the 193 commemorative Masonic stones that lined the interior of the monument. Seavers, however, knew from a secret DARPA report filed during the Griffin Yeats regime that there were really 194 stones. He had yet to figure out which stone was omitted from the official count, let alone unlock its significance. But at this point, he concluded none of that Masonic nonsense mattered anymore.

As the group stepped inside the glass elevator, Dr. Ling shook his head. "My wife is never going to believe this."

"Don't worry, I'll take your picture," Seavers said, holding up his cell phone camera as the doors closed and the elevator began its ascent.

50

FEW OF THE Capitol Fourth concert-goers who sat on the white marble benches and low, curving granite walls ringing the Washington Monument knew that these amenities were actually part of a multimillion-dollar security upgrade in the wake of the attacks of Sept. 11, 2001.

The decorative walls, for example, were augmented by retractable posts that could spring up in an instant to stop any charging vehicle packed with explosives from ever reaching the monument itself. And fifty feet below the marble benches was a secret 17-foot-wide, 400-foot-long tunnel connecting the monument, which was closed to the public today, with an off-site screening facility near 15th Street.

But Conrad knew.

Soaked with scum he didn't want to think about, he emerged from the ruins of the Tiber Creek sewer into the tunnel he had been searching for—the only piece of an official underground visitors center for the Washington Monument that the National Planning Commission could never get approved but built anyway. The feds wanted any acts of terror to occur at the base of the site rather than in the upper level of the monument itself, where the walls weren't as thick and where a blast would cause the sides to peel away and the entire structure to collapse.

Unfortunately, Conrad realized, Max Seavers was in that most vulnerable part of the monument right now—more than 500 feet above him.

On the observation deck, Max Seavers hurriedly herded the Chinese delegation back into the glass elevator. The fireworks on the Mall were almost over, save for the grand finale, and some of the Chinese had started talking about walking down the stairwell to view the Masonic commemorative stones after the show. Seavers couldn't allow it.

"The ride down is two minutes and eighteen seconds," he said. "So you'll have plenty of time to view 45 of the 193 then. Plus, you'll get to see the grand finale over the Capitol Dome from our special private viewing area for you on the east side of the monument."

"Thank you so much, Dr. Seavers," said Dr. Ling as the doors began to close. "This has been fantastic. My wife will be . . ."

The doors shut and the elevator began its descent.

Seavers pulled out his cell phone, pressed the number 3 key twice and walked across the observation deck to the east window. He looked outside in wonder at the New World Order.

It is done, he thought.

The aerosol canister he had placed above the elevator cab's overhead compartment was slowly releasing its fine, imperceptible mist on the longer descent. He couldn't do it on the way up because of the shorter trip; his bird flu took a good two minutes of inhalation to guarantee infection.

By the time the Chinese walked outside and gawked at the last orgasmic gasp of Independence Day in the United States, they would be dead and they wouldn't even know it. Same for the republic.

His phone rang and he looked at the screen. It was a private number.

"Seavers," he answered.

"It's Yeats, you sick bastard. Your star-crossed plan failed. The Chinese aren't going to be spreading your germs after all."

The shock took a moment for Seavers to shake. *How did he escape?* Then a pit in his stomach formed. "How in hell did you get this number?"

The voice on the other end said: "I just ripped off the cell phone from your aerosol canister inside the elevator cab and returned the last call. By the way, I'm coming up for you right now."

Seavers shut the phone and frantically looked around the observation deck. He wasn't about to wait for the elevator doors to open and let Yeats take a shot at him. He was going to have to shoot first, and he knew he had less than a minute before the elevator reached the observation deck.

He ran past the gift shop a half-level below the observation deck and then bounded down the stone stairwell that lined the interior of the monument, several steps at a time. He had only made it to the 400-foot level before he saw the elevator coming up and positioned himself, bending down on one knee and aiming his Glock at the open air shaft.

The glass cab was coming up fast, its panel windows opaque. Seavers aimed carefully, his finger on the trigger as the glass began to clear.

But the elevator was empty.

Seavers's hands holding the gun wavered as he stared. Too late he saw Yeats hanging on to the bottom of the ascending cab with one arm, the other swinging up with a gun, firing.

The first bullet caught Seavers in the leg, spinning him back against the Masonic stone. He crouched in pain as he looked up and saw Yeats approaching the observation deck. He could hear shouts hundreds of feet below. Police would soon be swarming up the monument.

He fired twice at Yeats. A bullet bounced off the bottom of the elevator with a spark, and Yeats let go, falling into the darkness below. He heard a loud shout.

Seavers peered down and saw nothing. Then a bullet whizzed past his ear. Yeats had landed somewhere, hurt but alive and coming back up.

Seavers knew he had no choice now but to release the virus outside on the crowds below. And he wouldn't be walking out the front door of the monument now. He willed himself to stand and marched up the steps in the darkness, each footfall exploding in searing agony. He looked into the shattered cab at the top with caution and the empty observation deck. But he could hear footsteps coming up the stairwell.

"Game over, sport," he shouted. "You lose."

He unfastened the canister from the overhead compartment of the elevator. Thankfully, Yeats had only removed the remote detonator mechanism. The canister was still intact and full of the deadly virus.

If conditions were even remotely optimal outside, the virus could survive 24 hours after being sprayed like a small cloud into the air. Just one tiny droplet inhaled by one person on the Mall hundreds of feet below would start a time-delayed virulent chain reaction.

Seavers smashed the butt of his gun against one of the large reinforced observation windows, but the window wouldn't break. He would have to find some other means to release the virus outside.

He looked up at the ceiling above the observation deck and pulled a hidden latch to open a secret hatch door. A metal ladder like a fire escape telescoped down.

Seavers climbed up the ladder into the 55-foot-tall structure above the shaft called the "pyramidion," because of the way its four walls converged to form the point of the 555-foot-tall monument. It was packed with several banks of electrical machinery and classified surveillance equipment, but for the most part was as empty inside as a church steeple.

Slowly he began his ascent in the dark toward the capstone at the top of the pyramidion as he listened to the strains of the Capitol Fourth concert outside.

When Conrad reached the observation deck, it was empty. So was the elevator cab. Seavers had taken the canister with the virus. Conrad looked out the west window. A remote network television camera was stationed there, pointed out to capture the fireworks. From the east window he could hear the National Symphony Orchestra on the Mall reaching a crescendo.

He felt a stab of pain in the back, pushing him to the glass, blood smearing across it. The bullet passed right through his shoulder. Conrad heard two hollow clicks and looked up to see Seavers disappear through a hatch in the ceiling above the elevator shaft. He was out of ammo and had climbed up into the monument's pyramidion.

He's got the canister. The son of a bitch is going to release the virus.

Conrad knew the pyramidion was about 55 feet in height. So Seavers had another 40 feet to go to reach the capstone.

Forcing himself to stand up, Conrad put a hand to his shoulder, applying pressure on the gunshot wound. It felt like a heavy power drill, boring into him full blast. But he reached up, grabbed the ladder and pulled himself up with a gasp of pain.

"You've nothing to gain and everything to lose by stopping me," Seavers's voice called down from the dark. "Think about it. A new world order. No China. No religion . . ."

Conrad pointed his gun toward the sound of the voice. "You mean no Serena, you bastard."

Conrad paused. A thunderous boom outside from the cannons from the *1812* Overture sounded.

At that moment Seavers swung down from the dark feet first and struck Conrad in the shoulder full force, knocking the gun out of his hand. Conrad watched it clink against the wall and fall fifty feet to the floor of the observation deck.

Conrad was now clinging by his shot arm to a metal lightning rod that ran along the masonry wall, which was lined with tiny cracks.

He looked up at a square of starlight. Somehow Seavers had popped open the aluminum capstone at the top in order to release the aerosol form of the bird flu into the air. The square aperture framed the constellation Virgo, its alpha star Spica directly overhead, shimmering between bursts of fireworks and smoke.

The alignment, he thought. *It's happening right now. Seavers is actually going to release his global plague at the exact moment the Washington Monument locks with Virgo.*

Conrad climbed up the lightning rod toward Seavers, who was trying to raise the canister through the opening, but the base of the capstone was too small.

"Don't do it, Seavers!" Conrad shouted. "Think of all the people."

"This isn't a democracy, Yeats," Seavers shouted as he tried to force the aerosol canister through the aperture. "Your vote doesn't count. It never did. This is a republic. It was built to be run by elite overlords."

"Like the Alignment?" Conrad reached behind his back and pulled out the Masonic dagger that Seavers had lifted from old Herc before he killed him.

"Do you want to know why George Washington and the Founding Fathers wanted a representative government? Because they were the representatives!" Seavers shouted, finally forcing the canister through the aperture and lifting his finger to push the button. "They're the real Alignment. I'm the cure."

"Got a cure for this?" Conrad said and hurled the dagger across the air into Seavers's neck.

Seavers screamed and released his grip on the canister, which clanked down the pyramidion and disappeared into the darkness. Seavers himself began to lose his balance as he pulled the dagger from his neck and stared in fascination at the blade's Masonic markings coated with his own blood.

"Von Berg," he wheezed, gurgling up blood.

"What?" Conrad demanded. "Who?"

But Seavers's eyes rolled back into his head, his unconscious body wavering for a few seconds before it fell fifty feet to the observation deck below, killing him instantly.

Conrad reached up to the aluminum capstone, popped on its side like a hinge. It had been set atop the monument by Colonel Thomas Lincoln Casey, the same Mason responsible for the construction of the Library of Congress.

So close was Conrad that he could read the Latin letters engraved across the east face of the capstone, by design visible only to the heavens:

LAUS DEO

In Praise of God, Conrad repeated in English, and pulled it shut.

He climbed down the ladder and dropped down onto the floor of the observation deck. He leaned over Seavers's corpse and saw the twisted smile on his face. He then reached inside Seavers's jacket, removed the

Newburgh Treaty, and pocketed it. He was about to pick up the canister of lethal virus when the thunder of boots rumbled up the stairwell and Sergeant Randolph in her flak jacket reached the observation deck.

"Drop the gun!" she shouted. "Hands in the air!"

Behind her popped up two more CPs with M-4s. A dozen more NPS officers clamored up behind them and surrounded him.

Conrad slowly lay the Glock on the floor and put his hands up. His left shoulder blazed with pain.

Sergeant Randolph kicked the gun away.

"Dang, Yeats," she said. "You killed Max Seavers."

"Before he was about to kill millions. That's a canister of bird flu on the floor. He was about to release it over the Mall. You're going to need a Haz-Mat team."

"You're going to need a doctor," she said, looking at his blood-soaked shoulder.

Conrad shook his head. "No time," he said. "Serena. You've got to get me back to her."

"Sister Serghetti?" Sergeant Randolph said. "Don't tell me you dragged her into this, too?"

Minutes later, while fireworks and cannons exploded over the Mall, Conrad and Randolph's R.A.T.S. burst into the secret underground laboratories beneath L'Enfant Plaza and found the Alignment boardroom empty.

Serena was gone.

And so was the terrestrial globe.

The shock of her betrayal stabbed Conrad like a dagger through the heart.

51

THE WHITE HOUSE

JULY 5, 2008

It was just before nine the following evening when Conrad, his arm in a sling, was admitted in the Oval Office. The president was sitting on a sofa, sipping some Scotch, staring into the empty fireplace as a gentle rain drummed the windows behind him. To the right of the fireplace stood the celestial globe.

"You have the Newburgh Treaty, Dr. Yeats?"

"Yes, Mr. President."

Conrad sat down on the opposite sofa, eyes fixed on the globe, thinking of Serena, and wondering where she had gone. Above the fireplace mantle was a portrait of George Washington. Conrad almost felt like Washington was studying him as closely as the current president was. He wondered if the president knew that the East Wing of the White House was designed by architect I.M. Pei as a triangle to mirror the federal triangle, based on the slope of Pennsylvania Avenue as it intersects with Constitution Avenue and 16th Street. But now was not the time to bring it up.

"I suppose the other globe is safe inside the Vatican

by now," the president said. "Somewhere even we can't touch it. But these globes are meant to go together."

"I wanted to talk to you about that, Mr. President," Conrad said. "Sister Serghetti has already seen the signatures on the Treaty. The damage is done. I think we could make an exchange: the Treaty for the terrestrial globe."

The president looked him in the eye. "How about the Treaty for your freedom, Yeats, so I don't throw you in military lockup?"

Conrad handed it over.

The president calmly unfolded it and then pulled out a pair of reading glasses. For a crazy second Conrad wondered if the president would repeat Washington's famous line from Newburgh:

"Gentlemen, you will permit me to put on my spectacles, for I have not only grown gray but almost blind in the service of my country."

But the president simply looked over the Newburgh Treaty once, and then again. Finally, he sat back and stared at Conrad over his reading glasses. "Some of the signatures on this Treaty . . . it's beyond shocking."

"Like your ancestor John Marshall, Mr. President?" Conrad said. "It's the sixth name down if you need help finding it."

"I see it, thank you," the president said tersely. "And no, Dr. Yeats, like you I had no idea of the extent of my family's dealings with the Alignment. But as you discovered, when your roots go that far back in American history, it's probably unavoidable. Some of these names will turn up modern-day Alignment figures. Some won't. It will be a tricky but necessary ordeal to ferret them out. But we will."

"Like Senator Scarborough?"

Conrad knew the FBI had raided Scarborough's home in Virginia that morning. News reports said a federal grand jury was looking into his ties to a defense contractor—biotech billionaire Max Seavers.

"It appears Seavers funneled money to the senator," the president said, sounding genuinely shocked. "Scarborough's position in Congress, where he sits on the Armed Services Committee that controls the Pentagon budget, could have allowed him to influence the flow of contracts to Seavers's company, or even Seavers's appointment to DARPA."

So that's how it's going down, Conrad thought. "So the only reason you wanted the Newburgh Treaty was to take names?"

"Hell no, Yeats," the president said. "This is America. Nobody gives a damn what your ancestors did. Or shouldn't. We're judged by our fruits, not our roots. The sins of the fathers should not be visited on their sons. I should think you would appreciate that more than anybody else."

Conrad sighed at this none-too-subtle reminder of Antarctica and his father General Yeats.

"It's what the Newburgh Treaty and the Alignment represent that threatens our security," the president went on. "Science and technology have advanced more rapidly than the ability of politicians and generals to grasp their implications. That's what Plato implied was the real problem with Atlantis. Not the cataclysm that supposedly destroyed it. If we don't do any better in America, which Sir Francis Bacon prophesized to be the New Atlantis, we'll suffer the same fate. Hell, just a few years back I used to sweat over mass extinction from some terrorist biotoxin. Max Seavers was on the brink of bottling it as a vaccine with the label 'Made in the USA.' Thank God you stopped him."

"God?" Conrad repeated, wondering if the president really believed in America as "one nation under God" or was simply posing for Middle America at his prayer breakfast the other day.

The president gazed up at Washington over the fireplace.

"Washington's greatness lay in his readiness to surrender power and embrace his faith," the president said, a faraway look in his eyes. "He understood that true political freedom cannot exist without religious freedom. Sure, he bent over backwards not to favor any particular religion. But he instinctively grasped that Americans of religious faith are the true protectors of American liberty."

"He also gave his spies bags of gold, Mr. President."

The president paused for a moment, then pursed his lips and smiled at Yeats in a way that almost resembled a smirk. "You've done your part, Dr. Yeats, and America is grateful," he said. "Big time."

The president put the Treaty down on the table beside him and picked up a box. "There's more, don't worry," he said, holding the box out to him. "This is the Presidential Medal of Honor with Military Distinction.

The incredible truth is that you successfully carried out the orders of the commander-in-chief."

Conrad wasn't sure if the president was referring to himself or George Washington. But he felt an honest-to-goodness surge of pride as he opened the box and looked at the medal. It was a golden disc with a great white star on top of a red enamel pentagon. In the center of the star was a gold circle with blue enamel bearing thirteen gold stars. The medal hung from a blue ribbon with white edge stripes, white stars, and a golden American eagle with spread wings.

The president said, "Secretary Packard insisted you deserved no less and wanted me to tell you that he wants you back at DARPA."

"It's Danny Z and old Herc who deserve this," Conrad said and closed the box. "Along with that poor soul you buried in my father's tomb."

The president only said, "Take a lesson from Sister Serghetti, son, and stop mourning for those you're sure to follow shortly."

"None of this changes the fact that we have one globe and the Vatican has the other," Conrad pressed. "Or that you and Sister Serghetti and I saw the names on the Treaty with our own eyes."

"That girl is going to do what she's going to do," the president said. "I have to do what I have to do."

The president rose to his feet, picked up the Newburgh Treaty and stepped to the fireplace. He touched a lighter to the corner of the Treaty and placed the Treaty in the fireplace.

Conrad looked on as a corner curled into black and then burst into flame beneath the watchful eyes of George Washington. Within seconds more black holes like growing welts appeared all over the Treaty until it went up in smoke.

52

VATICAN CITY

STILL TORMENTED over her sudden abandonment and betrayal of Conrad, a resolute Serena marched into the office of Cardinal Tucci in the Governorate with the terrestrial globe and a plainclothes security detail of six Swiss Guards. Much like the American president's Secret Service, the centuries-old guards protected the pope both at home and abroad. Whether they would do the same for her now, well, she was about to find out.

Cardinal Tucci was seated in practically the same position she had last seen him weeks earlier, deep in his leather chair between two Bleau globes, echoes of the globes that Conrad had uncovered. Tucci held a glass of red wine in his hand. The silver Roman coin around his neck caught the morning light from the window beside him, warning her that he was the head of *Dominus Dei*.

She said, "A bit early in the morning for that, Your Eminence."

"Sister Serghetti, I see you brought me the globe," Tucci replied, "along with an entourage."

Serena turned to the captain of the guards and said,

"I'd like a private audience with His Eminence for a moment. Wait outside."

As the guards withdrew and closed the door behind them, Tucci took another sip of his wine. "I take it you disobeyed my direct orders and opened the globe?"

"I did, Your Eminence. Both of them."

"I see."

"So do I," Serena said. "And I see your mother's family in Boston among the names at the bottom of the Newburgh Treaty. You're Osiris. And *Dominus Dei* is the Alignment's cell within the Church. It always has been. Long before the Knights Templar. It's the Church that's in danger, not just America."

"Is that what you told Dr. Yeats?" Tucci said dismissively. "I'm sure he appreciated your sentiments. Tell me, did you sleep with him on your adventure?"

Serena pointed her finger at him. "You are the wolf in sheep's clothing, Tucci! You don't love the Church. You've never loved the Church. You and your kind have only used the Church for yourselves, to build a worldly empire for the Alignment."

"Well, if you bother to look around, Sister Serghetti, you'll find that there are plenty of others like me. Where God builds a church, the Devil builds a chapel, you know. I take it by the guards that you've told the Holy See?"

"I have, Your Eminence, and this is one chapel I'm closing."

"Only to build the Antichrist's cathedral." Tucci finished his wine. "Indeed, the federal city of the future, the world's capital city, is going up soon. Something to make Washington and the new Beijing pale in comparison."

"What are you getting at?" she demanded.

"America is inconsequential in the sweep of history—it doesn't even merit a mention in the Book of Revelation," Tucci said. "It was the globes all along and not the Newburgh Treaty that the international Alignment was interested in."

"The globes?"

"They're necessary for the construction of the Third Temple," Tucci said in triumph. "By uncovering the globes you have now ensured the rise of the last master civilization."

"You're insane," she said.

"Soon you'll be, too." He placed his empty wine glass down and nodded toward the door. "Shall we call your guards?"

Serena took a step toward the door and caught a blur of movement in the corner of her eye. She whirled around in time to see Tucci rush toward the window and hurl himself through the glass with a thunderous crash. She heard a scream outside, ran to the sill and looked down to see Tucci sprawled on the pavement below, two uniformed Swiss Guards pointing up at her in the window.

"No!" she gasped.

She heard the door behind her fling open as the guards burst in. She turned from the window to see the captain staring. But not at the broken window and terrible scene outside. He was staring at the *Dominus Dei* pendant on the floor. She stared at it, too. The chain was unbroken, as if Tucci had removed it first before he had leapt to his death.

"Is everything all right, Sister Serghetti?" he asked her.

"Cardinal Tucci is dead, Captain. Obviously everything is not all right."

Her heart was pounding as she watched the captain pick up the medallion off the floor with great reverence and hand it to her. He was practically genuflecting, as if he now answered to her.

Somehow he has it in his head that I'm the new head of the Dei.

She took the chain and stared at the ancient Roman coin. Only the pope could nominate the head of the Dei, she knew. But then she recalled the jokes of conspiracy buffs in the College of the Cardinals who said that it was Dei all these centuries who picked the popes.

"Cardinal Tucci was not well," the captain said suddenly, as if forming his story for the Vatican's press release about the incident. He clearly knew more than he was letting on. "Arrhythmia, you know. It is a shame his heart should fail while looking out the window."

"Thank you, Captain. You are dismissed."

"Very well," he said and knelt to kiss the medallion now wrapped around her fingers. "I will post guards outside your door and leave you to your privacy."

She watched him close the door behind him and sat down in Tucci's chair, suddenly feeling like a prisoner in a cell full of secrets.

She stared at the medallion in her hands, realizing that it was her only way out now. To protect the Church she would have to root out the Alignment, even if it meant joining the Dei. She mourned for Conrad, but knew in her heart that she couldn't abandon the Church to these predators. She had to find out what the Dei was up to.

I do those things I don't want to do, and don't do those things I want to do, she thought, paraphrasing St. Paul. *What a wretched woman I am.*

Slowly she put the chain with the Dominus Dei medallion around her neck, feeling the silver Roman coin press heavily on her heart.

EPILOGUE

THE DAY AFTER

ARLINGTON CEMETERY

THE RAIN CAME DOWN even harder as Conrad approached his father's tombstone in the dark of night, consumed by an obsession for the truth that the burning of the Newburgh Treaty had only inflamed.

He shined a light on the three-foot-tall obelisk and again read the inscription beneath the engraved cross:

GRIFFIN W. YEATS
BRIG GEN
US AIR FORCE
BORN
MAY 4 1945
KILLED IN ACTION
EAST ANTARCTICA
SEPT 21 2004

He could feel it all coming up now inside him: the anger, the betrayal, the loss—first his father, and now Serena, all over again.

He stared at the numerical strings on one side of the obelisk that had led him to the Stargazer text and the three constellations engraved on the other side that had revealed the secret alignment of America's key monuments.

For some reason he couldn't shake the same uneasy feeling creeping up his spine that he experienced the first time.

There must be more.

Conrad felt a surge of anger and frustration as he leaned back and gave the obelisk a hard kick.

The heavy tombstone barely budged.

Conrad gave it another kick, with feeling.

This time the obelisk, its base loosened from the rain, moved about an inch before it settled back into the muck.

"You goddamn bastard!" he shouted as he kicked it again.

At last the gravestone toppled over on its side in the wet grass.

Conrad stared.

There it was, inscribed in the bottom of the obelisk, now facing him like a picture in stone as the rain washed away the dirt:

A Crusader's cross.

It was an emblem of the Templar Crusaders, a single cross made up of four smaller crosses.

It was also a symbol of Jerusalem.

The cross's four arms were of equal length, symbolizing the four directions and the belief that Jerusalem was the spiritual center of the earth.

He remembered the two columns in the Savage portrait of Mount Vernon, along with the two pillars to the entrance of King Solomon's Temple in that Masonic mural under the Library of Congress. Then he recalled what sat on top of those two pillars—globes with terrestrial and celestial maps.

The globes belonged in Solomon's Temple. Not just the original Temple. But the next Temple. And if each globe was reputed to have originally contained the secrets of Genesis or "First Time," then it stood to reason that together the globes worked to reveal the secret of . . . the end of time.

He stared at the cross, the last secret symbol that his father had left him.

Did Serena know about it? Conrad wondered. She must.

Now he knew, too.

"See you there, Serena," he said to the pounding rain, and walked away into the night.

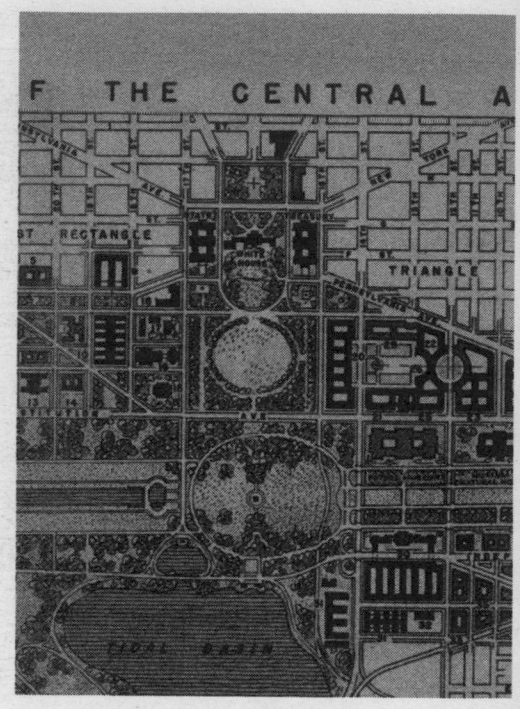

REA WEST AND EAST
MUNICIPAL CENTER AREA
MASSACHUSETTS
UNION STATION
CAPITOL AREA
SOUTHWEST AREA

BOÖTES
ARCTURUS
LEO
VIRGO
SPICA
REGULUS

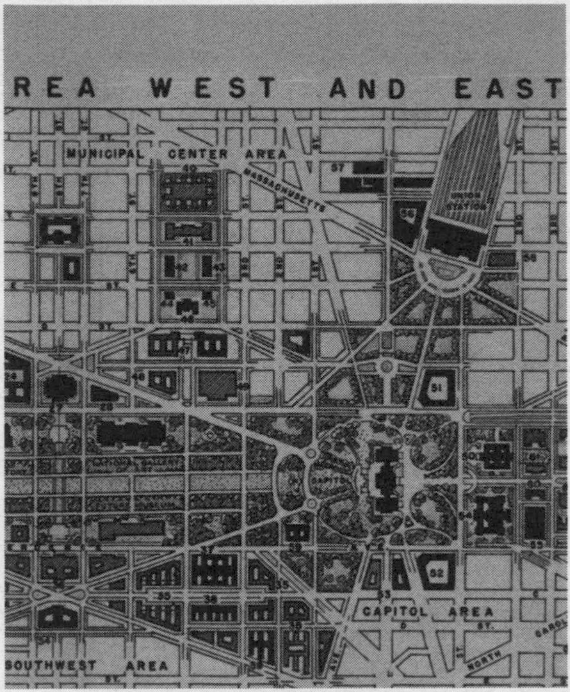

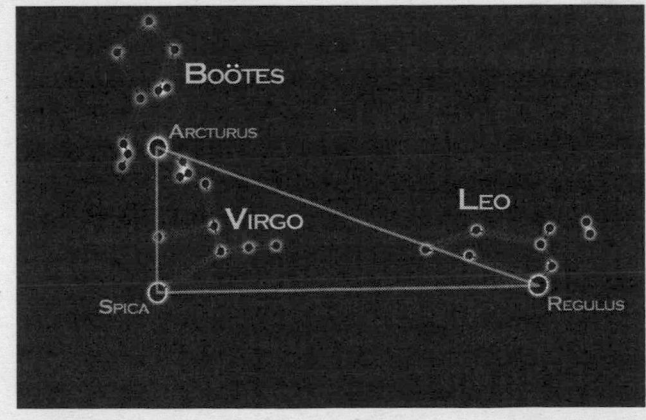

POCKET
BOOKS

Thomas Greanias
Raising Atlantis

Under the ice of Antarctica, a centuries-old mystery awaits . . .

In Antarctica, a glacial earthquake swallows up a team of scientists . . . and exposes a mysterious monument older than the Earth itself.

In Peru, archaeologist Dr Conrad Yeats is apprehended by US Special Forces . . . to unlock the final key to the origins of the human race.

In Rome, the Pope summons environmental activist Dr Serena Serghetti to the Vatican . . . and reveals a terrifying vision of apocalyptic disaster.

In space, a weather satellite reveals four massive storms forming around the South Pole . . . and three US spy satellites disappear from orbit.

These are the end times, when the legends of a lost civilization and the prophecies of the world's great religions lead a man and a woman to a shattering discovery that will change the fate of humankind. This is Raising Atlantis . . .

ISBN 978-1-4165-2232-4
PRICE £6.99